Mum's the Word

"This is the alarm notification center. Your alarm was triggered."

I gulped. Had Bloomers been burgled?

"I'm on my way right now." I shut the phone, stuffed it in my bag and practically sprinted to the car. Driving as fast as the weather allowed, I headed up the long, two-lane road that led back to town.

As I neared Maple Creek Bridge, headlights came up fast behind me. I tapped on my brakes to warn the driver to slow down, but he apparently didn't notice because he bumped me.

I honked my horn, but that seemed to make the speed-ster angry, because he bumped me again, harder this time. He'd had to speed up to do it, so I knew it was intentional.

Steering the Vette over to the side of the road, I was digging for my phone when he hit me again, pushing my car forward, so that the right front end was hanging off the narrow, sloping shoulder and I was staring down into muddy water. Fear prickled along my spine. What if this wasn't a case of road rage? What if someone was trying to kill me?

I heard the unmistakable sound of an engine being shifted into reverse. I glanced up at my mirror in horror.

He was getting his car positioned to ram me again.

MUM'S THE WORD

A Flower Shop Mystery

Kate Collins

A SIGNET BOOK

SIGNET
Published by New American Library, a division of
Penguin Group (USA) Inc., 375 Hudson Street,
New York, New York 10014, USA
Penguin Group (Canada), 90 Eglinton Avenue East, Suite 700, Toronto,
Ontario M4P 2Y3, Canada (a division of Pearson Penguin Canada Inc.)
Penguin Books Ltd., 80 Strand, London WC2R 0RL, England
Penguin Ireland, 25 St. Stephen's Green, Dublin 2,
Ireland (a division of Penguin Books Ltd.)
Penguin Group (Australia), 250 Camberwell Road, Camberwell, Victoria 3124,
Australia (a division of Pearson Australia Group Pty. Ltd.)
Penguin Books India Pvt. Ltd., 11 Community Centre, Panchsheel Park,
New Delhi - 110 017, India
Penguin Group (NZ), cnr Airborne and Rosedale Roads, Albany,
Auckland 1310, New Zealand (a division of Pearson New Zealand Ltd.)
Penguin Books (South Africa) (Pty.) Ltd., 24 Sturdee Avenue,
Rosebank, Johannesburg 2196, South Africa

Penguin Books Ltd., Registered Offices:
80 Strand, London WC2R 0RL, England

First published by Signet, an imprint of New American Library,
a division of Penguin Group (USA) Inc.

First Printing, November 2004
10 9 8 7

Copyright © Linda Tsoutsouris, 2004
All rights reserved

Ⓟ REGISTERED TRADEMARK—MARCA REGISTRADA

Printed in the United States of America

PUBLISHER'S NOTE
This is a work of fiction. Names, characters, places, and incidents either are
the product of the author's imagination or are used fictitiously, and any resem-
blance to actual persons, living or dead, business establishments, events, or
locales is entirely coincidental.

The publisher does not have any control over and does not assume any
responsibility for author or third-party Web sites or their content.

If you purchased this book without a cover you should be aware that this
book is stolen property. It was reported as "unsold and destroyed" to the
publisher and neither the author nor the publisher has received any payment
for this "stripped book."

To my husband, Jim, and my other two J's, Jason and Julie, and to my extended family and dear friends for tolerating me during deadline crunch, when I hide in the den like a mole, sticking my head out for food now and then. You deserve big hugs and lots of smooches. I couldn't do this without you.

To my friends Jim and Kenton at Hidden Gardens flower shop. I will spare you the smooches and simply thank you for letting me hang out and pester you with questions.

To my uncle Leon, who started my love of flowers and of all growing things by teaching a five-year-old about all the yucky bugs in the garden. Thanks, Unk!

CHAPTER ONE

Most people hate Mondays.

Not me. I see them as portals to untold prospects, gateways to golden opportunities, pristine canvases awaiting bold splashes of color. And this particular Monday seemed to epitomize all that was good about them. Robins warbled merrily in the maples along Franklin Street, a warm June sun glinted off the hood of my vintage 1960 yellow Corvette convertible, and I had nabbed a prime parking space right across the street from my shop.

Slinging my bag over one shoulder, I climbed out of the car, pulled off my tortoiseshell sunglasses, and regarded the wooden sign mounted above the door of the old redbrick building.

BLOOMERS

Every time I saw it, a thrill of pride raced through me. Me, Abby Knight, an entrepreneur! Penniless, perhaps, yet soundly devoted to my new profession. Who would have guessed when I flunked out of law school a year ago that I'd be standing here today in front of my own flower shop? Certainly not my parents, who were still shell-shocked.

I locked the car door and gave the Vette an affectionate pat before pocketing the keys. This car was my baby. I loved it with a passion I normally reserved for fine dark chocolate or a bathing suit that actually fit. It was a four-on-the-floor with a black ragtop roof, black leather seats that were cracked from age and wear, and a slightly scratched chrome-and-black dashboard. Originally, beneath a thick coat of grime and bird droppings, the body color had been white. Now, with its two-week-old paint job, the car was a bright, cheery banana yellow, my favorite color.

Hovering like a proud mother, I flicked a leaf off the hood and polished away a stray fingerprint with the hem of my white blouse. Out of the corner of my eye I noticed a man race from the alley between two buildings and hop into a black monster of an SUV parked in front of the Vette. I thought nothing of it until he gunned the motor. Then I looked up in surprise as he threw the vehicle into Reverse and backed into my car's front end. *Wham!*

I stood in the street with mouth agape as visions of the precious dollars I had just spent on the car winged fiendishly past. The SUV took off with a squeal of tires.

"Sixty-four apple David three—damn it!" He was too fast. I didn't have a chance to catch the whole license plate number.

"You're leaving the scene of an accident!" I shouted, shaking my fist at him as he sped away. "Come back here, coward!" He had his windows down; I knew he heard me.

"Go get 'im, honey," someone called from a city van. A tow truck driver honked his horn and gave me a thumbs-up.

I found a pen and scribbled the numbers on the back of my hand, then crouched in front of my car to inspect the damage. My stomach lurched at the horrible sight: shattered double headlights, dented chrome grill and hood. I stood up and glared in the direction he had gone. There was no way I would let an irresponsible moron get away with a hit-and-run on *my* car. No way. I hadn't grown up as the daughter of a cop for nothing, not to mention that if my insurance payments went up, I'd go broke.

As I dug in my purse for my cell phone, one of the warbling robins flew over and deposited a big white blob of bird poop on the trunk. With a shudder, I turned my back on the scene of the crime and called the police dispatcher, who promised to send someone out as soon as possible. My assistant, Lottie Dombowski, was watching me through Bloomers's window, a look of horror on her face. I signaled back to let her know I had everything under control.

This was not the colorful start I'd had in mind earlier that morning.

Lottie had to unlock the door for me since I was too rattled to find my keys and the shop didn't open for another hour. She was dressed in her usual summer getup— bright pink loafers, white denims that fit her size-fourteen body a little too snugly, a pink blouse that gaped where it stretched across her ample bosom, and a pink satin bow snuggled into the brassy curls above her left ear Shirley Temple style. Not exactly a trendy hairdo for the mother of seventeen-year-old quadruplets, but try to tell her that and she would hand you a hair dryer and tell you to knock yourself out. After raising those four boys, *nothing* fazed Lottie.

"Are you okay, sweetie?" she asked, looking me over from my shoulder-length bob to my open-toed black mules. "I saw that pond scum ram you."

"I'm fine, just angry is all."

"He was in some hurry, wasn't he? Come on back. I'm making breakfast."

Cooking was just one of Lottie's abilities. Besides being a true genius at floral design, she was also the one who put me on to my Corvette. And she knew just about everyone on the New Chapel town square—a boon to any business person, especially a novice like me.

I had met Lottie during the period of my fateful engagement to Pryce Osborne II, when Lottie owned Bloomers and I made deliveries for her—in between clerking for a lawyer. Holding two jobs was the only way I could afford law school. My grandfather's trust had covered my undergraduate expenses at Indiana University, a state college, but had not been enough to pay for three years of law school, even a local one that allowed me to live at home.

But the trust *had* been enough for a minimal down payment on a quaint flower shop in a small Midwestern college town.

The inhabitants of New Chapel, Indiana, were typical in that regard, tolerating the students that flocked to the cheap eateries, coffeehouses, and dollar stores during the school year, and bemoaning their absence during the summer months. The town square had the regulation limestone courthouse set amid a huge expanse of lawn, with a tall spire and huge clock face that proclaimed it ten minutes after four regardless of the real time, along with the standard compliment of family-owned restaurants, shops, and businesses flanking the courthouse square on all sides.

The town was unique only in its location—thirty minutes by car from the famed Indiana Dunes lakeshore on the southern tip of Lake Michigan, and an hour by train from Chicago, barring unforeseen weather conditions, such as, say, clouds. New Chapel was close enough to take advantage of the big-city highlights yet far enough away to escape the madness.

The population was eclectic—ranging from blue-collar workers employed by a nearby steel mill, to farmers in the outlying county, to businesspeople who commuted to the Loop, to the professors and students at New

Chapel University. The neighborhoods varied from sprawling areas of tract housing on former swampland, to square, flat blocks of identical ranch homes or bungalows on what had been grazing pastures, to fancy gated communities set in hilly, wooded areas, to dilapidated farmhouses that dotted the miles of rural roads connecting New Chapel to neighboring towns.

I had always loved the charm of Bloomers—with its two multipaned bay windows displaying a colorful array of flowers and its old-fashioned yellow-framed door with beveled glass center—but I never thought I would one day own it. After my disastrous year at law school and my breakup with Pryce, I had considered moving to Chicago to find work, but the thought of all that noise and traffic congestion made me queasy. Actually, I'm slightly claustrophobic.

My parents had urged me to stay in town. My mother was adamant about it being the best place to raise a family—like that was going to happen anytime soon—but I hadn't seen much in the way of career opportunities for someone with a creative bent and little money.

Then in stepped Lottie with an offer I couldn't refuse. She'd had a modestly successful floral business going, but her husband's enormous medical bills had wiped out her cash reserves. Since she was desperate to pay off her debts, and I was equally desperate to find *something* I could do well, I took a long hard look at my abilities and came to the conclusion that the only things I'd ever had any luck with were plants, so why not make a living from them?

"You can't be serious," my mother had said after I'd announced my intentions. "Why not resume your law studies? Take the dean a plate of brownies. He'll let you back in."

"Mother, endowing the dean with an entire brownie *company* would not make that happen. Besides, I don't want to be a lawyer."

"You can't keep changing your mind, Abigail, not at your age. Not if you want to make me a grandmother. How many times did you switch majors in college? Three, four?"

"Two. And it put me only a year behind."

"Why didn't you go for a medical degree? You always wanted to be a dermatologist."

"*You* always wanted me to be a dermatologist. I wanted to be a translator at the UN—until I found out I had to learn more than conversational French."

"But a florist, Abigail? A *florist?*"

It wasn't like I was the first person in the family to make a living from plants. My grandmother had raised a big family solely on the produce from her garden, along with a few turkeys here and there. From her I had learned how to cultivate flowers, grow vegetables, and sneak raspberries into my mouth without leaving behind telltale red stains.

But it was while working for Lottie that I actually began to dream about arranging flowers for a living. I'd loved the fragrance of fresh blossoms, the exhilaration of helping Lottie create beautiful bouquets, and the smiles on the faces of the people who received them. So I'd closed my eyes, made the leap, and became the proud owner of a huge mortgage. And Lottie, relieved of her financial burden, was able to do what she loved without the headaches. She swore she would be eternally in my debt, as I was in the bank's. The difference was that the bank wanted their debt paid back monthly.

The fly in the ointment was a big new floral and hobby shop that had opened on the main highway, where fresh flowers were sold in premade bouquets for rock-bottom prices and silk flowers were to be had in every color of the rainbow. For those on a budget it was a dream come true. For a small shop like Bloomers it was a disaster.

To curb the drain of customers, I had been trying various inexpensive promotional devices, including running a contest—What's My Vine?—handing out free flowers at grocery stores—A Mum for Your Mum!—and adding a coffee and tea parlor. So far, the coffee and tea parlor held the most promise.

"How many orders came in over the wires last night?" I asked Lottie, as I followed her through the shop into the workroom behind it.

"Three."

Three wasn't good. Seven was good. Seventeen was better. *Twenty*-seven would have me doing handsprings over the worktable.

We went through a doorway into the tiny, crowded kitchen at the rear of the building, where Lottie had already started preparing her traditional Monday-morning breakfast. Bloomers occupied the entire first floor of the deep, three-story, redbrick structure, from Franklin Street in front to the alley in back. Three apartments made up the second floor, accessible through a door and stairway to the left of our shop. The third floor was unfinished—full of dusty, discarded furniture and enough spiders to fuel my nightmares well into the next century, should I still be alive and kicking.

It was a wonderful old building from the turn of the century, when ceilings were a minimum of ten feet high and the brick walls inside were real. There were the added benefits of having the courthouse right across the street and the university five blocks south, another reason why I figured my coffee and tea parlor might fly.

Lottie tied on her black bib apron, took eggs from the old refrigerator, and cracked them on the side of a bowl. "How do you want 'em?"

"Scrambled." Just like my brain at that moment. I put my head in my hands and moaned at the thought of my poor car.

"How much damage?" she asked.

"Front end. Who knows how much it'll cost." With a heavy sigh, I pulled off my shades, dropped them in my slouchy leather bag—a bargain I'd found at Target—and perched on a stool at the narrow eating counter. "I'll find the maggot somehow. He had local plates."

"Call Justin about the car. He'll get you in right away."

Justin was Lottie's nephew. He ran Dunn's Body Shop and was a true genius when it came to fixing cars, though he could barely read the back of a cereal box. He'd bought my Vette from a widow who'd stored it in a barn for decades after her farmer husband died. Other than needing bodywork, new paint, and a rear bumper, the four-speed stick shift had been in relatively good shape. Most important, it had been cheap.

"Listen, sweetie," Lottie said, her back to me as she worked, "my cousin Pearl needs advice real bad, but she won't go see a lawyer, so I convinced her to talk to you."

That was the trouble with people who knew me: They assumed that since I'd attended law school, even for one year, I was practically a lawyer and therefore could advise them—for free. Combine their need for help with my intense hatred of injustice and a strong proclivity for untangling all those little quandaries people got themselves into and—well, let's just say I often found myself in rather *interesting* situations.

Although I knew better, I had to ask, "What's Pearl's problem?"

Lottie whipped the eggs with a wire whisk, then poured the batter into a sizzling skillet. "That lousy, son-of-a-bee husband of hers is the problem. Now we find out he's keeping a little doxy on the side, too. I told her to divorce him, but she's afraid."

The aroma wafting from the skillet made my stomach growl. "Afraid of a divorce or afraid of her husband?"

"Both. Tom Harding's an ornery cuss. I'm not fearful of many people, as you know, but he sure the hell scares me. I know you'll be able to talk some sense into Pearl."

I didn't want to *talk* a person into getting a divorce. I understood that not all lawyers shared my feelings, but maybe that was one of the reasons I'd flunked my law classes. "I think Pearl should see a marriage counselor, Lottie."

She put down the spatula, wiped her hands, and pulled up the stool next to mine. "Listen, baby, this man is abusing her and their boy, too. She's scared out of her wits. I'd never get her to a counselor. I'll be lucky to pry her out of the house to get her *here*. You've got to help, Abby. You're good at helping people."

"What does Pearl's husband do for a living?"

"He's a farmer."

Not good, financially. Most farmers barely managed to eke out a living and often worked two jobs. There wouldn't be much in the way of assets to split between them—*if* Lottie's cousin had the courage to proceed with the divorce. Something I had learned from my clerking days was that reluctant clients usually ended up dismissing their divorce actions.

"Good morning, all!" Grace Bingham called brightly in her meticulous British accent, poking her head into the kitchen. "How are we today?" Grace had left her nursing career behind ages ago, yet still spoke in first person plural.

"Other than having our car smashed by a reprobate in an SUV, we're fine," I said.

"Us, too," Lottie added.

Grace gave me a thorough once-over, just to be sure. "Shall I call Dunn's Body Shop and make an appointment for your car, dear?"

"Would you, please?"

Before coming to Bloomers, Grace had been a top-notch legal secretary for Dave Hammond, the lawyer for whom I had clerked. Several months ago Grace had decided to retire, and after ten agonizingly boring days of staring at her walls, realized her mistake. Now, as our girl Friday, she manned the cash register, answered the phone, and ran the coffee and tea parlor. In fact, the parlor had been her creation.

Brought here from England by her GI husband, Grace had always bemoaned that New Chapel had no tea parlor. It turned out that Grace was an expert tea brewer and a fast study on gourmet coffee, as well. Plus, she loved to bake scones and the little cookies she called biscuits, so we had decorated half of the store in a Victorian theme, installed equipment, put her in charge, and voila! Now, in addition to the fragrance of the flowers, the shop was scented with coffee, tea, and baked goods. In nice weather, we opened the door and let the aroma draw people in.

Grace was amazing. A widow for the last fifteen years, and well into her sixth decade, she climbed stairs without breaking a sweat, maintained her calm in any crisis, and bowled no less than two hundred twenty. She worked for me because she enjoyed it, not because she needed the money, which suited me just fine. She'd starve on what I could afford to pay.

Grace and Lottie worked well together—usually. Sometimes Grace's fussiness got under Lottie's skin. But then, Lottie's teasing irritated Grace, so they evened each other out.

"Listen, baby, will you talk to Pearl this afternoon?" Lottie asked, resuming our conversation. "I told her I'd take her to Wal-Mart during my lunch hour, but I'll bring her here instead. It'll be a surprise."

Some surprise.

"Abby, you're not dabbling in legalities again, are you?" Grace warned. "Remember what happened last time?"

"Yes, but the judge ended up seeing the humor in it."

"And the time before that?"

I hung my head. My aunt still hadn't forgiven me. For that matter, neither had my high-school homeroom teacher, who'd claimed I had a problem sticking my nose where it didn't belong. Also the middle-school principal, who had taken away my monitor's sash, the school bus driver with the *Playboy* magazines under his seat, the cafeteria lady with the walnut-sized wart on her nose and the funny cigarettes in her sock—but what was the sense of looking back?

"If you choose to meddle thus," Grace said, striking a Hamlet-esque pose, "then you must be prepared to face the consequences, whatever they are."

"Very good!" Lottie said, giving her a brief burst of applause. We were constantly awed by Grace's ability to find a quote to fit any situation.

She gave a regal nod of her head to acknowledge our praise. "Jimmy Sangster, British screenwriter."

"Don't worry, Grace," Lottie said. "Abby is only going to offer her advice this time. Aren't you, sweetie?"

I glanced at Grace, who was giving me a stern head shake.

"Lottie, I really think your cousin would be better off seeing a lawyer," I said, and Grace beamed at me.

"Sweetie, if I pull up in front of a law office, Pearl will bolt from the car and take off running. You have an honest face. She'll believe what you tell her. Then you can send her to Dave. What do you say?" Lottie slipped the steaming heap of buttery, golden eggs in front of me.

I was easily swayed by food. I took a scrumptious mouthful and muttered, "How about twelve thirty?" I could at least listen to her story. What harm would there be in that?

"I want it noted," Grace sang out as she retreated to the sanctity of her tea parlor, "I did warn you."

CHAPTER TWO

I finished the eggs and got a cup of Grace's coffee to sip while I designed a centerpiece of miniature roses for the Monday-afternoon ladies' poetry circle that met in the tea parlor. Holding meetings in the parlor was another of my schemes to drum up business. I'd plastered posters around town offering free use of the room for small groups, but, so far, only the poetesses had taken advantage of it.

As I settled on a stool at the worktable, Grace called from the front, "There's a bobby standing beside your automobile, dear."

A bobby?

A cop! I dashed out of the shop and across the street in the brilliant sunshine, squinting at the motorcycle cop in a black helmet and silver sunglasses who was busy writing in his notebook. I knew some of the younger ones from high school, but this guy didn't look familiar. Then again, New Chapel had grown a lot over the past five years, and a lot of disgruntled Chicagoans looking for small-town atmosphere and cheaper taxes had moved in.

"This yours?" he asked brusquely, nodding at my Vette.

"Yes." I sighed morosely as I ran my hand along the car's sleek side. "It was just painted."

"Shame. See who did it?"

"Just briefly. A man, mid-to-late twenties, dark brown curly hair, light gray T-shirt with some kind of logo on it, blue jeans, quite tall . . ." I tried to remember more, but couldn't.

The cop glanced at me, sizing up my five-foot-two frame. I knew what he was thinking: *Everyone looks tall to you, sweetheart.* It was a prejudice I'd battled since my freshman year in high school, when my growth had come to a screeching halt.

I read the license plate numbers off my hand. "That's all I got. Think you can find him?"

A muscle in the cop's jaw twitched, as though the question offended him. "I'll see what I can do." He took down my name and number, then looked at my name again and asked if I was related to Sergeant Jeffrey Knight.

"He's my father."

Motorcycle Cop looked at me with new respect. "He's a good guy. How's he doing?"

"Not bad, considering what he's been through."

The cop didn't say anything for a moment and neither did I. It was still a sore subject with me. Three years ago my dad had been hot on the trail of a drug dealer, not knowing he was heading into an ambush. He took a bullet in his thigh, ended up in emergency surgery, suffered a stroke on the table, and nearly died. My father will never leave his wheelchair, and the drug dealer is still out there, selling his poison. Where was the justice in that?

"Give him my regards," the cop said. "Name's Gordon. Pick up a copy of the accident report in five days."

"Thanks," I called, as he swaggered back to his cycle.

When I returned to the shop, Grace was in the parlor, humming as she set bud vases on the white wrought-iron tables. We had six tables with four chairs apiece, allowing us to serve up to twenty-four people at a time. All seats had a view from the big bay window, allowing customers to watch the happenings on the square.

"Would you do me a favor?" I asked, holding out my hand to display the blue scribbles. "This is the partial plate number of the moron who hit me. Would you see what you can find out about him?" Grace had good contacts, the result of working many years for Dave.

She eyed me suspiciously as she copied the digits onto her notepad using the little pen she kept on a chain around her neck. "Won't the police be handling it?"

"I thought I'd give them a little help."

She handed me two squares of paper, along with a look that said *You can't resist meddling, can you?* "These messages came in while you were outside."

I glanced at the slips as I headed for the workroom. Both were from my mother, reminding me about dinner at the country club on Friday. I dropped my purse on the small desk crammed into one corner of the room, tossed the messages in the waste can, and went back to work on the roses. At least she hadn't called to say she was bringing over a sculpture.

In addition to being a kindergarten teacher, my mother was also an artist. Her medium was clay, and at least once a week she showed up at the shop with her latest creation, which we dutifully displayed until someone bought it or, if it was too hideous, until Lottie could sneak it down to the basement and hide it among the stacks of clay pots.

At least my mother was trying to bring in business. It was quite a shift in attitude from the woman who used to remind me—daily—that she wanted only three things from life: that her children should marry well, become successful doctors and/or lawyers, and belong to the local country club—none of which I had done.

Growing up on a farm, my mother had fantasized about being in high society—not that New Chapel had any. The best it could cough up was a low to medium society, but it still translated into belonging to the country club, which, for the wife of a cop, was simply too expensive. For her children, however, all things had been possible, especially after my grandfather had died and his trust had kicked in.

Gramps had owned a huge parcel of valuable acreage, or at least the developer had thought so, because he'd paid a barrel of money for it. With that money and a healthy dose of scholarships my brothers, Jordan and Jonathan, had become surgeons, attached themselves to a thriving medical group with ties to a Chicago teaching hospital, married into good families, and, much to my mother's never ending happiness, joined the local country club.

Thank goodness for my brothers, because had it been left to me she would be unfulfilled as a mother. After having been publicly humiliated by my ex-fiancé's cancellation of our wedding, I might never find the courage to march down that petal-strewn aisle—even if I were to supply the petals. On top of that, country clubs gave me a nervous rash.

My brothers, on the other hand, with their classic good looks, long-boned bodies, Jaguars, Gucci golf bags, and stylish wives who shopped at Neiman Marcus Chicago, instantly took to country-club life. They ate portobello-mushroom-and-brie club sandwiches, for heaven's sake.

My style ran more to sub sandwiches than club sandwiches, and I'd rather have a tooth pulled than chase a dimpled white ball through sand traps, which was great because I couldn't have afforded the balls anyway. My father felt the same way, only he would never say so in front of my mother.

Bloomers was where I fit in. I loved it there, especially in the workroom. It smelled of roses, lavender, eucalyptus, and moist, tropical air, and even with no window it felt like a garden. Wreaths and swags hung from pegs on one ivory latticed wall, and rows of shelves above a

Formica counter and deep sink on another wall held all manner of vases and containers of dried flowers. A long, slate-covered worktable sat in the middle of the room, with drawers underneath for the floral knives and sheers, diagonals, awls, pruners, and other tools we used on a daily basis. A shelf at the bottom held foam, wire mesh, and papier mâché containers.

Dividing our workroom from the display room in front was a huge stainless-steel walk-in cooler where we stored fresh greenery and flowers and where, at that moment, Lottie was taking a daily inventory. As she stepped out and shut the heavy door, I held up the vase of roses. "Does this look full enough?"

"Maybe put a little more baby's breath in it. And a few more roses, too." The radio was on, tuned in to her favorite local station, and she paused to listen to the weather forecast. "Another scorcher," she said with a shake of her curls, and went to the phone beside the computer to place a call to the wholesaler.

I finished the arrangement and set it aside, then took an armful of multicolored daisies to the glass-fronted display cooler in front to replenish the supply. The bell jingled as three clerks from the courthouse came in to get their daily cappuccino fixes, and Grace went off to the parlor to make it for them. Lottie breezed past, calling that she was off to buy baskets, leaving me alone in the shop, where I cast longing looks at the telephone that sat stubbornly silent on the front counter.

Ring, I commanded silently. I had bills to pay. Lots of bills. I really needed some big orders to make ends meet.

After rearranging the floral display in the bay window I went outside to take a look at my handiwork. Three doors down, an elderly window washer was applying his squeegee to the wide plate glass of Down the Hatch Bar and Grill, which I had just learned from the owner of the realty next door was under new management.

I had met a few of the shop owners on the square.

Some I'd known because I'd gone to school with their children, but I hadn't yet met the bar's owner. With three gift boutiques, two restaurants, two ladies' clothing stores, one men's store, one children's shop, a shoe store, a deli, a hardware store, four banks, two realties, and six law offices, I had a way to go.

The phone was ringing as I stepped back inside. I crossed my fingers and chanted, mantralike, "Please let this be a big order."

Grace answered the call, then gave me a look of impending doom as she handed me the receiver. "It's your mother."

As I dashed back to the workroom to take the call at my desk, I changed my mantra to, "Please let this not be another sculpture."

"Am I interrupting anything?" my mother asked. "You sound breathless. You're all right, aren't you, Abigail? Did something happen?"

There was no way in the world I would tell her about the accident with my car. She'd been appalled that I'd actually paid money for it in the first place. "I was arranging the window display. What can I do for you?"

"I wanted to remind you about dinner at the country club Friday night."

She was nothing if not persistent. She lived for those dinners where she could show off her successful children to New Chapel society. Well, two of her children anyway. "Would I miss a family dinner?" I asked her. Actually, if my father didn't need an ally, I would.

"I'll see you then, Abigail. Don't forget to wear something nice."

As opposed to my usual rags? I bit my tongue and bid her a fond adieu.

"Abby," Grace said, "I called the Department of Motor Vehicles about that license plate number. As I suspected, even if they were to trace the plate, they won't give out names."

We both paused at the sound of a male clearing his throat. Grace looked at me in surprise. Neither of us had heard the bell over the door. She stepped through the curtain to see who it was, then returned with mouth pursed as though she'd just eaten something distasteful.

"There's a man here to see you, and I don't think he's a customer." She leaned closer. "He says he wants to proposition you."

"Probably a salesman."

"Not like any I've ever seen."

I followed Grace to the curtain. She opened it a crack and we both peered out, my head below hers. A man stood in the display room studying a large arrangement of silk flowers, one of my best creations yet—a striking combination of dwarf raspberry astilbe and royal blue spiderwort. But even that paled in comparison to the man beside it.

He had gleaming black hair, wore a black leather motorcycle jacket, blue denims that appeared to have been sprayed onto his long legs, and polished-to-a-sheen black boots. He turned his head toward the doorway and smiled, obviously spotting the two pairs of eyeballs gaping at him. He had olive-colored skin, dark eyes framed by darker eyebrows, and a cocky stance. He didn't appear to be a danger, but he did look dangerous. A woman would understand the difference.

I whispered to Grace, "I'll talk to him."

She looked down at me. "Are you certain? Look at him! Who wears leather in this heat?"

"I say we find out."

CHAPTER THREE

Grace opened the curtain and said crisply, "You may come in, sir."

As the man passed, she fixed him with a warning glance, then left, making sure to leave the curtain pulled back. I stood behind the worktable with my arms folded, the classic defense posture.

"Marco Salvare," he said, reaching across the table to shake my hand.

"Abby Knight. What can I do for you?" I saw his gaze dart to my bosom, another unfortunate aspect of my physique. I'm small *and* busty—a terrible combination for any female who has ever had aspirations of being taken seriously.

"It's what I can do for *you*, Abby." He lifted an eyebrow suggestively.

I gave his lean body a cool appraisal. He didn't look like a salesman, but he sounded like one. "What you can do for *me*, Mr. Salvare, is not call me Abby. It's Ms. Knight to you."

One corner of his mouth curved up. He unzipped his jacket and pulled a card from an inner pocket, revealing a black T-shirt stretched taut over a six-pack waist. I took the card and glanced at the script: DOWN THE HATCH BAR AND GRILL. *Marco V. Salvare, Owner.*

So this was the bar's new management. He was quite a hunk, actually, but way too cocky for his own good. Tossing his card on the desk behind me, I eyed him skeptically. "What can you do for me?"

"Get you the information you're looking for."

"How do you know I'm looking for information?"

His cocky grin dissolved, replaced by a somewhat sheepish look. "I overheard your conversation with your mother."

"She's not my mother."

"Sorry."

I brushed a stray lemon leaf off the table. "What kind of information?"

"Name and registration of the guy who hit your car."

"Did you see the accident?"

"Jingles told me about it."

"Jingles?" The image of a tiny man with pointed ears and turned-up shoes popped into my mind.

"The window washer. It's his nickname. He has a habit of jingling the coins in his pockets. If you want to know what's happening on the square, ask Jingles."

Why hadn't I known that?

"So," Marco said, folding his arms across that broad expanse of chest, "do you want my help or not?"

I'm not normally suspicious of people, but this guy was too smooth. "And just what is it you want in return, Mr. Salvare?"

"Flowers. One dozen."

That seemed a fair enough trade. "One dozen of what kind?"

He leaned across the table, so close I could smell his aftershave—a masculine, spicy scent that made my insides quiver. "You pick out something for me," he said in a husky voice.

It took a full minute of gazing into those spellbinding dark eyes for me to realize what was going on. He was hitting on me. "You didn't come down here for flowers," I scoffed.

"I didn't say there weren't additional reasons."

"Really? And what might they be?" I braced myself for his next line.

"I saw you outside with the cop. I thought you looked pretty, and I wanted to meet you."

Marco's frank response brought instant color to my cheeks. I muttered a hasty thanks, grabbed a pencil and my order pad, and began to write to cover my embarrassment. "Are these flowers for the bar, or for someone special, like a girlfriend, perhaps?" I didn't really need to know that last part, but I couldn't help myself.

"Someone special."

I pictured a tall, leggy blonde in a bikini stretched out on a chaise longue beside a pool, waiting eagerly for his call, while he flirted in the back of a flower shop with me. The cad! I was supremely flattered. "We can do long-stemmed roses or something summery like gerbera daisies or gladiolas—which would you prefer?"

"I'd like roses."

Of course he would. They were expensive. "Any particular color? Red, for instance, is for passion. White is for peace. Yellow is for— "

"How about mixed?"

No clue to the special person there. "Do you want them delivered?"

"Please. To the bar."

I finished writing the order and looked up. "You'll have them early this afternoon."

Marco seemed impressed. "How long have you owned this shop?"

"Two months. How about you?"

"A few weeks. How's business?"

I shrugged. "It could be better."

"That new floral and hobby store out on the highway must be making you nervous."

He couldn't begin to know how nervous. If I didn't make a go of this business, I'd be selling hot dogs on the corner. But would I admit it to him? "A bit nervous," I answered.

"I wouldn't worry. A babe like you will have men standing in line to buy your flowers."

Chauvinist! I gave him a scowl. "Thanks, but I'd like to think my talent will be the draw, not my *babe*ness."

"Think what you want, I know men." He winked at me and started toward the doorway, his scent lingering behind like a wispy finger beckoning me closer. It worked.

"Mr. Salvare," I called.

He sauntered back, leaned both hands on the table, and smiled ferally, revealing a handsome set of white teeth. "Call me Marco," he said in a voice that nearly melted my mules. I almost fanned my face. Had someone shut off the air conditioner?

I lowered my voice so Grace wouldn't hear. "How will you get the information?"

"I have my sources."

"Your *sources?*" I whispered. "What are you, a mafioso?"

"Ex-cop, slash, private investigator."

"Ex-*cop?*"

"Your old man is Sergeant Knight, isn't he? I was starting out when he took that hit. A real tragedy what happened afterward—and you don't like talking about it, do you?"

"It's a sensitive subject. So you gave up police work to run a bar and grill?"

"It's not just any bar and grill. It's Down the Hatch," he said, parroting the ad that had run on the radio for twenty years. "I only gave up the cop part. I still dabble in PI work. It's my hobby, so to speak. The bar pays my bills."

"And you gave up the cop part because?"

"Let's say it was a mutual decision that I should leave the force. I didn't always agree with their rules."

I liked him more and more. I held out my left hand to show him the numbers and said sotto voce, "Here's what I was able to get from the license plate."

"Why are we whispering?"

I glanced over Marco's shoulder, half expecting to see Grace standing at the curtain, shaking her head in admonishment. "I'd rather no one know about this."

"Gotcha." He gave me his wolf smile again and started for the doorway.

"Don't you want to write down the numbers?"

He tapped the side of his head. "They're up here. I'll let you know when I have something."

As soon as I heard the bell over the front door signal his departure, I scurried to the bay window to watch Marco stride across the street toward my Vette. He circled around it, looked at the damage, then glanced up and mouthed at me, "Nice wheels."

I was grateful for the spray of silk irises that hid my red face. How the heck had he known I'd be watching? He gave me a thumbs-up and headed back to Down the Hatch.

"Did that man say something offensive, dear?" Grace asked, coming to peer at me over her granny glasses. "You look a bit flustered."

I was saved from answering when Lottie came through the door, her arms loaded with baskets. "Did you hear the news?" she asked breathlessly. "There was a murder on Taylor Street this morning. The police have the area all sealed up. An eyewitness saw a man run from that old apartment building behind us and head up the alley alongside our shop."

The image of the jogging SUV owner flashed in my mind. "Did they say what time?"

"Around eight o'clock," she replied. Her eyes widened the same time mine did.

"I saw the murderer!" I called, and dashed out the door and into the alley, heading for Taylor Street.

CHAPTER FOUR

I came out of the alley to find four squad cars parked in front of the dilapidated Hampton Arms apartment building. Fifty years ago the brown brick building had been a showplace, but a neglectful owner had let it fall into disrepair. Now, other than a handful of senior citizens who'd been there a long time, it rented mostly by the month.

I approached one of the cops standing by the front door and identified myself. I didn't usually pay much attention to men a lot older than me, but this one caught my eye. He was a good-looking man of medium height, about forty years old, who displayed an air of confidence without the normal posturing. He had intelligent hazel eyes, good facial structure, brown hair starting to show a bit of white on the sides and, more important, no gut hanging over his belt. He took a closer look at me and said, "Is your father Sergeant Knight?"

"Yes, he is."

"Sean Reilly," he said, holding out a hand for me to shake. "Quite a guy, your old man. We worked together for several years. I liked him. He was honest, played by the rules."

"Right. And just look where it got him."

He eyed me skeptically. "Is that attitude why you didn't stick with law school?" Before I could answer, his radio squawked information. He paused to listen, then gave me a blank look. "Where was I?"

"You were getting ready to tell me about the murder."

"I didn't say there was a murder."

"You've got a dead body in an upstairs apartment, don't you?" Before he could backpedal, I started rattling off questions in that strictly female way of appearing cute and innocent while being incredibly nosy. "So it happened about eight o'clock this morning?"

"That's what the coroner said."

I sighed dramatically. "How sad. The elderly are such easy targets."

"This vic was just a boy, maybe twenty years old."

Two details in less than a minute. Not bad, but I could do better. "Now we've got a nut running around with a gun. It *was* a gun, right? I hope there were witnesses."

Reilly paused to tell a group of curious college students to stay back. "One witness so far, an elderly lady out walking her dog."

"And she saw a stranger run out of the building and cut through the alley heading toward Franklin?"

"That's what she says. We're checking for other witnesses now." It must have dawned on Reilly that I was gathering a lot of information. "Why all the questions?" he asked, peering closer at me. "Do you know something?"

"I *may* have seen something."

He was all ears. "Go on."

"A little before eight o'clock this morning I was parking my car on Franklin, across from the alley, when a guy came sprinting out, jumped into an SUV, and rammed my Vette in his haste to leave."

"Hold it. I think you'd better talk to the detective in charge." He walked to the propped-open door of the building and called up, "Al? I've got an eyewitness down here."

I called up the stairs, "A *potential* eyewitness," just as a harried-looking, balding, middle-aged man in a brown plaid sport coat and brown pants came trudging down the steps. At the bottom, he hiked his pants over his belly and stepped out into the sunlight, squinting at me.

"You're the eyewitness?"

"*Potential* eyewitness." I gave him a quick smile and held out my hand. "Abby Knight. My shop is on the next—"

"You're Sergeant Knight's kid, aren't ya?" he asked, pulling out a notebook. "How come you didn't become a doctor like your brothers?"

At least he hadn't asked about law school. "I like flowers."

He gave me a look of incredulity, then hiked up his pants again, making me want to clue him in on a great little invention called suspenders. Or put him on a diet.

"So what did you see?"

"I'm sorry, I didn't catch your name."

"Corbison. Detective Al Corbison."

I'd heard that name many times. New Chapel had two detectives on its police force, Al Corbison and Rob Williams, both of them paunchy, middle-aged, balding men, the type that blended into a crowd. Usually they investigated forgeries and petty theft. This murder was the big time for them.

I launched into my report as Corbison scribbled notes. "To be honest, Detective, I caught only a brief glimpse of this guy."

"You were how close to him?"

"I was standing beside the left front fender of my car, so maybe eight feet."

"Anything about this man that stands out in your mind? Anything out of the ordinary?"

I scrunched my eyes closed and tried to picture the scene. There was something hovering in my memory just beyond my grasp, but I couldn't reach it. "No. Sorry."

"Al?" Reilly called, striding up. "We've got another witness who says he saw Elvis Jones leave the building about eight o'clock this morning."

"Elvis doesn't live here anymore, does he?"

Reilly told him no and Corbison groaned. "Okay. Pick him up for questioning."

Elvis Jones was a notoriously mean drunk, in and out of jail and constantly in the news. He was an army veteran who'd served in Vietnam until he'd been discharged for psychological reasons. My ex-boss Dave Hammond had represented him pro bono a few times, which is how I'd learned Elvis's history. His name had been Bob, but he'd changed it to honor his hero Elvis Presley and still wore what was left of his hair in Presley style. He had a record of home robberies, store break-ins, and even a bank holdup, but he'd never murdered anyone that we knew of. Which didn't mean he wouldn't. But if he had, what about my SUV driver?

Corbison glanced at his notes. "Sorry for the interruption. What kind of SUV was it?"

"Black Cadillac, partial plate number sixty-four apple David three."

Something flashed in his eyes—shock? worry?—which he immediately suppressed. My ever-alert antennae went up. He knew something about that vehicle. Maybe there was a connection after all.

"Okay," he said, flipping his notebook closed. "We'll check it out. If you think of anything else, give me a call."

Wouldn't this put an interesting wrinkle in Marco Salvare's investigation? I mused as I headed back to Bloomers. In fact, the wrinkle seemed much too large for one person to iron. Marco was definitely going to need my help.

Lottie and Grace, who were waiting at the door, began firing questions the moment I stepped inside. I dutifully answered them all, filling them in on the details as I knew them.

"Wouldn't surprise me a bit if Elvis killed that boy," Lottie said. "You cross him and he'd just as soon shoot you as argue."

"The timing of your hit-and-run could have been a co-incidence," Grace said.

"A little too much of a coincidence, if you ask me," I said.

"Nevertheless, Abby, you did your part, the police are on it, and you can walk away with a clear conscience," Grace finished.

Lottie gave me a look that said *Grace doesn't have a clue, does she*? As we stepped into the workroom, she said quietly, "All right, what do you have up your sleeve?"

"I don't have anything up my sleeve." At her snort I said, "Okay, maybe one thing. I'm going to give the information to Marco Salvare, the new owner of Down the Hatch. He's offered to help me find the SUV driver. And that's all—for now. I swear."

"Is Marco good-looking?"

"That's not important."

"Listen to me, baby. It's *always* important."

I stopped short of pointing out that the heel I'd nearly married had been good-looking. And that Lottie's husband, while the dearest man on earth, resembled a platypus on growth hormones. Instead, I put together Marco's roses, wrapped them, and slipped out while Grace was busy with customers in the parlor. Otherwise I had the feeling she'd insist on going along as my chaperone.

Down the Hatch Bar and Grill was the town's local watering hole, a meeting place for the judges and attorneys from the courthouse across the street, as well as a suppertime hangout for a group of active senior citizens. Decorated in a corny fishing theme—complete with a fake carp mounted above the long, dark wood bar, a bright blue plastic anchor on the wall above the row of booths opposite the bar, a big brass bell near the cash register, and a fisherman's net hanging from the beamed ceiling — it screamed for a rehab.

As soon as my eyes adjusted to the dim interior, I saw Marco behind the bar having a serious discussion with a customer seated on a stool in front of him. One of his bartenders was filling a mug with beer, and a waitress was ringing up a bill at the old-fashioned cash register. Another waitress, Debby, a girl who'd been a few years ahead of me in high school, came up to greet me. "Hi, Abby. Here for lunch?"

I held up the roses. "Delivery for Marco."

"Isn't that sweet?" She cast a lovelorn look in Marco's direction. "He didn't forget his mother's birthday. Wait here. I'll get him."

The flowers were for his mother. So much for the leggy blonde in the bikini.

In a moment, Marco came toward me, walking in an easy, confident, all-male gait that almost took my breath away. "Here you go," I said, thrusting the parcel at him, hoping he couldn't hear the abnormally loud thumping sound coming from the region of my rib cage. "My part of the bargain is done. I even included a packet of Floral Life to extend the bloom life."

"Super. Come back to my office." He turned and walked straight through the restaurant without once checking to see if I was following. I had half a mind to walk out the door. Thank goodness the other half wouldn't let me.

Marco seated himself behind an ultramodern black-and-chrome desk and opened a drawer. "Have a seat," he said without looking up.

The decor of the room was so incongruous with the rest of the bar that all I could do was stand in the doorway and stare in amazement. The walls were painted dove gray with white trim, and the single window was covered by silver-gray miniblinds with a shiny black valance. The only other furnishings were a pair of very modern-looking black director's chairs with chrome legs, a tall, gunmetal-gray filing cabinet, and a flat-panel black TV mounted in a corner up near the ceiling. Other than a red-and-black poster advertisement of a Harley-Davidson motorcycle, the room was spare and held not a single clue to the man's identity.

Marco opened a checkbook and started writing. "What do I owe you?"

"I thought we were trading favors."

"We are. If I don't get you the information you need, fill in what I owe and cash the check."

I was impressed.

He slid the check across the desk toward me, returned his book to the drawer, and sat back, folding his arms across his chest. "Spit it out."

"Excuse me?"

"You're dying to tell me something. It's written all over your face."

"Okay, here's the thing," I said, perching on a corner of his desk. "Getting information on that vehicle may be a little tricky. You're going to need help."

"Let me guess—*your* help?"

"Did you hear about the murder?"

"It's the main topic of conversation in the bar."

"Did you also hear that a suspect ran *into* the alley alongside my shop at about the same time that oaf with the SUV ran *out* of the alley before ramming my car? Quite a coincidence, don't you think? So I may be a material witness in a murder investigation. Ergo, I should help you find him."

"Your logic is flawed."

Probably another reason I hadn't cut it in law school.

"Besides, I thought Elvis Jones was their suspect," he said.

"Trust me. The guy I saw come out of the alley wasn't Elvis. But he *is* involved, I'm certain of it. When I gave

Corbison a description of the SUV, I saw *fear* in his face."

"Fear?" Marco asked skeptically.

"Fear. I happen to know how to read faces, too, *Mr. Salvare.*"

"Really?" He scraped back his chair and came around the desk to where I was perched. "What is my face telling you now?"

Most guys couldn't stand to be studied at close range, but Marco didn't bat an eye as I examined his rugged features. In fact, it seemed our closeness was affecting only me. I had to clear my throat to speak. "I give up. What is your face telling me?"

"Don't borrow trouble." He shook his head. "Some face reader you are."

"I *know* what I saw in that detective's eyes. Corbison recognized that SUV."

"And because of that, you think the driver is involved in the murder and I need your help to find him?"

I nodded enthusiastically.

"You like to meddle, don't you?"

As I was sputtering a halfhearted denial, Marco said, "Do you know what I think happened? Your Corvette was rammed by some teenager borrowing his dad's car—one of the local politico's kids, most likely. Not many people drive an expensive sucker like that around town. Corbison probably cringed because he recognized the car's description and knew Mr. Bigwig would throw a fit when he found out."

"First of all, this guy wasn't a teenager. Second, that doesn't explain why the imbecile was in such a hurry that he had to hit my car. I *know* there's a connection with the murder. I have a sixth sense about these things. And if you're right about the driver being Mr. Bigwig's son, we need to make sure he doesn't get special treatment from the police. All crimes must be punished, especially murderous ones, no matter who commits them."

Marco waggled an index finger at me. "You're not out to solve a murder. All you want to do is find the guy who hit your car."

"But what if it's the same guy?"

"Listen to me, sunshine, let the detectives work the murder case and you keep your pert little nose out of it."

Sunshine? I gave him a resigned sigh, mostly to appease him. Anyone who called my nose pert deserved to be appeased. "So where do we go from here?"

"You mean where do *I* go. First stop, the police department to see if I can get them to divulge a tidbit or two. Second stop, the Department of Motor Vehicles. I've made a friend there, and with a little luck and the famous Salvare charm, I should be able to wheedle some information from her on the driver's identity."

"Her?"

Marco smiled. "You didn't think it'd be a *him,* did you?"

"And what do you want me to do?"

It was his turn to study my features. I didn't flinch either, but I did curl my toes. "What I want you to do is go back to selling flowers and stay out of trouble."

Frustrated, I slid off the desk and headed for the door. Marco had a lot to learn about me.

CHAPTER FIVE

At twelve thirty sharp, just moments after I had finished my turkey sandwich, Lottie hauled in her cousin Pearl the Reluctant and plunked her down on a stool across from me at the worktable, which still held snips of leaves and traces of stephanotis from Marco's bouquet.

"Abby, this is my cousin Pearl Harding. See, Pearlie, don't Abby and I look like mother and daughter?" Lottie threw an arm around my shoulders and smiled broadly. Because we both had red hair she liked to tell people we were related. The thing was, mine was natural.

Pearl didn't crack a smile. She was a short, plump, drab woman with fearful eyes, a hopeless, hangdog expression, and a permed cut in a style dating back to the eighties.

"Go ahead, Pearlie," Lottie directed, hovering at her shoulder. "Tell Abby about that no-good husband of yours."

"I think I should go home," Pearl said in a meek voice, ready to slip off the stool.

"Pearlie, look at Abby," Lottie directed. "Look at that sweet baby face. Is that a face you can trust? Now, tell Abby what Tom does when you disobey him."

Pearl glanced down at her hands lying limply on her lap. "He takes away my grocery money and my car keys."

I could tell that Pearl's self-esteem was so low she probably figured she deserved the punishment. She played right into the bully's hands.

"Guess why I'm driving her around," Lottie said, practically wiggling in her eagerness to share. "Pearl bought a different brand of potato chips. Tom doesn't like her making decisions."

He was punishing her over potato chips? "How long has he been doing this?"

"About"—Pearl paused to count on her fingers—"fifteen years."

I was appalled. "And you've been married how long?"

"Fifteen years. It's my second marriage, Tom's third."

How could she have lived like that for *fifteen years?* All I could do was shake my head in disbelief. "Have you tried counseling?"

"He says he don't need it. I'm the one causing problems."

As Pearl's story slowly unfolded, I found myself making an attitude adjustment. This woman did need a divorce, whether she thought so or not. Thomas Harding was a bully. He not only controlled the money, but also monitored her activities, berated her daily, banned her friends and most of her family, and ignored their child— a twelve-year-old boy who'd suffered brain and spinal cord damage at birth, causing a paralysis in his legs and slowness of speech. Little Tommy, as the boy was called, wore braces on his legs, used crutches to walk, and needed lots of special education, which Harding provided grudgingly.

I drummed my fingers on the tabletop, wondering how much advice to give. She needed to see a real lawyer, but first I had to convince her of that. "Pearl, you do understand he's abusing you, don't you?"

She seemed startled. "He don't beat me up."

"Maybe not physically—yet—but he beats you up mentally. That has to stop."

She shrugged unhappily. "I s'pose."

"The first thing you have to do is get Tom out of the house."

Lottie slapped her thigh. "That's what I told her!"

"But it's Tom's house," Pearl replied with a stricken look. "He'll never leave it. His father gave it to him. How can I make him leave his own house?"

"With a protective order. Trust me, it's better if Tom finds another place to stay." I almost said, *like with his girlfriend,* but thought better of it. Pearl was in enough misery.

Pearl glanced at her cousin, stark panic in her eyes. "I can't kick him out, Lottie. I'm afraid of what he'll do."

Lottie waved a finger in her face. "You listen to me, Pearlie. That bastard has walked on you long enough. Don't you want better for Little Tommy?"

Pearl's eyes filled with tears. "Yes," she whispered raggedly.

"Then let Abby help you. Okay?"

"I can't do any legal work for you," I reminded her, "but I have a friend who can."

Grace joined us in the workroom, bringing in a cup of black coffee for Pearl, although the poor woman looked like she could've used something much stronger. Pearl sniffled back tears and took a sip. "If I go see a lawyer, Tom will cut off my money."

"You'll have a court order that will make him pay the bills and give you grocery money just like he's been doing," I assured her. "But you'll need to make a list of your assets and debts. Where do you bank?"

"Tom does the banking—I don't know where. He doesn't tell me anything."

My blood was really boiling now. "Then we'll just have to do a little digging." I glanced at Grace's frowning face and quickly amended my statement. "I mean your *lawyer* will have to do a little digging. We'll get you in to see Dave Hammond. I used to work for him and I know he'll do a great job for you."

"How much will he charge?" Pearl asked.

"To start with, you'll need a hundred dollars for the court's filing fee."

She removed her wallet and looked inside. "All I have is fifty-three dollars."

"Shoot, I'll pay it," Lottie offered. "Anything to get that jackass off your back. You can pay me later, Pearlie, after you get your settlement."

I started to pick up the phone, but noticed Pearl's white-knuckled grasp on her purse and I knew it wouldn't take much to make her bolt. I replaced the receiver, scribbled my home phone number on a Post-it note, and handed it to her. "In case you need to talk," I said. Then I put my hands on her shoulders and bent down to look her in the eye. "You're going to be okay, Pearl. I promise."

Pearl lifted her gaze, and for the first time I saw a glimmer of hope there. "Thank you," she said in a choked voice.

"See, Pearlie? I told you Abby would take care of you," Lottie exclaimed proudly.

I risked a quick peek at Grace, who was rolling her eyes.

I was able to get Pearl an appointment with my former boss at ten thirty the next morning. It took a little flattery to get his secretary to squeeze Pearl in, but I did it. I hoped Pearl didn't change her mind overnight.

An hour later I returned from making a delivery and found the Monday-afternoon ladies' poetry circle meeting in full swing, its twelve members occupying three of the white wrought-iron tables. Grace was in her glory— brewing tea, serving crisp biscuits, buttery scones, and little pots of jam, and bustling quietly among the tables as the women shared their sonnets. I'd sat in on a meeting once, when the parlor first opened, and had nearly dozed off listening to odes about grass, hiccups, varicose veins, and dust bunnies. Now I just greeted the ladies cheerfully and beat a hasty retreat.

Since the meeting was already in progress, I tiptoed past the door and headed for the workroom, where Lottie was busy putting together a floral arrangement of pink vanda miniorchids and green birch buds in a pink-frosted glass vase. It was a beauty.

"We got some contest entries in the mail," Lottie told me as she expertly slid in another orchid. "I put them on your desk. And we have a customer coming in tomorrow to discuss funeral flowers. A nice little old lady named Martha Schmidt."

"I remember Martha," I told her as I scanned the short stack of entries. "She lived down the street from my parents. At Halloween she would hand out popcorn balls that smelled like soap and tasted like soggy cardboard. Did her husband pass away?"

"Several years ago. The flowers are for *her* funeral. She's very organized."

In my opinion that was carrying organization a bit too far.

Over the next few hours Lottie and I put together six floral pieces and a dried-flower wreath, and tried to devise more ways to promote Bloomers. The contest hadn't pulled in as many entries as I'd hoped, and I couldn't afford to buy ad space in the newspaper, but I had to come up with something. I had bills due the fifteenth and not much money to cover them.

I left early to drop my car at the body shop and pick up the old blue Ford Escort Lottie's nephew was lending me; then I headed for home—a two bedroom apartment I shared with my best friend, Nikki Hiduke. We lived near the hospital, where she worked afternoon shifts as an X-ray technician. Our schedules meshed perfectly: I was out of her hair during the day and she was out of mine during the evening.

Nikki and I went all the way back to fourth grade. We had met over the summer, shortly after my family had moved onto her street. She Rollerbladed past my house, took a dive, and skinned her knee. My mom bandaged her. I carried her skates home, and we'd been fast friends ever since.

My parents still lived in the old neighborhood, an area of modest, aluminum-sided bungalows in the standard three colors of white, beige, and blue. The houses all had small front yards with sidewalks, big back yards, garages facing the back alley, lots of giant oak and maple trees, and kids everywhere. It had been a great place to grow up.

I pulled into the covered lot by building C, let myself into the vestibule, and checked the mailbox, dumping all but one envelope into the trash container. I took the steps to the second floor and headed for the last door on the left. Across the hall from us lived the Samples, a middle-aged, childless couple, and their annoying little Chihuahua, Peewee, a dog that shivered even when bundled into his red wool plaid sweater, booties, and tam, and barked at anything that moved, including blowing leaves, caterpillars, and his own reflection.

The three of them were just coming out as I unlocked my door. "Look who's home, Peewee," Mrs. Sample cooed to him.

"Nice to see you," I said, smiling politely while dodging Peewee's sharp teeth. No matter how many doggie treats I gave him, the mutt still went for my ankles.

I opened the door and was promptly greeted by Simon, Nikki's two-year-old white cat, who arched his back and hissed a warning at Peewee, causing the dog to back away shivering harder than usual. Having performed his duty as guard cat, Simon turned his back on the door with a haughty sniff and followed me to the kitchen, meowing loud enough to wake the dead. *Danger is over. You are safe. Feed me.*

Simon was fearless when it came to other animals. Big,

small, shaggy, poodled, Simon was undaunted. He would hiss and spit and look evil enough to send them all running, tail between their legs. His only real fears were loud noises, bees, and small, colorful rugs, which he took pains to avoid. The noises and bees I could understand, but throw rugs?

Nikki and I felt it was inhumane to treat an animal as a prisoner serving a life sentence, never able to experience the joys of nature, so we took him outside on a regular basis to let him indulge in his favorite activity: eating grass and throwing it up. Since we also didn't want him to become a pile of fur in the road, we made him wear a harness on a rope. He'd rebelled at first, bucking like a horse on speed, but now he put each paw into it as if donning a jacket.

"Sorry I'm late," I said, stooping to scratch behind his ears. "Someone hit my car this morning and I had to take it to the body shop."

As I peeled off the lid of his cat food it occurred to me I was talking to Simon just like Mrs. Sample talked to Peewee. The difference was, I assured myself, that Simon really did understand.

Our kitchen was a typical, cramped galley kitchen, positioned to the right of the front door off the center hallway. The narrow living room/dining room was on the left, and the two bedrooms and the bathroom were on the right, past the kitchen. The roomy bathroom, the apartment's one true luxury, had an actual bathtub *and* a shower. At the far end of the center hall was a window, outside of which was our fire escape. Nikki and I had squeezed out that window and sat on the tiny, wrought-iron balcony on many a hot summer night, crunching strawberry popsicles and singing to the radio.

I fixed myself a grilled-cheese sandwich and a bowl of tomato soup—my comfort food—grabbed a can of V8 Splash and took them to the living room to watch the six o'clock news. Simon hopped onto the green plaid sofa beside me and dropped a rubber band on my knee. This was his signal that he had finished his dinner and was now ready for play. "Here you go," I said, and tossed it across the room.

Simon leaped down, snagged the rubber band, and brought it back. Fetching rubber bands and plastic straws was his favorite sport—also plotting the death of the squirrel that taunted him from a tree outside our window.

I threw it again and resumed eating only to have him return, drop the saliva-coated band on my plate, and look at me expectantly. After ten more tosses, I finally placed it behind me. "No more, Simon. You got to eat your dinner; now it's my turn."

Scolding never phased him. He merely began to wash his face, as if that's what he'd planned to do all along. He stopped only once, when I offered him a fingertip of melted cheese, which he sniffed first, just in case I had poisoned it.

When the phone rang, Simon leaped off the sofa and scampered down the hallway. "Coward," I called, and grabbed the receiver. "Hello?"

A click followed. Wrong number, I assured myself, and took the last bite of my sandwich. The phone rang again. Another click. Could have been a mistake. The third hang-up was no mistake. I took the phone off the hook and buried it under the pillow until bedtime. That'd show him.

The phone rang again in the middle of the night. Normally I let the machine pick it up after midnight, but this time I was in such a deep sleep that I automatically reached for it. "Hello?" I rasped.

"You'd be smart to mind your own business," a voice whispered. I hung up immediately, then sat there with my heart pounding, trying to decide if I knew that whisper or not. Was it a prank? Was it a threat? Should I report it or ignore it?

Wide-awake now, and angry to boot, I padded barefoot

to the kitchen to pour myself a glass of calcium-fortified chocolate soy milk. It was my latest concession to my mother's incessant harping about the dangers of osteoporosis. Plus it was chocolate.

"Who called?" Nikki asked groggily, shuffling into the kitchen in her pink cotton pj's and furry purple slippers. Her short dishwater-blond hair stuck out at odd angles around her pixie face. Unlike me, Nikki was tall and lanky and always searching for Mr. Right, whereas I clung to my fairytale belief that *my* hero would come riding up on a white charger and sweep me off my feet, thus sparing me the search effort. I no longer trusted my instincts when it came to picking potential spouses anyway.

I decided not to bother Nikki with the whisperer, assuring myself it was a prank call and nothing more. "Wrong number. Want some chocolate milk?"

She wrinkled her nose. "That's not real milk." She leaned against the counter and tucked one foot behind her like a stork, her hazel eyes brightening. "I met this gorgeous doctor today—a gynecologist. I think he's going to ask me out."

"Is he married?" I routinely asked her this question. Nikki had had her heart broken by too many men pretending to be single.

"He wasn't wearing a ring," she said hopefully.

"No good. Get more info." I finished the milk down to the last swirl of chocolate and set the glass in the sink.

"I thought maybe you could do that for me. Didn't you say you hadn't had a checkup in a long time?"

"You want me to be naked in front of your potential boyfriend?"

"Please?"

"Nikki, I'd do just about anything for you, but not that. I'm going to bed."

She followed me to my door. "Fine. I'll make an appointment for myself."

"You wouldn't."

She looked brave for about two seconds. Then her face crumpled into hopelessness. "You're right, I wouldn't."

"Can't you just ask his nurse if he's married?"

"And let her know I'm interested? What if she's interested, too? What if she's his wife? What if she tells him? Well, that wouldn't be so bad."

"Tell him you're throwing a party for some hospital friends and you'd like to invite him and his wife. Then let him take it from there."

She pursed her lips. "But then I really have to throw a party."

"Yes, but if he says he doesn't have a wife, you can make it a very intimate party." I wiggled one eyebrow.

"Abby, you're a genius. I'll do it!" She hustled back to her room, where I was sure she made plans well into the morning.

My alarm went off at six o'clock a.m., and I was out the door by six thirty, heading for Community Park and the exercise track that circled it. That was another difference between my brothers and me. They went to fitness centers; I preferred the outdoors. Mosquitoes, rain, wind, whatever, it was better than being cooped in a big room with a bunch of sweaty people in designer exercise outfits, not that I could have afforded any of it.

I pulled the Escort into the lot, bunched my hair into a short ponytail and topped it with a Chicago Cubs baseball hat. After a few good stretches, I was off on a power walk.

At that time of the morning the track was usually empty, which was how I liked it. Unfortunately, on my third lap, Deputy Prosecutor Gregory F. Morgan came trotting out from the opposite direction, wearing a tank top and running shorts, displaying his fantastic physique.

Greg Morgan was the only glitch in an otherwise seamless relationship between Lottie and me. For some reason she firmly believed a higher power had ordained her to relaunch my love life. To that end she had set me up with a dozen chance meetings with Morgan even though I'd told her that after being wounded by Pryce I wasn't ready for a love life, especially not with Morgan, who had managed to go through four years of high school without even once acknowledging my existence. Not that I hadn't done what I could to get his attention. A besotted teenager will suffer many degradations to get the object of her adoration to notice her.

The ultimate humiliation came just after our graduation ceremony, when I finally worked up the courage to ask Morgan to sign my yearbook. *To Ally,* he wrote, *with breast wishes.*

It still stung.

Morgan had been hired by the prosecutor's office as soon as he'd passed the bar. He went from being the high-school hunk to the law school lothario to the courthouse staffs' golden boy, reeking of charm, good looks, and a modicum of intelligence. He wasn't tall, but he had a toned body that looked great in either a suit or jeans, chestnut-colored hair with blond glints women would kill for, blue eyes that made you swear he'd stashed a halo somewhere, and a flawless smile that smacked of braces.

Lottie insisted there was a lot going on beneath his model-perfect surface, but I had yet to see proof of it. Now he flashed his dimpled smile as he circled around me. "If it isn't our new florist out for some exercise."

"That's what I like about small towns," I quipped. "If you don't know what you're doing, someone else does."

His gaze took in my black-and-yellow sports bra and black spandex shorts, sale items from Wal-Mart. "I didn't know florists could look so hot."

I searched for a witty comeback, but the blush spreading up my neck seemed to have thrown up some kind of mental block. I had to settle for a haughty look. He laughed and sped up.

"Hey, Morgan," I called, causing him to circle back. "Are they close to solving the murder case?"

"Very close." He rubbed his hands together, his blue eyes snapping with anticipation. "I can't wait until they nab the bastard."

"Elvis?"

He shrugged, not willing to admit it. "Will you get the case?" I asked.

"Looks like it," he boasted. "I have a briefing this morning."

"Have you heard anything about a suspect leaving the scene in a Cadillac SUV?"

He came to a stop, looking genuinely perplexed. "I hadn't heard that one."

"Ask Corbison about it. He has the details." I snickered to myself. That ought to rattle some cages in the detective bureau.

"Will do," he called, and jogged off. Morgan prided himself on having his finger on the pulse of New Chapel.

I returned home to shower, change into white cotton slacks and yellow T, and grab a quick bowl of cereal. At the kitchen table, I opened the morning paper to a headline that screamed MURDER AT THE HAMPTON. A smaller headline beneath it said POLICE SEEK ELVIS JONES.

According to the article, the victim had been a nineteen-year-old white male, a cocaine user who'd rented the apartment two weeks prior to the murder. He'd been shot once in the chest by an unknown assailant. No name was given because at the time the paper went to press the family hadn't been notified. The police were looking for Elvis. There was no mention of any other suspect.

Poor nameless boy, I thought. Poor grieving parents. Whoever the killer was, he needed to be caught and punished.

"Good morning. How are we today?" Grace chirped when I stepped inside the shop.

"Great. Any messages?" I was hoping Marco had called with information.

"None."

Lottie came out of the workroom carrying a large arrangement for a display table. "Did you see the newspaper article about the murder? Looks like Elvis is in trouble big time."

"I still think the hit-and-run driver is connected," I said.

"In any case, it's a terrible tragedy," Grace remarked. "The boy was a mere nineteen years old. He had his whole future ahead of him. Now his life is over."

We were all musing on that point when the phone rang. I began to mutter my mantra as Grace answered it.

"That was Martha Schmidt," she announced, replacing the receiver. "She'll be here at nine thirty to pick out her funeral flowers."

Martha Schmidt was a frail, white-haired, ninety-three-year-old woman who still drove her own car—a 1982 blue Buick. She came in with a notebook in which she had listed the flowers she wanted for her casket. Martha didn't leave anything to chance. We seated her in the parlor, and Grace made her a cup of English Breakfast tea.

Martha watched me closely as I tallied up her order. "How much?" she asked in her thin, warbling voice.

I glanced at her small, hunched body and wrinkled face with its faded blue eyes and trembling mouth, and remembered how kind she'd always been to the neighborhood kids—even the ones who'd climbed her apple trees and helped themselves to a snack. No way could I charge her the standard markup. I gave her a wholesale price instead, as though I could actually afford to be generous. "Two hundred dollars."

She gave me a grateful smile. What was money anyway?

"Your mother told me you went to law school," she said, turning a page in the notebook. "This," she said, tapping the writing on the page, "is my last will and testament. Would you mind looking it over?"

I glanced over her head at Grace, who was shaking her head furiously. "I'm not a lawyer, Mrs. Schmidt. You need a lawyer."

"My heavens, I don't like lawyers," Martha replied. "My late husband tangled with one back in 1963, and I haven't trusted them since. You seem like an honest young woman, though I must say I had my doubts about how you'd turn out when you kept stealing my apples." She smiled sweetly. "Won't you just take a peek at it?"

How long could it take? Pretending not to see Grace scowling at me in the background, I read the first and second page, then began to flip through the pages that followed—lots and lots of them—onto which she had listed all her possessions and who should get them, down to the last throw pillow on her sofa. "Everything seems to be in order," I told her.

"Now if you'll just type that up for me," she said with a sweet smile.

As my mouth opened in astonishment, Grace suddenly materialized at my side. "I'd be delighted to type it up for you, Mrs. Schmidt. I'm an excellent typist, you know. Come back in two days and we'll see that you're well taken care of."

My mouth dropped open even further. Was this the same woman who had scolded me earlier for dabbling in the law?

"Could I trouble you for more tea?" Martha asked dulcetly, holding out the china cup.

"I'll brew you a fresh batch," Grace promised and whisked the cup from her hands.

I followed Grace back to her coffee counter and whispered, "Did I hear you volunteer to type up a will?"

"Don't get your knickers in a twist, dear. When Martha returns in two days, I shall give her the typed papers and walk her over to the law office, where she will have an appointment with David. You won't need to meddle at all."

"I don't meddle."

She patted my arm. "That's not what your aunt says. Why don't you keep Martha company while I fix her tea?"

"You know," Martha said, her forehead wrinkling even more as I seated myself across from her, "now that I think about it, I'm not sure I should leave the Chinese lamp to my niece."

She retrieved the notebook, turned to page nine, and tapped a yellowed fingernail on it. "Here it is: 'Lamp, Chinese.' Mary loves Oriental furniture, but she's a terrible housekeeper. I wouldn't want my precious lamp sitting in dust. My husband bought it for me on our second anniversary."

I glanced at the clock. Five minutes to brew tea. Five long minutes.

"On the other hand, my grandson's wife—what is her name? Darna, Darla, Karla. Now *she* keeps a clean house." Martha gazed past me, deep in thought. "She's a modern gal, though. Probably wouldn't care for Oriental."

I stared at the clock on the wall as Martha flipped through notebook pages, muttering to herself. That second hand seemed to creep around with excruciating slowness. Couldn't a customer come into the shop just about now? Or Marco? What was taking him so long anyway? Maybe that "old Salvare charm" hadn't worked after all.

The phone rang, and I jumped up just as Lottie called, "I've got it." I sank down again.

Mercifully, Grace glided over moments later, cup in hand. "Here you go, dear."

I excused myself from the table and headed for the workroom, where Lottie said, "That was Detective Corbison. His number is on the pad on your desk."

I called the station and was told I'd just missed him. "But he called here minutes ago," I protested.

"And?" came the grumpy reply.

"And now he's gone?"

"That's what I said, lady."

"Okay. Have him call me tomorrow."

There was a pause before he replied, "Detective Corbison left on vacation."

"Just now?"

"Yes, ma'am."

In the middle of a big murder investigation?

CHAPTER SIX

I tried to pump the officer on the phone for any recent news on the case, but if he knew anything, he was keeping mum. If I had questions I would have to talk to Detective Williams. Did I want his number?

Yes, as a matter of fact I did. Unfortunately, Williams had no idea why Corbison had phoned me, nor did he feel the need to share any facts about the case. Did I have anything else to report? No? Then thanks for the call.

I hung up and stared at Corbison's number on the pad. Why had he phoned? If I let my imagination run, I'd think he had learned something about the SUV owner that had put his life in jeopardy, and that's why he'd suddenly left town. And I hadn't been available.

I debated about calling my dad, but since he'd had that stroke we didn't like to upset him. Telling him about my hit-and-run would definitely upset him. Who else might know what was going on? Greg Morgan. The only problem was that he'd never divulge it willingly. I'd have to devise a subtle approach.

Lottie came bustling in, her cheeks flushed from the heat. "Well, she did it! Pearl filed for divorce. I just took her back home."

"How is she?"

"Nervous as a cat. She swears Tom's been having her followed. He goaded her all evening yesterday and again this morning." Lottie shook her head. "Wait till he gets those papers tomorrow. He'll be madder than a wet hen."

"Is the sheriff going to serve him at the house?" I had a frightening image of Pearl being trapped there with Tom Harding after he took a look at the divorce summons.

"He works at the greenhouse Tuesdays, Thursdays, and Fridays."

"Is the greenhouse on their property?"

"No, baby. He owns Tom's Green Thumb."

I blinked, absorbing the surprising news. Tom's Green Thumb was a huge landscape center out on the main highway. There were even big billboards on the highway with Tom's picture on them. This guy had more money than I thought. "You told me he was a farmer."

"He is a farmer. Before I forget, I had to give Pearl your home number again. She lost that slip of paper you gave her."

"How did she like Dave?"

"She was edgy at first, but Dave, bless his heart, calmed her right down. He made sure to get a protective order filed for her, too."

I hoped she wouldn't need it. I gave Lottie an update on the flower orders; then we both settled down to work.

I was still figuring out a way to pump Greg Morgan for information when I stepped out of the shop a little before noon to get a sandwich. I glanced over at the blue Escort and saw a ticket fluttering under the windshield wiper. On closer inspection, it claimed I had violated the two-hour parking limit.

I checked my watch. As I thought, I had fifteen minutes to spare. A glance up and down the street did not produce any sign of a parking cop or any other ticketed cars, though I distinctly remembered seeing that very same silver Honda parked in front of me when I pulled in.

Since I refused to let a miscarriage of justice go unpunished, I headed straight for the traffic clerk's office to lodge a protest. The office was in the basement of the courthouse, a cold, damp, windowless area that seemed to suck the life out of the people who worked there. A bored, overweight, pale woman took my ticket and examined it for all of three seconds. "Twenty dollars. No personal checks."

"I'm appealing this."

She gave me a deer-in-the-headlights look, as if no one had ever attempted such a feat.

"My time wasn't up," I explained politely. "And there was a car parked in front of mine that had been there longer, yet *it* didn't get ticketed."

Without saying a word, she stepped away from the window and returned with a form, which she slid across the old wooden counter toward me. "Fill this out."

As I penned in my information, I said to her, "I'd like an explanation from the officer as to why I got the ticket."

"Put your complaint on the form."

I searched the paper for a comment section, or at least an inch of free space. "Where?" I finally asked.

"On the back." She covered her mouth and yawned.

I wrote *See back* at the bottom, then flipped the form over and scribbled a paragraph outlining my complaint. "When will I hear something?"

"Two, three weeks." She stapled the form to my ticket, stuffed them in a shoe box, and threw it beneath her counter.

Bureaucracy! I made a bet with myself that no one would even bother to read the back. Huffing in indignation, I headed to the deli on the other side of the square. Sitting at an outside table, I crunched potato chips and tore bites off my turkey sandwich while scouring the area for the parking cop. No one stopped to say hello. I'm sure my mood was written all over my face.

Suddenly, a hand reached across my shoulder and snatched one of my chips. I swiveled around and found Marco calmly munching the purloined potato. He had on a khaki colored T-shirt, blue jeans, and his ever-present black boots, along with that spicy aftershave and a heavy dose of animal magnetism.

"Hey, Ms. Sunshine. How's the world's gloomiest flower girl?" He turned a chair opposite mine to straddle it.

"Angry. I got a parking ticket and I still had time left."

"Fight it."

"I did." I grabbed a chip and bit into it with a vengeance.

He tweaked my nose. "You're cute when you're irate."

I batted his hand aside, secretly flattered. "How would you be if you'd received an unjust ticket?"

"Not cute, that's for damn sure." He stole another chip and inserted it into that handsome mouth of his.

How could I stay angry under the force of such magnetism? "Are you here for lunch or did you just stop by to steal my food?" was my halfhearted attempt.

Marco picked out a curly chip and folded it neatly into his mouth. "I stopped by the station to have a chat with the boys in blue about your accident, but they got touchy when I started asking questions."

"How is that any different than usual?"

"You have a point. Anyway, they said it would be best if you just filed a claim with your insurance and let it go at that."

"Let it *go?* Well, they're not paying the premium!" I stabbed the air with a chip. "I smell something rotten."

"Maybe it's the turkey."

"I'm serious, Marco. Listen to this." I scooted my chair closer. "Detective Corbison phoned me this morning. When I called him back, I was told he had left suddenly on vacation."

Marco lifted a skeptical eyebrow. "They used the word *suddenly?*"

"They implied it." I shooed a fly away from my sandwich and ignored his snicker. "Anyway, it couldn't have been more than ten minutes between the time he phoned and I called him back."

"He could have stopped by the station to wrap up a few loose ends before he left for a trip—which could have been planned long before the murder. They should have told you that."

"Coulda, shoulda, woulda." I crossed my arms and sat back. I'd match my quips to Grace's any day. "I still say there's something fishy going on. I talked to Detective Williams, and he had no idea why Corbison had called me. This is a big crime, Marco. Shouldn't they be working together to solve it?"

"How do you know they're not?"

"Because Williams didn't know why Corbison had called me."

"You're getting yourself into a stew over nothing, sunshine. It takes time to work a case. Corbison will get back to you."

I took a breath and let it out. Marco was right. Besides, I had my own problems. "So where are we on the SUV investigation? You're not giving up on it, are you?"

"I never give up." In one smooth move, he nabbed the last chip from my fingers, popped it whole into his mouth, and rose. "I'll keep you posted," he said, and strode across the street toward Down the Hatch.

"Hey, what about your date with your friend at the DMV?" I called.

"Tonight," he replied over his shoulder.

I drummed my fingers on the table, part of my brain watching his well-formed backside, the other part busy thinking. What if Marco's hot date turned out to be a dud? What if she didn't come through with the information after all? Could I count on the police to find the culprit?

Grace always says, *If you want something done right, do it yourself.* It was one saying I totally believed. While Marco was wining and dining the girl from the DMV, I could be doing a little investigating of my own.

I started back toward the shop, pausing in the middle of Franklin to let a red pickup truck pass. As it drove by, the window rolled down, and a middle-aged, horse-faced farmer in a blue denim shirt, red suspenders, and red John Deere hat glared out at me.

"You're making a big mistake, bitch," he jeered.

I knew that face; I'd seen it on billboards. It was Tom Harding.

Someone behind him honked, causing him to issue a string of oaths and drive away, but not before he threw me one last menacing look. He didn't intimidate *me,* but I was very glad Dave had gotten Pearl a protective order.

When I walked into Bloomers, Grace was at the front counter, taking payment from a young couple buying a frothy fern. A gentleman stood behind them, waiting to pay for his purchase, two middle-aged ladies were admiring the floral wreaths on the opposite wall, and at least five people were sipping beverages in the parlor. We had customers!

I waited on the gentleman while Grace finished with the young couple. Then she handed me a stack of orders. "Eleven arrangements for Billy Ryan's funeral. The showing is tomorrow."

"Eleven!" I was so happy I threw my arms around her and gave her a big hug. Then I asked, "Who is Billy Ryan?"

"The young man who was murdered."

That sobered me. The victim now had a name—Billy. As we headed to the workroom I imagined a little boy with a missing front tooth and a sprinkle of freckles across his stubby nose, and then wondered how his life had ended so tragically. "Who's handling the viewing?"

"Happy Dreams. Lottie doesn't know yet. She took a late lunch to meet Herman."

Herman was Lottie's husband, an affable, teddy bear of a man whose heart had been impaired due to a congenital defect. Since his latest surgery, a quintuple bypass, his job was to keep house for Lottie and the quads—Jimmy, Joey, Johnny, and Karl. (Lottie had been too exhausted to think of any more *J* names by the time she'd pushed Karl out, so he was named after the brand of overhead light used in the delivery room.) Out of the four, Karl was the only one to give them headaches, but on the whole, the boys were polite and respectful. And they all held down jobs to help with household expenses.

"Herman had a coupon from Rosie's Diner for ten percent off any hamburger and fries platter," Grace explained.

"He can't eat greasy food."

"That's why Lottie went. She had to keep him honest."

"Then what's the point of going to Rosie's?"

"He had a coupon." Grace threw up her hands and went back to the shop, muttering, "I don't begin to understand you Yanks."

A coupon! That was what I could do to bring in more customers.

At three o'clock that afternoon the phone rang and Lottie reached for it, answering in her booming voice, "Bloomers."

She listened to the person on the other end, emitting a few choice words here and there, then finally held her hand over the mouthpiece and said quietly, "It's Pearl. She's scared half to death. Tom badgered her into admitting she filed for divorce and now he's calling her every five minutes, threatening to make life ugly for her and the boy if she goes ahead with it. What should she do?"

"Did she call the police?"

Lottie repeated my question into the phone, then shook her head at me.

"Okay, first, tell her the protective order forbids harassment of any type, including phone calls. Second, tell her she needs to alert the police immediately. Third, tell her to stop answering her phone. And fourth, tell her to call Dave so he can phone Tom's lawyer and threaten his client with arrest."

Lottie tried to give her the instructions, but Pearl was hysterical. Lottie covered the mouthpiece and said softly, "She thinks Tom is on his way over there. She's in a panic and wants me to come get her and Little Tommy. I'd send Herman, but he's gone for a stress test, and the boys are at work."

"Why don't you bring Pearl and Tommy here for the rest of the day?" I suggested.

Lottie repeated my offer to Pearl, assured her she'd be there within ten minutes, and hung up. "I hate to think what this is doing to Little Tommy. The kid has enough to deal with, what with all his handicaps. I still say that boy suffered brain damage *before* he was born, probably from when that brute Tom pushed Pearl over a wheelbarrow when she was four months along."

"Surely Tom wouldn't hurt his own son, would he?"

"It's hard to say." Lottie grabbed her purse and headed for the door. "All I know is Tom Harding is not a guy you'd want to mess with."

Half an hour later, I heard Grace call in a panic from the front of the shop, "Abby, come out here. Hurry!"

I jumped off the stool, dashed through the curtain, and followed Grace outside. Across the street, Pearl was backed up against Lottie's car, Harding was shaking his fist in her face, Lottie was tugging on his arm, and Little Tommy was huddled in the backseat, moaning and rocking, his arms crossed over his head.

"Call the police," I said to Grace, and raced across the street.

"Hey, moron!" I yelled to Harding, striding up to him, trying to draw his attention away from Pearl. "What do you think you're doing?"

He ignored me and snarled at Pearl, "Get that boy and get in the truck!"

I put my arm in front of her. "You can't order her around, Harding. She's got a protective order. The judge signed it this morning."

"You think I care? Pearl is *my* wife and I'm taking her and the boy home."

"They're not going anywhere with you."

"Abby, be careful!" Lottie warned, at the same moment that Harding shoved me aside so hard that I stumbled up over the curb and crashed against a tree trunk. Slightly dazed, I righted myself, rubbing my injured shoulder, and saw Harding grab Pearl's arm and drag her toward his truck. She didn't even fight him. All she did was whimper.

But I could fight him, and there was no way I was letting her get into that vehicle. Neither could I afford to wait for the police, so I ran after them, calling to the onlookers that had gathered, "Someone call 911!" which was more to scare Harding than anything else. I wrapped my arms around Pearl's waist and hung on, trying to pull her away from Harding. Lottie got behind me and the two of us pulled even harder. Grace joined the fray and began to take swipes at Harding's face with a fern frond, making him so furious he was foaming at the mouth, but he still wouldn't let his wife go.

I could feel Pearl start to go limp, and I said in her ear, "Hold on, Pearl."

"You bitches are crazy!" Harding bellowed, releasing his grip. We all fell back, Pearl landing on top of me, and me on Lottie, and Lottie on the curb. And before we could get up, there was Harding, right in Pearl's face again, his hand on her wrist.

"Get up and get into this goddamn truck!"

At that moment, a police motorcycle roared to a halt, and then Marco came racing across the street. The cop got off, and Harding instantly stepped back, holding his hands up, palm forward, as if to say, "It's not my fault. *They* started it."

I helped Pearl up, brushed off the seat of my pants, and said to the cop, "This woman has a restraining order, and that man is breaking it."

"I don't know anything about a restraining order!" Harding fairly spit out. "I was having a discussion with my wife and these bitches butted in."

"Do you have a restraining order, ma'am?" the unfazed cop asked Pearl.

I glanced at her, but she looked frozen. "She does," I told him. "She's too frightened of Mr. Harding to say so. The judge issued it today when she filed for divorce."

At that point Harding murmured something beneath his breath and stamped around to the driver's side of his truck.

"Hold it a minute," Motorcycle Cop called, and went after him.

I put my arm around Pearl and she sagged against me. Lottie took over and ushered her back to the shop, and Grace opened the back door of the car to help Little Tommy out.

"Are you all right?" Marco asked me, giving me a quick once-over.

"I'm fine, other than wanting to kick that man in the— Hey!" I called, as Harding drove off. I turned to the cop, who was getting on his cycle. "You're just going to let him go?"

"I gave him a warning."

"A *warning?* That's it? You're kidding, right?"

He glowered at me. "No, I'm not kidding. He hasn't even been served his papers yet."

"Yes, but I warned him about the order and he still pushed her around."

"Look, the guy just found out his wife is divorcing him. Sometimes they go a little nuts when they get news like that."

"Sometimes they go a little *nuts?* Would you be saying that if he'd *shot* her?"

"It's okay," Marco said, trying to calm me. "He didn't shoot her, and he's gone."

"For now. A lot of good the protective order did. Or the cops!" I added, giving Motorcycle Man a glare as he pulled away.

"Let me tell you something, sunshine," Marco said. "A protective order is only as good as the person it's served on. If he's decent and law-abiding, it works. Otherwise, it's just a piece of paper."

What a comfort.

When I got back to the shop, Little Tommy was in the parlor with Grace, contentedly eating scones, but back in the workroom Pearl was having a meltdown. Lottie and I took turns giving her pep talks to keep her from calling off the divorce, and finally calmed her down by assuring her that Herman and one of the quadruplets would stay at her house for the next few nights, just in case Harding tried anything else.

By the time we finished the funeral flowers and closed up shop, it was after six o'clock and I was drained. Dealing with Harding had taken its toll on my nerves. I couldn't begin to understand what kind of hell Pearl had gone through the last fifteen years. I opened the Escort's door and heat poured out from baking in the sun all afternoon. The interior was so hot to the touch I could barely hold the steering wheel. The engine turned over on the fourth attempt, and then the air conditioner would crank out only hot air, so by the time I got home, I was tired, sticky, hungry, and annoyed.

The answering machine was flashing, so I punched the

button and picked up a pen, ignoring Simon momentarily as he rubbed against my leg.

A disguised voice rasped harshly, "Mind your own business, bitch, or you'll be sorry."

I stabbed the Delete button, then picked up Simon and hugged him against me. It had to be Harding.

CHAPTER SEVEN

Having failed to gain my attention through conventional methods, Simon stood on his hind legs and patted my arm with a paw. It took several pats and finally a swipe to jerk my thoughts away from that ugly phone message.

"That was Harding's voice," I told Simon, as I swept him up in my arms. "Who else's business am I minding? Who else has such a vicious snarl? And believe me, Simon, he does have a vicious snarl. He didn't fool me by whispering."

In reply Simon butted my chin with his cold nose, which meant, *You think you've got problems? That crazy squirrel harassed me all day. Feed me.*

I was awake half the night fretting over that message. I wasn't too concerned about my own safety because I knew bullies liked to intimidate but rarely used force on anyone other than their immediate family. But I was concerned about Pearl and Little Tommy. Lottie's husband and sons couldn't be with them around the clock. If Harding wanted to hurt them, he could find a way.

The other half of my night was occupied by nightmares of Tom Harding chasing me down in a black SUV, and that annoyed me even more than the phone call. How dare he invade my dreams! But a good breakfast and an early power walk helped clear my head, so that by the time I got to the shop I was wide-awake and calm. Still, my first question when I stepped inside was, "How's Pearl?"

Lottie had arrived shortly before me and was sipping a cup of instant coffee. Grace wasn't there yet or Lottie would never have dared to tear open a packet of powdered java. "She's doing okay. Herman will be there all day today."

I sighed in relief. One worry off the list.

"Good morning, all!" Grace called from the front of the shop. Lottie immediately hustled back to the kitchen to gulp down the instant coffee and hide the evidence.

"How are we today?" Grace took a look at me and her eyes wrinkled in a sympathetic frown. "Didn't sleep well, dear?"

"How did you know?"

"Those telltale circles under your eyes."

I grabbed a shiny copper pot and peered at my reflection. Other than enlarging my pert nose, the pot didn't reveal any dark circles.

"Let's get the flowers down to the funeral home," Lottie said, emerging from the kitchen. "'Morning, Grace," she called, careful not to breathe coffee fumes on her. She picked up one of the shallow cardboard boxes loaded with arrangements and headed for the alley exit. She'd backed her old station wagon up to the door, so we slid the boxes in the back of the car and made the one-block trip down the alley and around the corner to the funeral home.

Maxwell and Delilah Dove owned Happy Dreams Funeral Home, a huge cream-colored Victorian clapboard house with dark green and light green trim and accents of mauve—a style commonly known as a painted lady. It had a reception area in front and a parlor on each side, running from the front to the back, joined by a small, common kitchen. A curving staircase at the right rear of the foyer led upstairs to the family's living area, which I'd heard was quite spacious. The basement was where the bodies were prepared.

The business had been in the Dove family for three generations and would undoubtedly be passed along to their only son, Daniel, who was still in college. Daniel worked at the funeral home during his summer breaks, whereas their daughter, Daisy, sold cosmetics in Chicago and wanted nothing to do with the family business. She swore it frightened away boyfriends.

Max held the door open while Lottie and I carried the flowers into parlor A. Max was a slightly built man with thinning brown hair, a narrow face, and a big, warm smile. He always wore a red bow tie and a three-piece suit. His wife, Delilah, was a petite, genteel Southern lady with a soft-spoken voice and impeccable manners. She and Max loved to bowl and were both in Grace's league.

While Max arranged the flowers, Delilah served us mint iced tea in the kitchen, something of a ritual for us. "Isn't it just dreadful about this murder?" she asked.

"My boys knew Billy Ryan from school," Lottie said, shaking her head.

"How are Billy's parents doing?" I asked Delilah.

"They're devastated. Billy was their only child. They were good parents, you know. Spent oodles of time with him, took him on a great vacation every summer, gave him every advantage, and still he got mixed up with a bad crowd. It just broke their hearts."

"They tried everything to get that boy off drugs," Max added, as he took a seat at the table. "Rehab, therapy, you name it. He'd straighten out for a while, and then those drug dealing friends of his would come sneaking around and he'd go right back on it."

Drug dealing friends. What every kid needs. I felt that

old burning in my stomach, the pain I always got when I remembered how my father had fought so hard to rid our community of the drug dealers that had been oozing in from Chicago. He believed that teens in New Chapel were easy targets for the wily dealers because they had too much free time and spending money with few parents at home to supervise. And the number of kids using drugs was growing as fast as New Chapel expanded.

Neither my brothers nor I had tried drugs. Our parents had insisted we have after-school jobs and household chores, and we were lectured constantly about the dangers of drug use. On top of that they watched us like hawks. But the truth was that our father had put his life on the line so that we wouldn't have to face those dangers, and *that's* what had really kept us away.

I thought about the dead boy and the battle his parents had fought to keep him from harm and wondered what else they could have done for him. The drug dealers had won again.

But maybe not all of them—not if one happened to be my hit-and-run driver. If I could find the driver and connect him to the murder, maybe I could score one for the good guys, especially for my father.

"You all right, sweetie?" Lottie asked, patting my arm. She knew how the subject bothered me.

"I'm fine. Thanks, Lottie." To Max I said, "Did the parents say anything to you about who they think might have shot their son?"

"Not to me. How about you, Mommy?"

"Not to me either," Delilah replied with a sigh. She collected our glasses and took them to the sink. "We'd better get busy, Daddy. We've got only a few hours before the viewing."

My ears perked up. "What time is the viewing?" I asked Max.

"Four o'clock."

The parents would most likely arrive around three

thirty. I'd have to make sure I had more flowers to deliver, even if I had to donate them. I couldn't pass up an opportunity to talk to the Ryans.

After a quick lunch at the deli, I started back toward the shop, then glanced at the blue Escort parked near Down the Hatch and spotted another rectangle of paper fluttering from beneath one wiper blade. Muttering under my breath, I marched down to the car and snatched it out. My crime this time: parking too far from the curb.

"Afternoon, sunshine. Get another ticket?"

I looked around at Marco, who was coming out of his bar, and flapped the yellow paper at him. "Have you ever heard of such a ridiculous charge?"

He looked at the ticket, then walked completely around the Escort to have a look. "Stay right there." He disappeared inside for a few moments and returned with a Polaroid camera and the front page of our local newspaper, the *New Chapel News*. He had me stand beside the car holding the paper and his bold-faced watch. Then he crouched in front and took a close-up. He took another shot from the rear and another from the sidewalk. "Now you have evidence," he said, handing me the photos. "Appeal it."

I squinted at the blurry copy. "I can't make out the name on the ticket."

"Doesn't matter. They'll figure it out."

"Why is this happening? Am I being targeted?"

"Nah! Just an overzealous parking cop. Probably a trainee."

I was on the verge of telling him about Harding's threat when I remembered I didn't like women who whined. Dave Hammond had a good philosophy about whining: Either do something about the problem or shut up. So I changed the topic. "How did your date go last night?"

The corner of Marco's mouth lifted in a half grin. "Very well."

Why did that make me jealous? I reminded the green-
eyed she monster inside my brain that I wasn't interested
in Marco and gave her a sharp kick in the ribs for good
measure. "What did you find out?"

"Nothing yet." He glanced at his watch. "But the day
is still young."

And so was his DMV date, I was betting. *Meow.*

The same traffic clerk came to the window to greet me.
"Can I help you?" she asked in a tone that said she'd
rather not.

I passed the ticket to her along with the photos. "As
you can see, I wasn't parked far from the curb. I was almost on *top* of the curb."

"All I know is what it says on the ticket," she droned
in a monotone.

"What's the regulation?"

She sighed heavily and reached for a thick green book.
After running a one-inch fuschia fingernail down the
index, she turned to a page and read, "One foot."

"Look at these pictures. There is no way I was parked
more than a foot away!"

"You gonna pay this or not?"

"Not." I snatched one of the photos, turned, and
marched out. Let them come after me. I welcomed the
fight.

As I was leaving, I met Dave Hammond on his way to
court and decided to walk with him to the fourth floor
courtroom.

Dave was a great lawyer and an even greater human
being. A short, pudgy man in his late fifties, he had a keen
mind, refused to charge by the billable nanosecond, loved
to skewer insurance companies, and made minced meat
out of sleazy attorneys who hadn't done their homework.
His only failing was that he had a hard time collecting his
fees. His clients would promise to pay him on payday and
then they would disappear.

As a result, Dave hadn't made a lot of money over the course of his twenty-five-year career. He wore cheap suits, lived with his wife in the same small bungalow where they'd raised three daughters, and drove a 1995 Honda with two hundred thousand miles on it.

"What do you think of Pearl Harding's case?" I asked.

"It's going to be a tough one. Her husband hired Sol Feinberg."

Ouch. Feinberg was known as the *pit bull* in legal circles. He would do anything to win a case, legally or otherwise.

"I've sent subpoenas to the banks in town to see what kind of assets Harding has," Dave told me, "but my guess is that he's already hidden everything. In the meantime, we have an emergency provisional hearing set for next Tuesday. That will get her some temporary funds, at least."

We stopped outside the judge's chambers. "Have you ever been out to Harding's landscape center?" I asked.

"No, but I've heard about it."

"He has a lot of money, Dave. That place is always busy."

"I'm sure you're right. It's just a matter of finding those accounts." He glanced at his watch and grimaced. "I've got to run, Abby. Thanks for referring the case."

"If you need any help, let me know."

He winked at me and went inside.

Nine more orders for funeral flowers came in during lunch. Nine! I would have shown more excitement, but I didn't think it was proper under the circumstances. Lottie and I finished them in record time and brought them down to Happy Dreams by three thirty. There was no time for iced tea this time. Max and Delilah were ready for the viewing.

"I'm going to stay a bit," I told Lottie, seeing Billy Ryan's parents pull up.

I waited in the foyer while the Ryans met in parlor A with Max. I had serious qualms about intruding during their burial proceedings, but I wanted to help them, and I wasn't sure how receptive they'd be to my questions if I showed up at their door. At least this way I had a reason for being here. Time was another factor in my decision. I'd seen too many TV shows not to know that the murder trail could get cold quickly.

Both parents emerged red eyed. Mrs. Ryan had tissues balled up in each fist. Mr. Ryan, his jaw set firmly, had an arm around her shoulders, as though afraid she would collapse at any moment. For me it was a flashback, and suddenly I was in the hospital waiting room, watching my brothers help my mother over to a sofa after the doctor had given her the news about my dad's condition. I remembered wanting to curl up into a ball and drop into the nearest hole, and at the same time, wanting to get my dad's police revolver and go find myself a few drug dealers.

I took a deep breath and barreled straight over to the Ryans to introduce myself and offer my condolences. Then I told them about the hit-and-run and the possibility of a connection to their son's murder. The news of this new suspect seemed to take them by surprise, which didn't make them very happy with the police.

"Does the description of the man I saw sound familiar at all?" I asked.

Mrs. Ryan shook her head, her chin trembling as she fought back tears. "We don't know who Billy was associating with. He cut off his ties with us because he—"

She turned her head away as she began to cry, so Mr. Ryan finished for her. "He didn't want us to know whom he was associating with because of their drug connections. He had a bad cocaine habit."

"I'm so sorry. I know this is painful for you, but I want to help you find Billy's killer. Would you mind answering a few questions?"

Mr. Ryan gazed at me skeptically. "Why do you want to help us?"

"My father was a cop. He was shot by a drug dealer and now he's paralyzed, so it's an issue with me. Was Billy going to school?"

"He dropped out after his first semester of college," Mr. Ryan replied. "Then we sent him to a new rehab facility for a month's stay, and when he came out he said he had a job and could support himself. He moved out of the house a few weeks ago. We hadn't seen him since."

"Where did Billy work?"

"Tom's Green Thumb," Mr. Ryan answered.

I shouldn't have been surprised; Tom's Green Thumb was a popular place for kids to work. I'd have to check it out. Someone there was bound to know something about Billy.

Mrs. Ryan wiped her eyes and said in a choked, bitter voice, "Billy wasn't a bad boy. It was those delinquents he hung out with. *They* got him hooked. Why aren't *they* dead? Why couldn't it have been them instead of Billy? Do you know he never forgot my birthday? Or his dad's? I just don't understand. Why Billy? Why would someone want to kill him?"

Mr. Ryan hugged her as she sobbed anew. "It's okay, hon. The police will find the son of a bitch who did this and punish him."

Good luck, I wanted to tell them. I watched him console her, putting up a brave front for her, and my heart ached for them both. "I'll do whatever I can to help," I promised, my own voice hoarse and tight.

Mrs. Ryan reached for my hands. "Billy was my only child. I loved him more than I can say, but I couldn't help him. I hope you can."

"It's time," Max said gently from the doorway. The Ryans looked at each other, as though gathering strength, then followed him inside, hand in hand, to take their place in front of their child's coffin. I knew only a fraction of the

pain they were suffering, and it made me more determined than ever to help them find that killer.

Sniffling back my own tears, I left as the first wave of
mourners came up the front walk. I made a quick detour
to Down the Hatch to tell Marco what I'd learned, but
he'd gone on an errand, so I scratched out a note for him
to call me and went back to the shop.

That evening, I was stretched out on the sofa reading a
book on Oriental flower arranging when Simon leaped
onto my stomach and dropped a well-chewed plastic
straw on my neck. After I'd regained my breath I plucked
the wet straw off my skin and tossed it toward the doorway, where it skittered down the hall with the cat close
behind.

Knowing this was the beginning of a long game—we
always played until Simon grew tired of it—I sat up and
closed the book. "Okay, Simon. Bring it on."

With kittenlike glee he galloped across the room and
hurled himself onto the sofa, straw clamped between his
jaws. He had just relinquished it to me when suddenly his
body tensed and his ears perked as he aimed his wide-
eyed gaze at the hallway.

Simon had a sixth sense about things. He knew when
Nikki was home before she pulled into the parking lot.
He knew when my mother was coming and hid under the
bed. He had even known when Pryce was on his way
over. He'd run to the kitchen and gobble dry food so he'd
have plenty to puke up on Pryce's Ferragamo shoes.

Now Simon made a low growling noise as he focused
on something I could neither see nor hear. This was not
his normal response to a visitor, and my heart sped up ac-
cordingly. I tiptoed to the doorway and peered around the
corner, where I had a clear view of the front door and the
back fire escape. Both were closed. I moved to the eye-
hole in the front door and peered out. The hall outside
was empty.

Feeling a bit more secure, I did a quick search of the apartment. As I cupped my hands to see through the fire escape window, Simon began to sniff along the bottom of the front door, and then to howl. I peered out the peephole once again, yet still saw no one. But Simon's persistent howling unnerved me enough that I grabbed the pepper spray from my purse and slowly opened the door, using my foot to hold back the cat.

On the hall carpet lay a dead rat, its neck twisted as only human hands could do.

Someone had sent me a message.

CHAPTER EIGHT

Shuddering hard, I shut the door and leaned against it. The rat was clearly meant as a threat, and my guess was that Tom Harding had left it. I scooped up Simon to get him away from the door and sat down on the chair to think, stroking his velvety fur as my mind raced. Was I in danger? Should I call the police?

I was sitting in that same position when Nikki came home, although Simon had deserted me.

"Omigod, omigod!" she shrieked from the outside hallway. The door opened and slammed shut. "Abby?"

"In here."

"There's a dead rat in front of our door!"

"I know," I answered in a flat voice.

She peered into the living room, took one look at me, and ran for the kitchen. "I'll get the wine."

We sat huddled on the sofa, sipping red wine, as I told her about Pearl Harding and her nasty husband. Nikki wanted me to call the police, but I kept imagining a cop scratching his head and saying, "What are we supposed to do, fingerprint the rat?"

Speaking of rats, that creature was still lying outside. I donned my yellow rubber kitchen gloves, grabbed a paper bag, and cautiously opened the front door. Finding the hallway clear, I picked up the rodent by the tail, dropped it in the bag and, with a shudder, sent the whole works, gloves and all, down the garbage chute in the hall trash room.

"So what are we going to do?" Nikki wanted to know.

"I'll call Marco and see what he says. Personally, I think Tom Harding is one of those guys who likes to bully those he knows he can push around. Once he learns he can't bully me, he'll back off." At least I hoped so. I swallowed the last of my wine and rinsed the glass. "Thanks for listening, Nik. I'm going to bed."

"And in return for listening?"

I paused at the doorway to give her a cautious glance. "What?"

"You have to help me with my party."

"What party?"

"Remember that ingenious idea you had about inviting Dr. Gorgeous to a party? Well, guess what? He accepted—with his wife. *That* party."

I phoned Marco, but he didn't answer, so I left a brief message telling him I needed advice. I didn't sleep well that night, and got up so early that it was dark when I hit the track. The air was heavy and still, as though a storm was coming in, and smelled of worms and wet grass. For the first time I didn't feel safe there, and kept looking over my shoulder, expecting to see a dark shape spring out of the trees. At least I had my pepper spray clipped to my waistband.

I arrived at the shop well before Grace or Lottie, so I went to the kitchen to make instant coffee. I didn't mess with Grace's beans. As I sipped the brew, I heard one of them come in. "I'm in the kitchen," I called. I rinsed my spoon and turned, then jumped three feet straight up.

Marco leaned against the doorjamb, arms folded over his chest. He had on a blue T-shirt, jeans, and black boots, and though he was clean shaven, he still had the swarthy air of a pirate.

"Salvare, you idiot! Are you trying to scare me to death? Don't ever do that again."

"Don't leave your door unlocked when you're here alone. It's not safe."

"Not with creeps like you hanging around."

"Got an extra cup?"

Scowling at him, I took a spare mug from the cabinet, added hot water, and stirred in a spoonful of instant granules. "You don't get any sugar."

"I don't need any sugar."

We stood nearly toe to toe, he towering above me so that I had to crank my neck back, yet standing close enough that I could see gold flecks in his eyes. I felt my pulse quicken and stepped around him. He had way too much animal magnetism for so early in the day.

"You left me a message to call you," he said, following me into the workroom. He slid onto a stool beside me just as Grace arrived.

"Good morning," she called in her usual singsong voice, poking her head through the curtain. "How are we to—" She stopped and frowned.

"'Morning," he said with a friendly nod.

Grace returned the nod, along with a warning glare. "I'll be right outside if you need me, Abby." She pulled open the curtains.

"You'll never need to hire a bodyguard with her around," Marco noted.

"Not at the shop anyway."

He lifted an eyebrow. "And that is supposed to mean . . . ?"

"Someone left me a present on my doorstep last night: a dead rat with its neck broken."

Marco grew very still. "Any note with it?"

"Nothing."

"Any idea who it might be? Old boyfriend? Irate customer?"

"I gave a woman some advice about divorcing her husband, and he's not taking it too well. Also, he's the abusive type."

"What kind of locks do you have on your door?"

"Standard key lock and a chain."

"Not good enough. The lock can be picked and the chain is easy to break. Install a dead bolt."

He was dead serious, and that frightened me more than the presence of the rat. Did he suspect that Harding, or whoever left the creature, might come back to wring *my* neck?

"Did you call the police about the rat?" he asked.

I shrugged. "What's the point?"

"The point, Miss Not-Quite-an-Attorney, is to get it on record so when you find out who's behind it, you can file harassment charges."

"How did you know I went to law school?"

"I heard it at the bar."

"People are talking about me?" I wasn't sure whether to be flattered or indignant.

"People talk about everything and everyone at a bar."

I leaned on my elbows and stared into those gorgeous, sexy eyes. "What else did you learn about me?"

He leaned even closer, his aftershave enveloping me in a cloud of raw male sensuality, turning my insides to jelly. Just when I was about to melt down the sides of the stool, he tweaked my nose. "That you're an inveterate busybody."

I straightened with a huff. "That's totally wrong. I just like to help people. And what about you, Mr. Salvare? Did your hot date ever pan out?"

"You'll get your information, don't worry. I'm a man of my word." He unfolded those long, lean legs and started for the door, pausing to say, "Get that lock."

I had to stick my face in the cooler to chill down. Marco Salvare was a man of his word, all right. *All* man.

Grace came up behind me. "Abby, did I hear correctly?

There was a dead rat at your door? Why are you standing inside the cooler?"

"Just doing a spot inventory," I replied, stepping out. "Not only was there a dead rat, but I also got a nasty telephone message. And we're low on daisies."

"I was afraid something like that would happen."

"Running out of daisies?"

Grace opened the phone book on my desk and began thumbing through the yellow pages. "I'm going to have an alarm system installed. I've been wanting to get one since we opened. It'll be my treat."

"The rat happened at home, Grace. We're not in danger *here.*"

"Do you know that for certain?"

Point taken. "Anyway, I can't let you pay for it."

"I work here, too, don't I? Besides, I know someone who will give us a good deal. I'll have him give you a price for your apartment, as well."

I gazed at Grace in awe as she pecked out a number on the phone. Marco was right. Grace was as good as any bodyguard.

Justin, bless his simple little heart, fixed my Corvette in record time, no doubt due to some prodding from Aunt Lottie. I skipped lunch to get my banana beauty, wincing as I counted out those precious twenties I'd pulled from the ATM, then took the Vette for a test run.

The air was still heavy with impending rain, but the sun was bright as I left the town behind. I turned off the highway to zip along a country road that stretched out in front of me like gray satin ribbon, passing corn rows and wheat fields and acres of soybeans, sighing blissfully at the feel of the steering wheel in my hands. For some reason I do my best thinking when I'm driving, as if the freedom of the open road also frees my thoughts.

Ahead, a farmer in a big tractor pulled out onto the

road and lumbered along, forcing me to a crawl behind him. I did a three-point turn and headed back to town, and as I did, my thoughts turned to Billy Ryan's murder. I wished I knew how the investigation was going. The article in the newspaper that morning had said only that Elvis Jones had thus far managed to elude police. There was still no mention of another suspect. I'd have to pay a visit to Greg Morgan to see if he knew more.

As I turned back onto the highway, I noticed that a dark cloud had billowed up from the west. Before I could get back to town, the skies opened up. I pulled off the pavement, unlatched the top, and lifted it over my head, but not before I got a good drenching.

Muttering curses, I put on my turn signal to get back on the road, squinting through the downpour to see if other cars were coming. Suddenly, headlights loomed out of the grayness coming straight at me. My stomach clenched as I threw the car into Reverse, jammed my foot on the pedal, and backed up, spinning my tires in the gravel, and nearly backing off the shoulder in the process. The car, big and dark colored, swerved off the road exactly where my car had been seconds before, and came to a stop.

I sat there for a moment, heart thundering beneath my ribs, wondering if the other driver had taken ill. A City Gas and Electric truck pulled alongside me, and the driver rolled down his window. "Everything all right?" he shouted through the rain.

I cracked my window to call, "I'm okay. I'm not sure about the other guy."

At once, the dark car took off with a squeal of tires. "I guess he's all right," the City worker called.

I thanked him for stopping, and he touched his fingers to his forehead and drove away. I sat for a moment to let my heart resume its normal pace, then carefully pulled onto the road and headed into town, assuring myself that it had been nothing more than a freak occurrence.

To think otherwise was to believe someone was out to hurt me.

Grace and Lottie took one look at my soggy locks and rain-darkened blouse, and said in unison, "You have your car back!"

I was on the verge of telling them about my near accident, but I knew from experience that they would worry me to death with it, and I was doing enough of that on my own. I dropped my purse on the desk and ran my fingers through my hair. "Your nephew is a wonder, Lottie."

"Can't spell his own name," she said with a laugh, "but he sure can fix a car."

"I should run home to change clothes. How much work do we have?"

"Eight arrangements to finish by five o'clock," Lottie told me. "Another funeral at Happy Dreams."

Eight arrangements meant eight payments and that was fantastic news, but I could scratch going home to change. I'd just have to stay out of the cooler.

"I'll pop down to the drugstore and buy a travel-sized hair dryer," Grace volunteered. "We should have one here for emergencies anyway."

"Take money from the business account."

"No, dear, not for a twenty-dollar dryer." She opened the door and left.

"How is Pearl?" I asked Lottie, settling on a stool while I waited for Grace's return.

"Sick with worry. We moved her and Little Tommy into our house so she'd feel safer."

I knew that would be a squeeze. Lottie and Herman lived in a very old two-story house near the town square. It had three small bedrooms—two upstairs and one down—two tiny bathrooms, a farm-style kitchen, and a front parlor. It had bundles of charm, but not much room.

"Has Harding given her any money yet?"

"Not a dime. And Dave hasn't had any luck finding Tom's bank accounts. Pearl says Tom goes up to Michigan every Saturday, so he could be banking his money there."

"He doesn't own a big, dark-colored car, does he?"

Lottie shrugged. "I've never seen one at their house. Why?"

"Just curious. Do you know where he goes in Michigan?"

"No, but someone at the greenhouse might have an answer."

That greenhouse kept popping up in conversation. "I think I may have to drop by Tom's Green Thumb and see what I can find out."

Lottie frowned. "Just be careful, sweetie. Tom may look like a simple farmer, but he's got a mind like a mean ol' bear trap, and I don't want you getting caught in those sharp teeth."

I was in the bathroom repairing my frizzed hair when I heard a familiar, "Yoo-hoo! Abigail!"

My mother had arrived.

Maureen Barnett Knight—Mo to her friends—popped around the corner a few seconds later, dressed in black slacks and a colorful print shirt, her trim, size-six body a model of what middle age should look like, her light brown hair swept up in a loose bun and clipped with a strange-looking pin, probably of her own creation.

"Your blouse is damp, Abigail. Did you get caught in the rain?" She turned me around to take a look. Tsk-tsking, she grabbed a tissue, spit on it, and tried to dab it under my eyes.

"Mother!" I said, dodging her hand. "Yuck."

"What? You have mascara under your eyes."

After I'd wiped the smudges off with my fingers, she took my arm and led me to the workroom, where she sat me on a stool and ordered me to cover my eyes. "All right, Lottie, put it on the table," she commanded.

I heard a loud thunk, and then my mother said, "Open your eyes, Abigail."

I blinked at the brightness that greeted me. It was a—thing.

"Well?" she asked breathlessly, her voice quivering with excitement.

The *thing* was two feet tall, a glossy neon green, partly cylindrical, and caved in on one side, as though someone had karate chopped its midsection. There was a bright orange spout-like lip on the upper opening and another spout, lemon yellow in color, on the other side about one-third of the way down. I turned it and sure enough, closer to the bottom there was yet another spout, hot pink this time.

I knew one thing for sure: It wasn't a pitcher.

I glanced at Lottie to get her reaction, but she had conveniently slipped into the cooler.

"It's—stunning," I replied.

"How much should I ask for it?"

Someone please shoot me. Over my mother's shoulder I saw Lottie, who had stepped out in time to hear the question, laughing in hysterical silence, both hands clapped over her mouth.

"I'm not sure," I said at last. "What do other such—objects—go for?"

"You would know that better than I, Abigail." My mother admired it for a few more moments, then turned to give me a big smile. "I've got to run. See you tomorrow evening at the club. And don't forget to figure the cost of the ivies to put in it," she called over her shoulder.

Ivies?

Ha! I had it.

"I give up," Lottie whispered, in case my mother was still within earshot. "What is it?"

I held it up and turned it around so she could get a better view. "A strawberry pot. Or, in this case, an ivy pot."

Lottie laughed so hard tears rolled down her cheeks. Her peals brought Grace in.

"Oh, good heavens!" Grace exclaimed in horror as she beheld the pot.

"Price?" I asked them.

Grace just shuddered.

"How much would an ordinary—strawberry pot—go for?" Lottie asked, trying to arrange her face.

I had a sudden brainstorm. "Maybe I should run out to Tom's Green Thumb after work and find out."

Tom's Green Thumb was located at the southern edge of town on a busy county highway. The enormous greenhouse hunkered in the middle of a giant outdoor garden filled with blooming plants, with several acres of land devoted to trees and shrubs.

I parked in the gravel lot in front and walked to the double automatic doors, which whooshed open to let me into the main building. The greenhouse had a high glass ceiling and wide aisles that led through rows of every possible type of plant and seedling—flower, herb, or vegetable.

I had two main objectives: to speak to someone who knew Billy Ryan and to find out what bank Harding's business used. I decided to tackle the Ryan question first. I wandered down a few aisles, stopping to sniff lemon balm and pinch a peppermint leaf, waiting for a young male employee to happen by. The only one I spotted was carrying boxes from what appeared to be a stockroom at the back of the greenhouse to a room off the side that held a collection of pots, small fountains, tools, boxed fertilizers, and anything else a home gardener could need.

As soon as he left, I aimed myself at the side room to wait for his return, figuring it was my best bet for talking to him privately. I trolled the aisles and spotted a good-sized clay strawberry pot priced at forty-five dollars. Would anyone pay that much for a Maureen Knight exclusive? Fat chance.

The boy returned, and I found him in the next aisle unloading a box of beetle spray. He was tall and gangly and sported six tiny silver ear hoops along each lobe and one shiny lip ring.

I tapped him on the arm. "Excuse me, do you carry strawberry pots?"

He stopped and gave me a blank look, so I described what I already knew they had. He led me back to the strawberry pots and started to walk away.

"Hey, that's really sad about Billy," I said.

He turned around, his pale eyebrows drawn together. "Billy?"

"Billy Ryan."

"Oh, right. You mean Will. Yeah, he was cool."

I followed him back to the half-unloaded box. "Did you go to school with Will?" I asked in an offhand manner, pretending to examine a can of repellant.

"Nope. I met him here."

"Did he have a lot of friends here?"

The kid shrugged. "Not really. He and Buzz used to hang out, though."

"Buzz?"

"He's the store manager."

"Ah. The head cheese."

"The what?"

"Chief honcho."

Another blank look. My attempt at talking his language wasn't working. Had I been out of high school that long? I gave it another try. "The man."

"Nah! Buzz is just the boss. Mr. Harding—now *he's* the man."

"Got it." I swiveled to look around the room. "This place must be a gold mine for Mr. Harding. I'll bet he owns some pricey wheels."

The kid stared at me.

"Expensive cars," I clarified.

He snorted. "Pricey wheels. I like that."

"What kind of wheels does he drive—if you know?"

He finished unloading his carton. "I don't know if I should be talking to you about Mr. Harding's cars."

"You're right. Sorry. I have a thing for cars. Got a Vette, myself."

"Dude! What year?"

"Sixty, with a ragtop."

He snorted again, but this time with new respect. "Way cool."

"Daryl!"

I turned toward the doorway, where a medium-sized, burly bodied man stood glowering at Daryl. He looked to be around thirty years old, with bulging biceps and a closely shaved head, the light brown hair cut flat across the top—or maybe that was the shape of his skull.

"Hey, man, what the hell are you doing? We've got a truck to unload."

I was betting this was Buzz. If so, then he was the guy I needed to question.

"Dude, I'm coming," Daryl called. Then, as he hoisted the empty box to his shoulder, he said to me in an undertone, "I gotta get going."

I racked my brain for something I hadn't seen in the room, something for which he would have to check with Buzz. "One quick question, Daryl. Do you have any espaliers?"

He tugged at his lip ring, torn between his duty to assist me and wanting to please his boss. "Let me find out," he finally said and shuffled away, muttering to Buzz as he passed, "The lady needs help."

Lady? Not girl? I *had* been out of high school a long time.

Buzz swaggered toward me, giving me a very slow once-over. "Tell me what I can do to make your day," he said, leering at me.

How about sticking your finger in an electric socket? I gave him a bright smile. "Tell me you have espaliers."

His smile faded. "Sorry. All out."

As if he knew what they were! I sighed dramatically. "I was hoping to surprise my friend. She's in serious need of cheering up. She just lost her son. . . . You probably knew him. He worked here. Will Ryan."

Buzz screwed up his face. "Yeah, I knew him. A shame what happened, huh?"

"Quite a shame. The funeral is tomorrow. I suppose some of your employees will be attending."

Buzz studied his right biceps, flexing and stretching the muscle. "Beats me. I don't associate with the kids. It's my personal policy."

Either he was lying, or Daryl was. I stepped closer, watching for a betraying twitch or shift of the eyes. "So you never associated with Will?"

"Nope."

"You never even had a conversation with him?"

Buzz scratched his chest, as though uncomfortable. "I didn't say that. Look, what are you, a cop?"

"Me?" I said, forcing a laugh. "I was just curious."

His eyes narrowed into pinpricks of distrust. "I think you'd better leave."

I was thinking the same thing myself. "No problem," I said lightly. "Sorry to bother you."

I tucked the pot under my arm and walked away. Buzz followed me all the way to the checkout counters, then veered off and headed for a door marked PRIVATE on the side wall, no doubt Harding's office.

There were six cashier stations along the front of the store. I picked the one farthest from the office door, then waited my turn behind three customers while trying to decide how best to get the cashier to reveal the name of the store's bank.

Suddenly, over the store's intercom I heard, "Mr. Harding, would you come to station five, please?"

Tom Harding was in the building.

Panicked, I glanced around as a big, horse-faced man in a blue shirt and red suspenders stepped out of the door. Ducking my head, I tried to blend into the crowd, but my red hair tended to stand out like a beacon. I peeked over my shoulder and locked eyes with *the man* himself. Harding's face contorted and, like a charging bull, he made straight for me.

Every nerve in my body screamed for me to run. But that would have been cowardly, and just what a bully would have loved. So I decided to stand my ground—and hoped I lived to tell about it.

CHAPTER NINE

My knees shook so hard I thought they might crumple under me. I put the strawberry pot down on the floor and turned to face him, putting on the biggest act of bravado of my life.

"You!" he bellowed from about ten feet away, startling the customers around me. They all parted to let the big man through. "Get the hell out of my store!"

"It's a free country," I retorted, but as he descended upon me, I decided it might be wise to get out of his way anyway. Unfortunately, someone had set a rosebush on the floor behind me and, as I stepped back, my heel struck it and I lost my balance. My arms windmilled as I fell. I tipped over the rose and landed hard on my seat.

Harding's face turned an ugly purple as he stood directly over me. "This here's *my* property," he shouted, spittle flying, "and I want your ass off it now or I'll throw it off."

I glanced up at his large, heavy hands clenching and unclenching at his sides, then up at his angry face, and I didn't doubt for a moment that he'd pick me up and heave me through the glass doors. I also doubted the threat of a civil suit would stop him.

"I was just about to leave anyway," I said, scrambling shakily to my feet and brushing off my backside. "There's no need to be rude." I left the strawberry pot where I'd set it and tried to stride casually toward the door without betraying my quivering legs. Once there I turned to call back, "I wouldn't buy anything here, anyway. Not with that ugly fungus on your plants."

Seeing the horrified looks on the customers' faces, I turned with a satisfied smile and marched to my car, making sure to lock the doors as soon as I was inside.

All in all, my mission was not a success.

That evening, I was on the floor wrestling Simon to the carpet so I could wash something sticky out of his fur—he liked to tip over the garbage can and see what rolled out—when his ears perked forward and he stared in the direction of the front door. My heart began to thud anxiously as visions of Harding returning to wring my neck flashed through my brain. I let Simon go and crawled across the room to reach my purse on a small table in the hall. Then, armed with pepper spray, I peered out the peephole just as a shadowy figure moved across my line of vision.

Quickly, I flung open the door with a loud karate yell and aimed the spray.

"Hey!" Marco yelled, grabbing my wrist and jerking it up over my head. "Watch it!"

"Damn it, Salvare! Why didn't you knock?"

He released his hold. "I was just about to. Damn, woman! You nearly sprayed me."

"Serves you right for scaring me."

Marco followed me inside and locked the door behind him. Dressed in black from neck to toe, and sporting quite a dashing five o'clock shadow, he looked dangerous and sexy. He bent down to stroke Simon, who was rubbing against his leg and purring loudly. This was the cat that hated men. "Where's your new dead bolt?"

"I'll pick it up on Saturday. And just so you know, Grace is pricing an alarm system for me."

He took in my mint green T-shirt and denim shorts. "What are you doing tonight?"

"Obviously not going to a ball. Why?"

"I got a name and address on the SUV, and I want to make sure it's accurate. I thought you might want to keep me company on a stakeout."

Alone in a dark car for hours with Marco?

"Give me a minute to change," I called as I dashed for my room.

"Who's Nikki?" he called back, obviously looking at the framed photos on the end table.

"My roommate."

"She's cute. Single?"

"Yes. Why do you want to know?" And why was I jealous again?

"I'm conducting a survey," he said dryly.

I emerged wearing black jeans, a black T-shirt, and a black baseball cap, with my red hair tucked safely away. "Very clever. Why really?"

He put back a photo of Nikki and me taken at Christmas. "I'm an investigator, remember? It's just something I ask."

Like I believed that line. "For future reference," I told him, "Nikki has her sights set on a doctor."

His eyes crinkled at the corners as if he found me amusing. I huffed to the kitchen, grabbed two bottles of Splash and my bag and met him at the front door.

"Friendly cat," he said, giving Simon one last scratch under the chin. Simon gave me a smug look.

"You," I said, pointing at Simon, "have a date with a bath."

He sashayed away with a disdainful sniff. Simon preferred to do his own bathing.

Marco had parked a tan Jeep in the alley behind the building. I climbed in beside him, buckled myself in, and sat back. "Nice vehicle. Where are we going?"

"Commissioner Vertucci's house."

I nearly choked. Louis Vertucci was one of five county commissioners, a big shot with a big ego and a mouth to match. "*His* SUV hit me?"

"Could be. I've got two possibilities."

"But the guy I saw was young."

"That doesn't mean Vertucci couldn't have bought the vehicle for a family member."

"Does he have sons?"

"A nephew—who just happens to be staying with him. Let's go see if we can rule him out."

We took the highway north toward Lake Michigan, then exited onto a road that dipped and climbed through a forest of ancient hardwood trees, leading into a neighborhood of expensive homes bordering the Indiana Dunes. Most homes were hidden from the road, with only their roofs visible. We drove past one such house, with four chimneys jutting from a steep slate roof and a black Cadillac parked at the top of the long brick driveway.

"Here we go," Marco said, backing up. He parked on the shoulder and turned off the motor and lights. "Now we wait to see who comes out."

"He owns a black Caddy," I pointed out. "I probably should have mentioned that I was almost the victim of a hit-and-run by a big black car the other day."

I could see Marco's eyes narrow in the darkness. "Yeah, you probably should have."

"I'm sure it was just a freak accident."

"Did you get a look at the driver?"

"It was pouring rain. Like I said, just a freak accident." I hoped.

We sat in silence for a good fifteen minutes, until I felt compelled to make conversation. "So," I said slowly, "you were a cop."

He grunted.

This wasn't the conversation opener I'd hoped it would be. "Did you go to college?"

"Indiana U."

This was surprising news. I'd figured him to be the straight-from-high-school-onto-the-force kind of guy. "What did you major in?"

"Political science."

"No kidding?" At last, something to discuss. "Did you want to be a lawyer?"

He laughed. "Hell, no."

"Then why did you major in poli sci?"

"I wanted to be a political scientist." One corner of his mouth curved up.

"Very funny." I pulled out the bottles of Splash and offered him one.

"No, thanks. Don't want to fill the bladder." His gaze suddenly shifted toward the house. "Get down," he whispered.

We scooted down in our seats. I heard the sound of a motor starting, then of a car coming toward us. I started to raise my head, but Marco pushed it back down. After several long moments, he lifted his head and looked out the back window.

"It was the Cadillac," he said, straightening.

"Shouldn't we follow it?"

"Why? We're looking for the SUV."

We sat quietly for several more minutes, but nobody else came out. Marco pulled out a pack of peppermint gum and offered me a stick. As I unwrapped a piece, he stuck one in his mouth, put the pack in his chest pocket, and leaned against his door, studying me. "Is your brother the heart doctor?"

"My oldest brother, yes."

"My old man was his patient."

"Was?"

"He had a heart attack during surgery and died."

Great! I was sitting in the dark on a fairly deserted road

with the son of a man my brother had killed on the operating table. "I'm sorry," I muttered, sinking down in my seat.

"He smoked three packs a day. What did he expect?"

"Probably not to die."

"Yeah. Well, no one expects that."

"How old were you?" I asked.

"Twenty-three. I'd just finished a stint in the army."

I was gaining a whole new image of Marco Salvare. "So you were a soldier before you went to college?"

"Gave the government three years of my life and went to school on the GI bill. My mother wouldn't have been able to afford to send me otherwise."

"Do you have siblings?"

"Five."

Five! I thought our family was large with three kids. "I don't remember any Salvares in school."

"Probably because we lived one county east."

"And your father came all the way to New Chapel for his surgery?"

"You have better medical facilities. Your brother was good to my dad, by the way."

"Jonathan is a skilled surgeon. A so-so brother, but what can you expect from a guy?"

"He doesn't like your meddling either, does he?"

I ignored Marco's gibe. "So getting back to your siblings, are they younger or older than you?"

"Both. Most of them have left the area, but my youngest sister lives close by." He grinned, thinking about her. "She's feisty. Has a baby now, a little boy named Christopher."

I could see Marco dangling a baby on his knee. I was betting he was great with kids. The thought ran through my mind that he might already have kids. And a wife. I was just about to ask when he grabbed my shoulders and pulled me down.

"The garage door is opening," he whispered in my ear.

We were both leaning toward the middle, his left arm across my back to keep me from popping up. He waited a few moments, then slowly raised his head.

"What do you see?" I whispered.

"Be patient . . . Another minute . . ." He let out a quiet whistle.

"What?" I tried to raise my head, but he kept me down.

"It's a black SUV. Okay, lift your head just enough to see. . . . He's going to pass in a second. Get a good look at the driver."

I raised my head. When the vehicle turned onto the road, Marco pulled me down again as the SUV's headlights lit up the Jeep. Had we not been in such a tense situation, I could have been highly aroused. The scent Marco was wearing was turning my insides into a quivering mound of chocolate mousse.

"Okay, now!" he ordered.

I peeked over the door, saw the driver, and my heart sank. "It's not the same man."

CHAPTER TEN

"You're sure he's not the guy?" Marco asked.

"Not unless he suddenly went bald and gained fifty pounds. Yes, I'm sure. Looks like your girlfriend at the DMV gave you bad information." I tucked stray wisps of hair under my cap as Marco started the motor. "Maybe that famous Salvare charm didn't work as well as you thought it would."

He shot me a bemused look. "I don't think that was it. Maybe the bald guy borrowed the vehicle. And I still have a second SUV to check out."

That little green-eyed monster inside made me say, "So, she liked you, did she?"

"My friend at the DMV? What's not to like?"

The ego of this man! "Your swaggering macho walk, for one thing."

"Shows how much you know. The ladies love my walk."

He was right; he had a great walk. "Does your wife think so, too?"

At that, Marco threw back his head and gave a genuine laugh. "You are something else, Miz Abby Knight. No, my wife doesn't think so. I don't have a wife. Or kids. Anything else you want to know?"

"Yes. How did you end up so insufferable?"

"Practice." Marco turned to look over his shoulder as he backed up. Then he slammed on the brakes and muttered something under his breath. I swiveled around and saw police lights come up behind us.

He gave me a warning look. "Don't say a word. I'll do the talking."

Two cops got out of the car and came toward us, one on each side. Marco rolled down the glass and said to the stocky, square-jawed man outside, "Is there a problem?"

The cop shined his flashlight at us, then said to his partner with a sneer, "Doesn't that just figure? It's Salvare." To Marco he said, "We got a call that someone was harassing the commissioner."

"Is that what you think we're doing?" Marco reached over and rubbed my knee suggestively, saying in that husky voice of his, for their benefit, "Boy, have they got that wrong, haven't they, babe?"

As if anyone would dress like we were for a make-out session. I gave him a coy smile and stayed mute, as difficult as that was. The temperature of my knee had risen twenty degrees where his hand lay.

"Besides," Marco said as he revved the engine, "as far as I know, it's not illegal to park on a public road. So either step back, Blasko, or charge me with something."

Blasko took off his hat to wipe his forehead, revealing a military-style haircut, short on the sides and longer on top. "Okay, listen up, smart-ass," he said, replacing the hat. "Get this pile of tin out of here or I'll find a reason to haul in you and Vampira here."

Vampira! That did it. I could take only so much from a sneering idiot. As the cop started back to his squad car, I climbed over Marco to stick my head out the window. "Listen, you pasty-faced primate, my father *mphff*—"

Marco clapped his hand over my mouth and wrestled me back to my seat. "Didn't I tell you not to talk?"

I pried off his fingers to cry, "He called me Vampira!"

"And you think antagonizing him is going to make him apologize?"

I huffed and sat back, straightening my T-shirt and cap as Marco put the car in gear and slowly pulled out behind them. "Who are those two morons, anyway? I don't remember seeing them before."

"Reed and Blasko, both fairly new to the force. Reed does whatever Blasko tells him to do, and Blasko's an arrogant jerk."

"Are they on private patrol here?"

"My guess is the Cadillac driver called to report a suspicious vehicle near the commissioner's property."

"You'd think he had something to hide. What are we going to do about it?"

Marco gave me a dark look, which pretty much ended that topic of conversation for the evening. When we pulled up in front of my apartment building, he got out and came around to open the door for me. Another point in Marco's favor. Not many guys were that well mannered.

"I'm coming up," he told me. "I want to check over your place."

"Not necessary. I have my pepper spray." At his snort I added, "Fine, check it out."

He waited while I opened the door. Then he climbed the stairs in front of me to the second floor. As he led the way down the hall, the Samples came out of their apartment to take Peewee for his nightly stroll.

"'Evening," he said with a nod.

As soon as the little beast saw me, he whined and wiggled so hard Mrs. Sample let him down. To my astonishment, he went for Marco instead, but rather than clamping those sharp teeth on the tender skin of Marco's ankle, the dog wagged his tail and stood on his hind legs, begging for attention. I wanted to smack one of them, probably Peewee.

Taking no chances that the little rat would change his mind, I used Marco as a doggie diversion to unlock the door and jump inside. Simon had been waiting there for his chance to terrify Peewee, but at my hurried entrance, he scooted off for parts unknown.

"I'll be out of your way shortly," Marco said, shutting the door behind him.

He strode off toward the bedrooms, and I pulled off my hat and ran my fingers through my hair. "No need to look in my closet," I called, and then heard the sound of doors being folded back. Damn. In my haste to dress for the stakeout, I had tossed a few garments on the floor. That was in addition to the pile of laundry waiting to be washed.

Marco was back in a few minutes, but made no comment on the state of my closet. I handed him a glass of red wine. "You're off duty now."

He took the glass and clinked the rim to mine. "To the sunshine girl."

I savored the wine, as well as the company, who was looking particularly sexy at that moment, with his head tipped back and that liquid moving down his throat. I could get very used to being around Marco. "What do we need to do next?"

"I'll follow up on the other name and address. No one was home when I tried earlier. With any luck we'll be able to rule out one of the two. Then you can turn the information over to your insurance agent and let him do the rest."

I didn't bother to correct him. No need for Marco to know my intentions.

"There's something I've been wondering all evening," I said, studying him over the rim. "How did you know where I live?"

"You're in the phone book."

I had been hoping for something a little more romantic, such as that he'd followed me home because he was curious about where a gorgeous woman like me would reside. I took another sip, wondering if he had any romantic thoughts at all in that handsome head. The closest he had come to flirting was that hand on my knee in the car, but that had been purely an act for the cops.

"When does Nikki get home?" he asked, eyeing her photo.

Damn that photo. She looked absolutely adorable in it. I downed the wine and took my glass to rinse it in the sink. "After midnight. Why? Do you want to wait for her?"

He reached around me to take the glass out of my hands, then turned me around and tilted my chin up. My heart did a jig as his lips came down on mine. I closed my eyes and let myself savor the experience: firm lips that tasted of grapes, the slight scratch of his beard against my chin, that heady, masculine scent. When I opened them again, he was at the door.

"Dead bolt, don't forget," he said, and then the door shut behind him.

I let out my breath and steadied myself on the counter. What had that been about?

Simon sat in the hallway, head tilted in wonderment. I picked him up and cuddled him. "Thank goodness you're not a human male, Simon, or I wouldn't understand you at all."

Simon didn't much care what he was, as long as I fed him.

Friday morning, Lottie and Grace were both hard at work when I arrived. Grace handed me a cup of coffee and followed me to the workroom. "Tell me what you think."

We played this game whenever Grace came up with a new blend. She never divulged her recipes, but she always made us guess anyway. It drove Lottie crazy, which might be why Grace did it. I took a tentative sip, then a bigger one, then drank the rest and handed the cup and saucer to her. "It's delicious. What's in it? Hazelnut?"

"Chocolate," Lottie announced triumphantly. "I saw her add it. Ha!"

Rather than admit Lottie was right, Grace sang out, "That's not all I put in *your* cup," and headed back to the parlor. I could hear her chortling as she set up the tables.

"Grace is in a good mood today," I remarked, taking a look at the orders that had come in over the wire. There were exactly three. That didn't do much for my mood.

"She had a date last night."

"No!" I pulled up a stool next to Lottie. "Tell me about it."

"You'll have to ask her yourself. She won't tell me a thing." Lottie clipped two inches off the stem of a yellow rose and stuck it in a rectangular glass vase. "Did you make it out to the greenhouse?"

"I barely made it out *of* the greenhouse. Harding wasn't exactly thrilled to see me there. Unfortunately, I had to leave before I could talk to the cashiers, so I still don't know where he's banking his money. The only thing I can do is follow Harding up to Michigan tomorrow to see if I can learn anything there." I pulled an order and started to gather the supplies I'd need.

"Baby, I know you want to help Pearl, and normally I'd tell you to go for it, but you'd better leave this for Dave to handle."

"Dave doesn't have the resources to hire a PI, and he can't go himself. Saturdays are his pro bono days at the university's legal clinic. But if it makes you feel better, I'll call him and tell him what I've got planned. And by the way, I don't mind following Harding up there—it's a beautiful drive and I can put the top down—as long as you'll be here to manage the shop."

"You've got it." Lottie stripped another rose of its

thorns and stuck it in the water. "What are you going to tell Grace?"

"That I'm taking a day trip in my convertible."

Lottie worked silently across from me, and I could tell something else was on her mind, but I didn't press. She'd get to it in her own good time. In the meantime, I had sketched out my coupons—ten percent off any purchase of twenty dollars or more—so I phoned Pronto Printer down the block, negotiated a reduced price by offering an arrangement for their counter, and was told the flyers would be ready Monday afternoon.

"I'll have my boys distribute them," Lottie said. "They're usually home from work a little after four o'clock."

"That works for me." I finished an arrangement, wrapped it in cellophane, and went to grab a cup of coffee. Grace was serving lattes to two bank tellers whom I'd known from high school, so I stopped to chat. When I got back, Lottie was ready to talk.

"I need to apologize for something, Abby. When I brought Pearl in, I didn't expect her to make so much trouble for you. I'm sure you've got better things to do on your Saturday than follow that jackass Harding around Michigan."

"Painfully, I don't."

"I want you to know I understand if you don't want to involve yourself any further. You know I always look out for your welfare." With a gleam in her eye that I found highly suspect, she stuck the last rose in the vase, wrapped it with green tissue paper, and handed it to me. "Would you mind running this across the street to the prosecutors' offices? It's a rush delivery—a gift for the chief prosecutor's wife."

So *that's* what was going on. Lottie was back to her matchmaking tricks. I didn't tell her that she was actually doing me a favor. No sense encouraging her.

*   *   *

The prosecutors' offices were located on the court-house's second floor. I bypassed the ancient elevator in favor of the wide center staircase and marched into their outer office, where I encountered a chicly dressed woman in her early thirties. "I have a delivery for the prosecuting attorney," I announced.

She sized me up through blue-tinted glasses, then held out her hands. "I'll take it." Her high, nasally voice did not match her looks.

"Is Greg Morgan here, by any chance?"

She put the vase on her desk and reached for the phone. "I can check. Who shall I say is calling?"

"Abby Knight—not calling, here in person."

"You're a client, Miss Knight?"

"A florist." I pointed at the flowers. "Those are mine."

"A florist is here to see you," she twanged into the phone. It was a good bet that her IQ and that of her blue glasses was approximately the same. "Have a seat," she told me, and left with the flowers.

I glanced around, saw straight-backed chairs against the wall, and sat down, feeling suddenly like a little girl waiting to see the principal. Miss Blue Tints returned and pointed toward a door. "Mr. Morgan will see you now."

Ancient and cramped, Morgan's office had stacks of files everywhere—on filing cabinets, spilling out of boxes, and sitting on an old wooden chair in front of a beat-up desk.

"Hi," I said, with a little wave.

"Abby!" He rose from an antiquated chair, surprised. "Come in!"

Morgan actually seemed embarrassed as I looked around for a place to sit. "I'll just move these," he said, grunting as he lifted a stack off the chair. He turned around twice trying to find a place to put the files, and finally set them on the floor beside his desk, making it necessary to climb back over the files to reach his seat. He leaned back on the creaky old springs and gave me that charmingly suave grin, then nearly tipped backward. I had to cough to hide a laugh.

"So," he said, flashing his dimpled grin, "what can I do you for?"

"I was just curious as to how the murder investigation was coming."

"It's—coming."

I didn't think he'd give up information that easily. Time to resort to flattery. I started with stage one: the subtle approach. "Congratulations on being given the case, Mr. Prosecutor. You deserve it."

Morgan tried to blush, but his ego was too strong. "Well," he said, with a self-deprecating smile, stroking the manila file folder in front of him, "you didn't hear it from me."

I leaned forward and said with a conspiratorial wink, "Mum's the word." I tried to read the label on the folder, but, unfortunately, his hand was covering it.

Moving on to stage two: "I *am* puzzled about one thing, and I'm sure you can clear it up, since you're *in the know.*" (Cross leg over knee and tilt head to one side. This worked best in a skirt.) "Why did Detective Corbison decide to take his vacation now? Considering that this kind of case comes around so seldom, it's a tad odd, don't you think?"

Morgan didn't even lift an eyebrow, making me think he was either clueless or a good actor. "It was a planned vacation."

"Right." I gave him another wink, again hoping to prompt some response that might indicate there was more going on. But he seemed merely puzzled by all the eye gesturing.

Morgan's phone rang; he picked it up, listened, and said, "I'll be right over."

I rose. "Sorry. I didn't mean to keep you from your work."

"No problem." He climbed over the files and headed for the door. "Stay there. I'll be back in two minutes. I want to ask you something."

I waited until his footsteps receded, then quickly grabbed the manila folder. Eureka! The name on the label read *Ryan*.

CHAPTER ELEVEN

Keeping an ear open for footsteps, I flipped open the file cover and skimmed like mad. First page was the official police report of the murder. I read it, noting that a slug determined to be from a large-caliber weapon, possibly a forty-five, had been taken from Billy's body. More testing would be conducted to determine the exact size.

Second page was the victim's information—name, background, employer—nothing I didn't already know, except for one item that said the victim had been known to the police department from a prior conviction for theft. Not too unusual if Billy had a drug habit.

Third page was marked *Inventory*, with a list of items found in Billy's apartment. I scanned the list, looking for anything unusual. Below the standard appliances— refrigerator and oven—the police had typed:

Wooden kitchen table
Wooden chairs (2)
Pink silk sofa
Twin-sized mattress
Brown wool blanket
Electric coffeemaker

Safety razor
Shaving cream
Electric fan
Potted plants (2)
Box of plant fertilizer, dimensions 4"x 6"x 2"
Leftover pizza in cardboard container
Beer cans (7)
Stainless-steel teaspoon (residue sent to state crime lab)
Box of kitchen matches
Syringes (2) (residue sent to state crime lab)
White plastic garbage can (contents sent to state crime lab)
Blue jeans (one pair)
White T-shirts (2)
Green cotton shirt (button-down)

That was it, the sum total of the last two weeks of Billy's life: one column on a single sheet of white paper. There should be more to a young man's life than that.

Before I could flip the page I heard someone coming. I slipped the folder back where I'd found it and turned, leaning my backside against the desk.

Morgan came through the doorway and smiled. "Good. You waited."

"So what's up?"

"Have dinner with me tomorrow night."

I locked my jaw to keep it from dropping. "Dinner?" I sputtered.

"I'll pick you up at six and whisk you away to Chicago for pasta at the Italian Village."

My mind did a few cartwheels. Greg Morgan had finally noticed me. I had the strongest urge to run over to New Chapel High and post it on the bulletin board.

But, wait; I wasn't that geeky, adoring high schooler anymore. I didn't need Morgan's attention. And I certainly wasn't about to let him see that I was flattered. So I pretended to ponder, drawing out the suspense, wishing

I could extend it for, oh, say, four years. "How about seven o'clock?"

"How about six thirty?"

Was he bargaining with me? I walked to the doorway, glanced at him over my shoulder, and in my best imitation of a sultry siren said, "Six forty-five and you've got a deal."

"Done. Wear something hot," he called as I left.

I glanced over at his secretary and saw her staring at me with new interest.

"He wants me to wear something hot," I told her in a stage whisper. I glided into the hall positively glowing, then came to an abrupt halt by the stairs. Why was I so happy? I didn't really want to go out with Greg Morgan. I had accepted that invitation because my ego had enjoyed it.

At least it would give me a chance to question him about the murder. With a bottle of wine to help, I was certain I could get him to loosen up. Besides, I knew Nikki would flip when she heard the news.

Grace and Lottie pounced on me as soon as I walked into the shop.

"Well?" Lottie asked. "When are you and that doll-faced prosecutor going out?"

I couldn't resist teasing her. "Where did you get the idea that Morgan was going to ask me out?"

Lottie's smile drooped. "He *didn't* ask you?" She turned with a sigh and went back to the workroom, where I heard her mutter, "I must be losing my touch."

I followed Grace into the coffee parlor. "Got any more of your special brew?"

"Coming right up, dear. What time is Mr. Morgan picking you up?"

There was no fooling Grace. I leaned my elbows on the counter and smiled at her. "Tell me about your date first."

"Blackmail, is it?" She handed me a cup and saucer, her eyes twinkling. "It's Mr. Davis."

"Richard Davis? The man who looks like Michael Caine? The man who owns the bowling alley *and* the miniature golf course, and drives a 1971 fire-engine-red Eldorado Biarritz Cadillac convertible with monster fins on the back?"

"Mind you, we only went bowling."

I couldn't stop smiling. Among Grace's peers Richard Davis was considered the catch of the century. However, he was also Grace's exact opposite in terms of temperament and breeding. Picturing the two of them on a date was a stretch of the imagination.

"Don't tell a soul, Abby. And by soul, I mean Lottie. You know how she can be."

"I won't say a word." Still shaking my head in wonder, I took the coffee to the workroom, where Lottie was putting together an arrangement of lavender and lilac phlox, blue wax flowers, and long, droopy wisps of mountain grass. "How is Pearl?" I asked her.

"Miserable. She doesn't like imposing on me, but she's scared to death that jackass is going to come after her." Lottie turned the ceramic pot in a circle, checking the arrangement from all angles, then put it aside and came over to put her arms around me. "I'm sorry I sent you over to the courthouse, baby. I have half a notion to go over there and smack that young man into next week for being such an idiot. Here you are, a treasure, right under his nose, and he's too blind to see it."

"I don't think you should do that."

She leaned back to look at me. "Why not?"

"He'd have a hard time driving me to the restaurant tomorrow night."

For a forty-five-year-old woman, Lottie had an amazing amount of upper-body strength. Of course, that's not what I was thinking as she lifted me in the air, whooping with delight.

*   *   *

I couldn't wait for Nikki to get home from work to tell her about my date, so as soon as I'd finished up at the shop, I called her at the hospital, hoping to catch her on her break.

I lucked out. "Nikki, you'll never guess who asked me out to dinner."

"Marco."

"Marco? You don't know Marco."

She waited until the loudspeaker in the background had finished paging a doctor to say, "I'm just going by what you've told me about him." She sounded hurt.

"Yes, but I never said I wanted to go out with him. Never mind. It's not Marco."

"Don't tell me it's Pryce!"

"That heel? Would I be excited if it were Pryce?"

"I give up. Who?"

"Greg Morgan."

"Nooooooo!" she breathed into the receiver. "You didn't accept, did you?"

"I did, on my terms."

She squealed in delight. "We have to find you something glamorous to wear on that date, Abby. And I have just the thing."

"Nikki, you're a head taller and a whole lot skinnier."

"Your boobs will take it up. Don't worry. I'll take care of it as soon as I get home."

Right. I hung up and ran to my closet. If only I had Candy Camford's telephone number. Would I love to let her know I was going out with her old boyfriend. Candy had been the head cheerleader at New Chapel High — perky personality, perfect body, gorgeous blond hair. The other cheerleaders had nicknamed her Candy Apple because of her love of sweets. I had another name for her: Crab Apple, for all the sour looks she used to give me. Last I'd heard of her, she had four kids, was on her second husband, and had eaten way too many gummy bears. There is, in some instances, justice in this world.

But what to do about my outfit for Saturday? I began yanking possibilities from the closet. Too baggy. Too old. Too passe. Too girlish. Too what-was-I-thinking. The drawers in my dresser held even fewer choices. I ended up with a cap-sleeved, black knit top and a pair of beige linen pants.

Standing in front of the mirror, holding them in front of me, I knew they'd never do. They weren't hot; they weren't even luke warm. They were *my mother.*

I finally gave up, deciding I'd have to let Nikki help after all. But first I had to get through dinner with the family.

For my evening at the club, I donned a sensible khaki skirt, white blouse, tan sling-backed heels, and put my hair up in a tidy little bun, held in place by a tortoiseshell plastic clip. I even used a spray of perfume, a light citrus fragrance I'd found at the local pharmacy, on a display that said, *If you like this famous designer's product, then try our brand.* So I did, knowing I no longer had to worry about my ex-fiancé's mother's sophisticated sniffer noticing the difference.

The weather was gorgeous, so I drove with the top down, tooling down the two-lane country road, slowing only to cross a narrow wooden bridge that spanned Maple Creek. I pulled into the parking lot of the New Chapel Country Club five minutes ahead of schedule and did a quick check of the other cars to see if my ex-fiancé's Beemer was there. It wasn't, and I prayed that he and the rest of his kin were out of town for the weekend. I was still uncomfortable eating in the same room with his family. They tended to glare at me a lot. Add Pryce to that mix and it made for a rough evening.

The country club sat on ten acres of land on the eastern border of the city in a beautiful hilly area surrounded by trees and edged on one side by the creek. The golf course was highly regarded in the sporting world, or so

my brothers said. The pool was olympic-sized and surrounded by aqua-colored lounge chairs and umbrella-
covered tables. The clubhouse was a tribute to what money
could buy.

The long brick and concrete structure sprawled across
the top of a hill, with the left wing devoted to banquets,
the center span holding offices, washrooms, and a coat-
room, and the right wing containing the kitchen, the bar,
and two adjoining dining rooms, complete with fireplaces
and soaring windows that looked out onto a flower and
shrub garden, with the golf course beyond it. Just outside
the windows was a patio for outdoor dining.

My brothers always declined the patio, where I'd be
more comfortable, in favor of the main dining room, a
huge room of white linen-covered tables, vanilla-scented
candles, hushed conversations, and air so icy in the summer that by the end of the evening icicles dangled from
my nose. In a separate section was the bar area, complete
with a polished mahogany bar with brass foot rails,
leather stools, ten round tables, and televisions mounted
on the walls.

The table where my brothers held court sat in front of
a window overlooking the gardens. As I strolled over I
heard loud male guffaws coming from the bar area. I
glanced around to see a big-bellied, middle-aged man entertaining friends with gestures and more guffaws. His
suit coat was off, his white shirtsleeves rolled back over
fat, hairy forearms, and his tie loosened. He had oiled
black hair, a thick salt-and-pepper mustache, a cigar in
one hand, and a martini glass in the other, and was using
his cigar to make his points. He looked familiar, but I
couldn't place him.

"Here's Abby," my father announced, smiling on the
side of his face that wasn't paralyzed. I walked over to his
wheelchair, gave him a hug, and sat down beside him.
Safety in numbers, that was my motto. My mother was
holding the occupants of a nearby table hostage with tales

of her sons' surgical marvels, but released them to join us.
I greeted my two brothers and their wives, noticing that
the chair usually occupied by my niece, Tara, sat empty
across from me. "Where's Tara tonight?" I asked.

Tara was the ten-year-old daughter of Jordan, the
younger of my brothers, and his wife, Kathy. Tara dressed
and talked like she was sixteen, and had one ambition in
life: to marry a prince so she could be an official princess.
Frankly, since Tara already had her parents jumping to
her commands, it wouldn't be much of a transition.

"Tara's at a birthday party," Kathy explained, her hazel
eyes sparkling with pride. "Her best friend's parents char-
tered a cruise on the Chicago River for the evening."

I was stunned. "For a tenth birthday?"

"You should have seen the party she went to last weekend," Kathy gushed. "The girl's parents rented an entire
water park for a whole day."

All I could do was gape at her. Whatever happened to
cake and ice cream, and sleepovers? When had a birthday
party turned into a contest to see who could throw the
most lavish bash? I'd hate to be the parents who had to
come up with weddings for those children.

My brother Jonathan and his wife, Portia, had opted
not to have kids. They preferred to spend their time,
money, and energy on other pursuits. For Portia that
meant finding *the* stylist to care for her fine, long, ash-
blond hair. She'd gone through a dozen already. With her
delicate frame and hipless, size-two body, I doubted Portia would have been able to stand the rigors of childbirth
anyway.

Kathy was the more normal of my sisters-in-law. She
came from a family of three kids, had a healthy size-ten
body complete with hips and thighs, and wore her dark
brown hair in a ponytail. Tonight it was clipped with a
gold barrette at her nape. Both women wore sweater sets,
Kathy's in powder blue, Portia's in—what else—black.
She liked the way it set off her pale hair. Personally, I

thought it made her look like an albino version of Morti-
cia Addams.

"Wine, honey?" my father asked as the waiter came
around with a bottle. "It's a California Cabernet."

"Absolutely." It never mattered to me whether it was
domestic or imported, white or red, as long as it had no
bubbles. I hated bubbles, which is why I shunned car-
bonated beverages and champagne, much to Pryce's parents' dismay. If my flunking out of law school hadn't
caused Pryce to cancel our wedding, my aversion to
champagne would have.

"Tell me it's not true, Pryce," his mother had said in a
near swoon after she'd found out. "*Everyone* drinks
champagne. Some people bathe in it. But absolutely *no
one* dislikes it."

"Fine, I'll bathe in it," I'd told Pryce, "but not during
the wedding."

It hadn't been a happy time.

"How is your car running?" my brother Jonathan
asked.

"Terrific."

He studied me over the rim of his glass. "One of the
nurses mentioned she saw you driving a beat-up Escort."

"Oh, that!" I replied, waving off the subject as if it
were a nasty smell. "I had to take my car in for service
and they gave me a loaner."

"What are you going to drive this winter?" Jonathan
asked. He still couldn't get over the fact that I'd bought
this car on a whim. Cars were researched, test-driven, and
mechanic-rated.

"My Vette, why?"

"Corvettes aren't winter cars. They're racing cars.
You'll slide all over the road."

"You know, Abigail, one shouldn't buy a car just for
show," Portia added.

I nearly decked her. She drove a Bentley.

"I'll worry about it when the snow flies," I answered

testily. I held up my wineglass to signal the waiter I needed more. This family could drive a saint to drink.

"So how's the shop?" Jordan asked, after we'd ordered our meals. He asked this same question every week, as though *the shop* were an actual living, breathing being.

"Dandy. How's medicine doing? All over the flu now?"

My father thought this was funny. No one else so much as cracked a smile. I reached for the bread basket and took a crusty slice of wheat berry. It was going to be a long evening.

I heard more loud laughter from the bar area and leaned over to say to my father, "Who's the fat man with the cigar? He looks familiar."

He turned his head to take a look. "That's Louis Vertucci, one of the county commissioners."

I almost choked on the bread. So that was the great and powerful Oz. I should have known. I'd seen his photos in the papers often enough.

"Odious man," my mother sniffed. "I hate the way people kowtow to him."

"Who's with him?" I asked.

"The balding man on his left runs his contracting business," my father said softly. "The white-haired man on his right is the head of Streets and Sanitation."

I kept my eye on Vertucci as we waited for our food. He and his friends took a table near the bar where they could watch the baseball game on TV. As our waiter delivered our salads, I happened to glance over at their table just as a younger man joined them.

My mouth fell open. It was the guy who hit me!

CHAPTER TWELVE

He was tall and lean, with the same dark curly hair I remembered. But could I say positively he was the SUV driver? No. What I really needed was for him to recognize *me*.

"Dad," I whispered, "look at Vertucci's table again. Who's the young guy?"

He glanced over. "I don't know."

"What are you two staring at?" Portia demanded, her head bobbing for a look as she tried to figure it out. Of course her remark made everyone else at the table turn to stare.

"Hey!" I said sharply, drawing their gazes back to me. "We are now the center of attention of the entire room. Will you all please resume eating?"

Throwing me chilly looks, they did.

"Excuse me," I said, and fled to the ladies' room, where I dug through my purse until I found Marco's card, then quickly punched in his number. His machine picked up. Damn! I left a message telling him where I was and who I saw, and asking him to meet me in an hour, when we'd be finished with dinner. Then I slipped out the front door to the parking lot and looked for the

SUV, with no luck. The big black Cadillac, however, was there.

"Are you all right?" my mother asked as I rejoined the table.

"Of course." I sat down and put my napkin on my lap.

"You look winded. Your cheeks are pink."

Another unfortunate aspect of being a redhead. My pale skin flushed easily. "That bathroom is colder than a meat locker." I shivered for effect, then glanced discreetly at the commissioner's table, hoping they would stay put until Marco arrived.

"Are you still running every morning?" my mother asked, picking at her poached salmon.

"I power walk, Mom."

"Jonathan and I have signed up for tai chi," Portia announced.

"Isn't that like karate?" my father asked.

Portia do karate? I nearly choked on a bite of steak as I envisioned her breaking a brick with her thin white hand, or hitting a two-by-four with her high, narrow forehead.

"Your brother and I are taking yoga lessons," Kathy announced proudly, giving Jordan a good-little-boy pat on the shoulder. My brother glanced at me as if hoping I wouldn't snicker.

"I'm into feng shui myself." I jabbed a fry into a pile of sweet red ketchup. The only thing I knew about feng shui was that Nikki had tried to arrange our apartment according to its principles, and we'd ended up with our sofa facing the hallway and our TV behind us. Obviously we didn't have a clue. My jest backfired; all three women gave me appreciative looks.

"Has it made a difference?" Portia asked eagerly, leaning forward.

I shrugged. "Take a look at me. What more can I say?"

"Oh, yes. I see it now," Portia said.

My father lifted his eyebrow. I slid a bite of steak in my

mouth and chewed hard to keep from laughing. I loved to yank Portia's chain.

At that moment, someone put his hands on my mother's shoulders. "Hi, Mom," my ex-fiancé said, casting me a smug glance.

"Pryce!" my mother exclaimed happily. "Abigail, look who's here!" She stood to give him a hug. Portia and Kathy greeted him like long-lost siblings. My dad shook his hand. No need to order dessert with all the sweetness flying.

It puzzled me how my family could be so warm to him, considering the shabby way he'd treated me. To think I'd once believed Pryce to be perfect husband material—employed by a respected law firm, responsible, close to his parents—but it turned out that his parents hadn't felt I was the perfect material for *him*. Or them. Mostly for them.

I'd met Pryce at a college basketball game during his last year of law school. After dating frat boys who had been more interested in my boobs than in me, a psychology major who had seen me as a research subject, and a drama major who had spent most of our dates trying to catch sight of his own reflection, Pryce had been a breath of fresh, very refined air. I'd instantly fallen for his classic good looks, keen mind, and silver BMW. Especially the BMW.

Pryce, in turn, had liked my spunk. But not enough to tell his parents about it. In fact, he'd kept our relationship a secret for almost two years, which should have been a big red flag, but I had been too blinded by his dazzle. So what if his parents weren't ready to meet me? They'd come around: When chickens grew teeth.

They had learned about me, finally, not from their son, but from Portia, who'd run into Pryce's mother on the golf course. Portia claimed she lost control of her cart, but I still wonder. While helping the woman up,

Portia had hit her again with the news of her son's secret girlfriend. For a ninety-six pound weakling, Portia packed one heck of a punch.

I should have realized from the outset that our relationship was doomed. We were the ultimate mismatch. Pryce had attended private schools, spent summers in Italian villas, and not only knew what *foie gras* was, but had eaten it as a child. I had gone to public schools, spent a week every July crowded into a ratty old camper, and thought goose liver spread was something that happened to old geese.

When I'd received the news that I'd been dropped from law school, I had automatically turned to the man to whom I intended to complain for the rest of his life. All I'd needed was a hug and a little moral support. What I got was the cold shoulder.

Pryce had told his parents about my dismissal, and they, in turn, had told him to tell me to take a hike. Not quite in those words. In Osborne-speak it would have been, "Considering that one must always uphold the high standards and traditions with which our family has long been associated, one must never settle for less. A wife who cannot maintain those standards must never bear the illustrious name of Osborne. So disentangle yourself, Pryce—unless you're not concerned about your rather substantial inheritance."

Pryce had been concerned all right, and not about my battered ego. So when he'd asked for his ring back two months before our wedding, I had adjusted the controls and brought Pryce into sharper focus. Perfect husband, no. Perfect jerk, most definitely.

He'd let himself off the hook by saying that he'd suddenly realized he hadn't been ready to commit after all, and he'd hoped I'd be a good sport about it. He'd even offered to pay for my wedding gown. Being a good sport, I'd let him.

"Would you rather have gone through with it and

learned later what a heel he was?" my father had said to console me.

"We still have to be nice to him," my mother had admonished. "It shows graciousness and good breeding. And his parents send lovely Christmas cards."

Forget that Pryce had trampled on my heart. Forget that his parents had snubbed me. We wouldn't want those cards to stop coming.

"Abigail," Pryce said in that stuffy tone of his. "How have you been?"

"Doing great," I said with as much enthusiasm as I could offer a cad. "And you?"

"Did you read about that million-dollar settlement we got for the IXE Corporation? That was my case."

"Well, congratulations," I said, wondering if my voice had sounded as flat to his ears as it had to mine.

"Oh, Pryce, how wonderful!" my mother gushed. "Why don't you sit down and tell us all about it? Tara's not here tonight. We have an extra chair. I'll pop over there, and you can sit beside Abigail."

"I'll just stay a few minutes," he said, settling in beside me. "My parents will be here soon." And he didn't dare ignore his parents.

I sipped my wine as Pryce glorified his part in settling the lawsuit. I knew perfectly well that one of the senior partners had looked over his shoulder; it was too big a case to let an unseasoned lawyer go it alone. But as usual, he had to impress everyone.

"So," he said, turning to me with that condescending smile on his face, "how's business?"

"Blooming," I deadpanned. Kathy and my father thought it was funny.

"Sounds like you're busy, then," Pryce said with a forced smile. Had we been alone, he would have said, "I really don't care for your attitude, Abigail. And must you dip your fries, for pity's sake?"

I dipped one right before his eyes and stuck it in my mouth.

"Your parents are here, Pryce," Portia called, as though she couldn't wait for the uncomfortable scene to end.

The Osbornes spotted us at the same time we saw them. Then again, it was hard not to see a table full of redheads. They gave a friendly wave, noticed me, and scampered into a far corner. Pryce said his good-byes, nodded to me stiffly, and left. As he walked away, I noted his expensive three-piece suit, manicured nails, and perfectly tonsured brown hair, and wondered what I'd ever seen in him.

"Abigail, you could have been kinder," my mother chided.

"I didn't say anything mean. Did I, Kathy?"

Kathy's eyes widened like a deer caught in headlights.

"One should never burn one's bridges," Portia chimed in, smoothing back a stray lock. She always had to add her two cents, although in her case it was more like a half cent. "One never knows when one will need to cross them again."

I narrowed my eyes at her, imagining Portia driving across one of those burning bridges. "You know, Portia . . ." I said, gearing up for a good argument.

"Dessert anyone?" Jordan piped up, signaling madly to the waiter like a drowning man going down for the third time. "Kathy, what would you like? How about that chocolate mousse, Abby? Looks good, huh?"

I ordered the mousse, then glanced over my shoulder to see that Pryce's family had stopped at Commissioner Vertucci's table, chatting with him as if they were old friends.

Aha! There was my introduction! I dug in my bag for a pen, hopped up, to the curious looks of my family, and barreled across the room, stopping just behind my former fiancé.

"Pryce," I said sweetly, mustering up all the Irish

charm I owned, "I found this on the floor beneath your chair. Did you drop it by any chance?"

He swung around to look at the Bic pen, then me, in disgust. "You know I use Montblancs."

"Silly me!" I said with a laugh. "Of course I do." Conversation halted as the rest turned to see who the newcomer was. I kept one eye on my suspect, but he didn't show any signs of recognition. "Good to see you again," I said, with a brief nod to his parents. I knew they'd have to introduce me now.

"You, too," his father said, with just a hint of pain. His mother merely gave me an icy smile. "Abigail Knight," his father began, "this is Commissioner Louis Vertucci, his nephew Tony Vertucci, Don Edwards, and Frank Jancich."

Tony Vertucci. I ran over the name twice to memorize it, then threw in the others for good measure. "How do you do?" I said, nodding to each of them. I patted Pryce's sleeve. "Pryce and I have known each other for *years.* In fact, we almost got married. Luckily, we realized what a mistake *that* would have been *before* we marched down the aisle."

There was an awkward moment of silence. Then his mother gave a nervous laugh, after which they resumed their conversation as though I'd suddenly become transparent. I saw the commissioner's nephew eyeing my boobs, so I turned my gaze on him, even going so far as to bat my lashes. "Hello—Tony, was it?"

"You got it, babe," he said with a wink, firing a mock pistol at me. "Have we met?"

Was that finger pistol a substitute for the real thing, say a .45, or just his idea of a suave move? I edged closer to him and away from the others. "I'm sure I would have remembered meeting *you,* Tony. You're not from around here, are you?"

He adjusted his collar and said in a slick voice, "I'm

from Chicago, west side, where a man knows how to treat a woman."

He had those cornball clichés down pat. "You left Chicago to move here?"

"Hard to believe, isn't it? My uncle asked me to do a favor for Mr. Jancich. He needed my expert help."

Sure he had. I inched closer yet, trying to get out of the others' earshot, and asked coquettishly, "What kind of expert are you?" I was so obvious I nearly laughed at myself. The only thing I hadn't done was walk my fingers up his shirtfront. The important thing was that Tony bought it.

"I'm a crew supervisor for CPC." He'd said it as though he were president of an international corporation.

"CPC?"

"County Paving Company." He leered at me and said in a suggestive voice, "I'm good at supervising. I like to watch."

"I'm sure you do."

He fired that finger pistol at me again. I couldn't believe men actually did that. "What do you say we lose this joint and head over to a real bar?"

Sure, Tony. I really want to get cozy with a suave guy like you. I motioned for him to lean down so I could whisper, "I wish I could, but it's almost time for another dose of antibiotics. Nasty little infection just won't go away."

He recoiled slightly, and his smile stiffened. "Some other time, then."

"What does a hip supervisor like you drive, Tony?" I asked nonchalantly.

His uncle materialized and affectionately rubbed Tony's curly head. "What does he drive? He drives me crazy, don't you, Tone?" Vertucci turned cold, assessing eyes my way. "Why do you want to know about my nephew's car?"

Obviously, he'd been eavesdropping. Didn't he trust

his nephew to keep his mouth shut? "I could have sworn I saw him at the Corvette show on the square last Sunday," I lied.

"I *wish* I had a Vette," Tony said, giving his uncle a pointed glance.

"You're a workingman, Tone," Vertucci replied, his smile still in place. "Save your money and buy yourself one."

It was clearly not the response Tony had hoped for. Vertucci led his nephew away, purportedly to meet an old friend of his. I suspected he wanted to get Tony away from me and my nosy questions.

"I wouldn't have picked him as your type," Pryce muttered near my ear.

I turned to glance at him in surprise. "What makes you think he's my type?"

"Perhaps it was the way you kept shoving your breasts in his face."

"In his face?" I sputtered, my fingers curling into my palms to stop myself from punching him. "First of all," I said, loud enough for the others to hear, "I'd have to be an amazon to pull off that trick, and second, it's none of your business what I do with my breasts." I turned to the others, who were gaping at Pryce, said, "Excuse me," and sashayed back to my table.

"What was that about?" Jonathan asked.

"A little matter I'm investigating." I sat down and dug into the mousse.

My mother gave me one of her chiding looks. "A matter like the one you investigated for Aunt Corrine?"

"No, not like the one I investigated for Aunt Corrine. Anyway, she forgave me."

"Then why does she bring it up in front of the entire family every Thanksgiving?"

"It's one of those treasured family stories." I smiled blithely, but she wasn't buying it.

"Abby, I hope your investigation doesn't include

Commissioner Vertucci," my father cautioned. "He holds a lot of sway in this county. You don't want to make an enemy of him."

"What will he do? Put me out of business?"

"If he wants to, and he'll do it without batting an eye. He's a cold man and he knows how to pull the right strings."

Exactly the kind of person I despised. Then again, I didn't trust politicians in general. If greed didn't suck them into the dark side, power would. Commissioner Vertucci was the type who would do whatever he could to protect his political power in the county, including cover up a horrendous crime. As the old quote goes, "Absolute power corrupts absolutely." It was one of Grace's favorites.

"Don't worry," I assured my dad. "I'll be careful."

I hoped those weren't famous last words.

I kept glancing at my watch as we finished our coffee, hoping Marco had received my message. What was he doing out of range of his cell phone anyway?

I had a sudden image of him and the girl from the DMV getting cozy on his sofa, and I quickly wiped it out of my head. I didn't even know if Marco *had* a sofa.

For some reason three words from the police inventory flashed in my mind: pink silk sofa. Odd choice for a nineteen-year-old. Billy could have purchased it from a secondhand shop, but still—pink silk? It struck me as odd enough to check out. Perhaps someone else had been living in that apartment with Billy—someone with feminine tastes. Someone who might have been a witness to the murder.

When we left, Vertucci and his nephew were still eating, which was good. As we crossed the parking lot, my brothers and their wives peeled off to their cars, then my parents headed for their specially designed van. I tagged along to help with Dad's chair.

"Be careful, Abigail," my mother cautioned. "There

are drunks out on the roads." This was her standard Friday-night admonition.

"Take care, baby," my dad said, as I leaned through the window to kiss his cheek.

I checked my watch as they pulled away. Where was Marco?

CHAPTER THIRTEEN

I was just about to slide into my car when Marco stepped out of the shadows. I jumped two inches. "I wish you wouldn't do that."

"Sorry." He gave me a glimmer of a smile, reminding me of the Cheshire cat from *Alice in Wonderland*. "Where's the SUV driver?"

"Follow me." I started for the clubhouse, with Marco fast on my heels. "What did you find out about the second car?"

"I checked out the address, but no one was home and newspapers were piled on the porch like they were out of town."

"I don't think we need to worry about them. I'm fairly certain I found the driver." We crouched outside the dining room and peered cautiously through a window in time to see Vertucci and his group rise from the table. "See the young guy? His name is Tony Vertucci. He's the commissioner's nephew."

I filled Marco in on the rest of the gang as we hid in the tall viburnums near the front door. We shadowed them to the parking lot and listened while Vertucci stopped to talk with his nephew, but all I could hear was a word here and there, none of which sounded like *murder* or *SUV.* Vertucci got into his Cadillac and drove off, while an obviously chastised Tony skulked over to a red Mustang. To my amazement, he drew back his foot and kicked the rear tire, muttering oaths that would have made a sailor blush. Then he got in the car and peeled rubber.

"I wouldn't want to be in front of him on that narrow road," I said to Marco.

"Let's see where he's going." Marco jogged away, weaving among cars to where he'd parked his Jeep on a golf cart trail. I followed as quickly as my high heels would allow, then climbed in the passenger side.

"What side of the car were you on when you saw the driver that morning?" he asked, pulling out of the parking lot.

"Left."

"Left it is."

We followed Tony into town, where the main streets were four lanes and Marco was able to pull closer to the Mustang's left side without being obvious.

"Okay, take a look at him. What do you think?"

"From this angle he's a dead ringer for the guy I saw. He even asked if we'd met before, although that might have been a really bad come-on. He didn't strike me as the brightest bulb on the tree." I fired a finger pistol at Marco.

"What's that about?"

"Part of Tony's shtick. I had a hard time keeping a straight face. He's staying with his uncle and working as a crew supervisor for a paving company. The commissioner got antsy when I started asking questions, especially when I asked what kind of car Tony drove. Suspicious, isn't it?"

When it became apparent that Tony was going back to the family compound, Marco slowed down, looking for a place to make a U-turn.

Suddenly, lights came up from behind—a car riding

our bumper. Marco glanced in his rearview mirror as the telltale red-and-blue lights of a police car began flashing. Swearing under his breath, he pulled over as the cop car came up even with his window.

"Well, well, look who's back again," Blasko sneered, glancing from Marco to me. He was by himself tonight.

"We've got to stop meeting like this," Marco said dryly.

Blasko was not up for Marco's wit. "You like being a PI, do ya, Salvare? Here's a tip for you: If you value your license, find another neighborhood to haunt."

Marco let out a long whistle. "Threats now, Blasko? What will you resort to next, breaking my kneecaps? Like I said before, it's a public road."

"You heard me," he yelled as Marco rolled up his window. "Both of you keep away from here."

"Is he watching us, or is he watching Vertucci?" I asked.

"Good question."

A light rain started, misting the windshield. Marco turned on the wipers and headed back for the highway. He didn't say anything for a long time, and I wondered if he was thinking he'd wasted a good evening. Maybe he'd even had to leave a hot date behind.

"Did you have your cell phone turned off this evening?" I asked, tracing a drip down the side window with my index finger.

"For a while."

"I hope I didn't pull you away from anything—important."

He gave me a sidelong glance, as if he knew exactly what I was hinting at. But rather than satisfying my curiosity, he said, "Now that you've found your SUV driver, you can give the information to your insurance company and let them take it from there. Case closed."

"My case, anyway."

"What other case is there?"

"The murder case."

"That's not your problem."

"But it is *a* problem." And I had promised the Ryans that I'd do whatever I could to help. Now that I had found my suspect, how could I turn my back on their need? The image of them walking hand in hand into that funeral parlor had imprinted itself in my mind. That boy had been their only child, and now he was gone because someone had decided Billy didn't need to live anymore.

"Actually," I said, studying a paper cut on my thumb, "I was thinking that it would be wise to find out where Tony Vertucci was the morning my car was hit—just to make sure I've got the right guy. Think how embarrassing it would be if it was the other SUV that hit me. But I can find that information myself, so thanks for your help, Marco. I'll tear up your check for the roses as soon as I get home."

"Back up, Miss Marple. You said this was your guy."

"He is! I think."

Marco gave me a you're-going-to-meddle-again-aren't-you? look. "Just how do you plan to get the information?"

I shrugged a shoulder. "Don't worry. I'll figure out something. I have a friend in the prosecutor's office."

He muttered a few choice words under his breath as he turned onto the highway. It wasn't until he had walked me to my door that he said, "I'll get the information for you. You keep your nose out of it."

When Nikki came home from work, I was sitting on my bed in my yellow print pajamas, thumbing through a Victoria's Secret catalog, bemoaning my body. I'd been endowed with breasts; why hadn't I been born with long legs, too? Where did they find these perfectly sculpted models?

"Implants," Nikki advised, leaning over my shoulder. "No skinny, tall woman has real boobs like that."

"I wish there were leg bone implants," I sighed.

"Femur."

"Whatever."

"Stay there," she said, and rushed to her room where I could hear plastic hangers clicking together. She came back carrying a spaghetti-strapped rayon dress in crimson. "You'll look taller in this."

"Tall? I'll look like a red fireplug!"

"Try it on before you start criticizing. Trust me; it looks different on."

I eyed the dress warily, then shrugged it on over my head, dropping my pj's as I wiggled the thing down over my breasts and then my hips. As I stood there, with the hem hanging midcalf, and the surplice top stretched so tight across my breasts that my nipples protruded, I threw up my hands in disgust. "See? I told you."

"Just wait," she said, making a few adjustments. She lifted the elastic waist to empire height, then grabbed my one and only pair of strappy black heels from the closet. "Step in."

I obeyed. And I had to admit the dress didn't look half-bad. But the other half . . .

"It's still too long. And the straps fall off my shoulders."

"I have two words for that: masking tape."

"I thought duct tape was what everyone used."

"Masking tape always works for me." She ran to the kitchen and returned with a roll, which she proceeded to use to tape up the hem to just the right length. She pulled the excess strap material inside the back of the dress and anchored it with more tape.

I swiveled to see the back, which had a deep V cut. Not bad. I had a nice back. And the front fit now, too. "Hey! I look kind of—"

"Hot," Nikki finished. "Definitely hot."

Saturday morning I was up early to prepare for my trip to Michigan to check out Tom Harding's bank. I chose a colorless outfit—white sleeveless shirt, khaki shorts, and sandals, and a tan baseball hat to cover my hair. I had already called Dave Hammond to inform him of my plan to follow Harding, and, at Dave's request, I'd also run it past Pearl to get her okay. Both had cautioned me to be careful.

I packed a lunch of peanut butter and grape jelly on whole wheat and a bottle of Splash, and grabbed my portable CD player and a few discs, since Corvettes didn't have radios or any other device that might take the driver's mind off the road. As my brother so helpfully pointed out, they were made for racing. Did I care about the lack of conveniences? Not when I had that 427-cubic-inch engine roaring down the highway with all 430 of its horsepower revved up. As for the winter, I'd deal with bad weather when it happened.

But once I had settled all my stuff into the car, I realized that if I were going to tail someone, the last thing I'd want to drive was a bright yellow convertible. So I loaded my arms with my equipment and trudged back up to the apartment, where I rummaged in the kitchen junk drawer for Nikki's spare keys. I wrote her a note explaining my purpose and leaving her my keys, then jogged down to her car, a 1998 white Toyota Corolla.

Lottie had given me the address of Tom Harding's girlfriend, so I arrived early and waited down the block. Half an hour later the woman's garage door opened and Harding's pickup truck rolled out. He was at the wheel with the girlfriend beside him, a woman with hair so big it looked like someone had pumped a hedgehog full of helium.

I gave them a two-block lead, then began to follow. The highway was deserted that early on a Saturday, making it necessary for me to keep my distance. Fortunately, as we crossed the state line into Michigan, traffic picked up and I was able to get closer.

An hour later, Harding veered off at a sign for Slinger

Lake, and I followed, winding through a tiny, nondescript village before turning onto a road that circled the lake. There were beach homes on both sides of the road, some modern, and some looking like they'd been there since the Ice Age. Harding drove halfway around the lake, then pulled into the short driveway on the backside of a huge, obviously pricey, cedar-sided home facing the lake.

As I inched past the house I could see a long sweep of green lawn that ran down to a private dock, where a motorboat was moored. I wrote down his address for reference, then retraced the road back to a village that consisted of a grocery/deli, marine supply store, upscale clothing store for the boating set, branch bank, gas station, and post office the size of a stamp. I parked at the marine supply store, diagonally across from the bank, then strolled casually across the street.

Two bank tellers, girls that couldn't have been out of high school more than a week, leaned against their counters chewing gum, twirling their hair, and generally looking bored. I sized them up and picked the girl most likely to gossip. "Hi, Susie," I said, reading the name posted on her counter. "Hey, love your eye shadow. What's the color?"

Susie preened, tossing her blond ponytail. "Icy violet. It, like, really sparkles at night."

"That is totally cool," I said, trying to seem deeply impressed. "Do you think it would look good on me? I'm not sure, with my hair color and all." I took off my hat and tucked it in my back pocket.

She leaned closer to study me. "I don't know. What do you think, Tami?"

Her colleague peered over her half wall. "She needs green."

"Yeah," Susie agreed. "Definitely green. Sea mist green."

"Sea mist. Thanks a lot." I started to turn, then smacked myself on the forehead. "I almost forgot why I came. I'm trying to find a man named Tom Harding. Do you know him?"

Tami wrinkled her nose. "We know him."

"The thing is," I said quietly, "his wife is a friend of mine, and she thinks he's cheating on her, hiding money, you know—being a total jerk."

The two tellers exchanged knowing looks. Susie spoke: "We're not supposed to give out information about our customers."

"That's what I was afraid of. I wish I knew where else to look. He left my friend without a car or money to care for their handicapped son—while he runs around!" I heaved a forlorn sigh. "Well, thanks anyway."

"Wait," Susie said, after first getting an encouraging nod from her cohort, "I can tell you one thing: Mr. Harding is a real dirtbag."

"He's like, 'Hey, girly, step on it,'" Tami chimed in, doing her impression of Harding. "He treats us like morons."

Susie glanced up at the clock on the wall, then leaned close to the window to whisper, "He comes in every Saturday before noon. If you want to see him, stick around."

"Thanks. I really appreciate your help." I took a brochure with the bank's name and address on it and walked across to the grocery/deli. It was ten thirty; I had time to kill.

I bought a cup of coffee and walked up and down the block, pretending to be fascinated by the contents of the store windows. At eleven, I remembered to put my hat on to hide my red mop, then decided I'd better find a place to sit before my feet started to throb. With no benches nearby, I ended up perched on the hood of Nikki's car, nursing a tall glass of lemonade in a paper cup and sweating rivulets between my breasts.

At eleven thirty Harding and his girlfriend pulled into a parking space in the bank lot, went inside, and emerged ten minutes later. I watched them walk up the street and enter a little café, so I waited a bit to make sure they were staying. Then I returned to the bank.

"Did you see them?" Susie whispered, when I finally stepped up to her window. "Isn't he, like, a total skag? Today he told me I would win first prize in the Most Stupid Teller contest." She snapped her gum with righteous indignation.

I leaned closer. "Want to help me get him?" At her enthusiastic nod, I said, "Tell me how much money is in his account."

At that Susie balked. "I'd like to help you, but I don't want to get in trouble. Maybe you could, like, talk to Mr. Keyes?" She nodded toward the glass windows of an inner office.

"Do you think he'd see me now?"

"Sure. Come with me. I'll introduce you. Hey, Tami, I'll be right back."

I followed Susie's bobbing ponytail into the branch manager's office. A man in his early thirties rose from his desk and gave me a long look.

"Mr. Keyes, this lady needs some information," Susie announced, and promptly left. So much for her introduction.

I quickly launched into my mission of mercy, using a lot of eyelash batting and hopeful smiles, then held my breath and prayed that it worked.

"You understand I'm not allowed to give out that information," he said.

"I was hoping that maybe you could accidentally let it slip somehow." *Blink, blink.*

Keyes typed something into the computer, then studied his screen. "Are you sure this is where Mr. Harding keeps his business account? All I see is a very modest personal account, unless he's using a different name. . . . Wait. What's this?" Again he typed. Then his eyebrows pulled together.

I was dying to jump up and run around for a look, but I forced myself to ask calmly, "Find something?"

He bit his lip, as though he couldn't decide what to do. Then he looked up at me and sighed. "I'm afraid I've told you all I can."

Time to haul out the blarney. I pulled off my hat, tucked it in my purse, and tossed my hair back flirtatiously. I leaned forward to rest my elbows on his desk. "Mr. Keyes," I began.

"Fred."

"Fred. I really need your help. If I can't find out where Harding is hiding his money, his poor wife won't be able to support their handicapped child." I turned the dial on my voice to sultry. I'm not above using feminine wiles to aid a person in need. "Will you help me, Fred?"

His gaze dropped to my bustline, and I could almost see the drool forming in the corners of his mouth. "I'd like to help you . . ." He paused, his eyes still on my chest. Then, as if he remembered there was a person attached to it, he shifted his gaze back to the screen, his face turning red. "I can't give you any information without a subpoena."

Double damn! Dave couldn't *issue* a subpoena unless he had the information. I had to find out in what other names Harding had opened accounts, or Pearl wouldn't get a dime of her husband's considerable income.

As I searched for something to say to make him change his mind, Fred turned the face of his monitor to the right side, so that if I leaned more to my left, I could read it. Then he swung his chair around and began to sort through papers on the credenza behind him. I took the hint and leaned.

There on the screen was the name Sapling Corporation.

"Thank you, Mr. Keyes. I won't trouble you any further."

I dashed to the car and dug out my cell phone. "Dave, you'll never guess where I am."

"Please tell me it's not the lockup." He listened quietly as I relayed the information, then said, "Harding didn't see you, did he?"

"He didn't see me. Can you issue that subpoena now?"

"You bet! Congratulations, Abby. Now we can find out what Harding is hiding."

I snapped my phone shut and turned on the ignition, imagining Harding's surprise when he found out his secret stash had been discovered. He'd be one furious farmer. Thank goodness he'd have no idea who Dave's source of information was. He was angry enough with me now.

As I pulled out of the parking lot, I glanced to my left, and there, not two yards from me, stood Tom Harding, glaring at me with murderous intent.

CHAPTER FOURTEEN

Harding's eyes were narrowed into tiny slits of fury. "You!" he bellowed, and I took off, tires squealing. My heart was pounding like a kettledrum as I drove onto the highway. I held tightly to the wheel and glanced in the rearview mirror every ten seconds, praying he wasn't hot on my heels. The more distance I put between us the more I was able to relax. By the time I reached the Indiana state line, I knew I was home free. This time my mission had been a success.

I pulled out my cell phone and called Lottie. "Tell Pearl she's going to be all right. We're this close to knowing where her husband is hiding his money."

"Sweetie, you're a wonder! Tom didn't see you, did he?"

"He might have caught a glimpse."

"Shoot! Abby, watch your back, you hear me?"

"I'll be fine. Gotta go. Big date tonight, remember?"

"With doll face? You didn't think I'd forget *that*, did you? One thing, Abby: I want your firstborn to be named after me, female *or* male."

When I arrived home at two o'clock that afternoon, Nikki was in the parking lot unloading groceries from the Vette.

"Wow! Did you get sunburned!" she said, as we carried bags of food up to our apartment.

I set the bags down and darted into the bathroom to check my reflection. Sure enough, my neck, shoulders, and arms were bright red. If there was any doubt about me looking like a red fireplug before, I'd certainly settled it now. I slathered on aloe lotion and went to help Nikki unpack.

"Did you get the information you needed?" she asked me.

"Oh, yeah. We're going to nail that bastard. I see you bought wine." I pulled out several bottles of pinot grigio and merlot.

"It's for my party. You *do* remember you're helping me throw a party, don't you? Have you decided what we're making yet?"

Her party! "How about Cheez Whiz on saltines?"

"How about some red pepper hummus on pita triangles, herbed goat cheese rolled in prosciutto slices, and melon balls for starters, then a main course of—"

"Hold it, Nik! This is a married man, remember? We don't need to impress him."

"But we do need to impress Scott. And besides, I bought some of the ingredients." She held up a container of goat cheese.

"Who's Scott?"

"He's the new male nurse in the ER." Nikki sighed dreamily. "Wait till you see him."

"Married?"

"Not. I swear."

"Okay, let's impress Scott, but not with a sit-down dinner. Let's just do an assortment of hors d'oeuvres and a couple choices of wine and beer."

She beamed. "Sounds great."

"When is this party?"

"A week from today. I've invited nine people already. Why don't you invite Greg Morgan and make it an even ten?"

I glanced down at my sizzling skin. "Let's see how the dinner goes this evening."

By the time Morgan arrived to pick me up, I was feeling the heat of my sunburn, but I looked good otherwise. Nikki had worked her masking tape magic on the dress, and in my strappy black heels, with my hair up in a twist, I actually felt tall.

"Slay him, tiger," Nikki whispered. "And don't forget the points."

We played this little game where we rated our dates by adding or subtracting points. Every guy started out with a zero and moved up or down from there. In Morgan's case, he earned two points for coming up to the door to get me instead of waiting in his car. I awarded him an additional two points for his outfit—a colorful Tommy Bahama–style silk shirt, neatly pressed off-white slacks, and tan loafers, no tassels.

I opened the door and let him have a look at me. His gaze swept down and up again. Then he nodded appreciatively. "Nice sunburn."

"Thanks, Morgan. You sure know how to make a girl feel special." That was a minus seven points. He was three in the hole. Not the best way to start a date.

The sultry evening air settled over my hot skin like a damp blanket as Morgan ushered me downstairs to his navy Volkswagen Jetta and opened my door. As I slid in and adjusted my dress, I noticed some of the tape starting to peel away from the hem, probably due to the humidity, and quickly pressed it back down. I heaved a sigh of relief when Morgan turned on the air-conditioning.

On the drive to Chicago we chatted about cars, the ever-present road construction, baseball scores, the state of our justice system, and red versus white pistachios. I gave him five points for liking the white ones. Basically, we chatted about everything *but* the murder case. I couldn't bring myself to pump him for information so early in the evening. I didn't want him to think that was my reason for agreeing to the dinner. My *sole* reason, at any rate.

Morgan pulled into a parking garage, gave the valet his keys, and escorted me across the street to the Italian Village. Women's heads turned to stare at us as we followed the waiter to our table, and I had to admit I felt flattered to be his date. He got ten points as a bonus.

And when Morgan started off the meal by ordering a 1994 Chianti, I was impressed enough to give him five more points. It wasn't often I found a guy who knew wine. Of course, I only knew about wine because Pryce had taught me. At least he'd contributed something to my life besides a resolve never to trust a male outside my immediate family.

Morgan toasted the success of both our careers. We clinked glasses, and I gazed at him admiringly over the rim as I sipped, thinking, *This guy could change my mind about men.* Then I heard the unmistakable *screetch* of masking tape separating from fabric. That was the moment my hem, as well as the evening, began to fall apart.

While discreetly trying to pinch the hem in place without giving the appearance that I had fleas, I noticed that my right spaghetti strap was starting to droop down my shoulder. I cursed inwardly, knowing it was only a matter of time until the left side followed suit. I excused myself and headed for the ladies' room, clutching my purse to my chest to hold up the straps, and weaving between tables rather than chancing the center aisle, where my state of dishabille would be more apparent. On my way, I nabbed a waitress, explained my situation, and sent her to find something with which to repair the dress.

She returned to the washroom with a handful of bobby pins and a roll of Scotch tape. I rejected the pins in favor of the tape, and ten minutes later walked back to the table with lots of crackling going on, making me sound like a bag of potato chips being opened, not to mention that my sunburn had deepened in color and intensity.

"Everything all right?" Morgan asked, rising from his seat. His gentlemanly gesture earned him another three points. He was now up to twenty.

"It's my sunburn," I said, forcing a smile.

For the next hour and a half I alternated between eating my dinner—spinach salad, linguini with marinara sauce, two pieces of crusty bread dipped in olive oil, and another glass of wine—and cooling off my hot face with my napkin, which I kept dipping in ice water. Morgan didn't notice because he was too busy telling me about every case he'd ever won, all his sports victories going all the way back to Little League, and every award and honor society he'd ever been invited to join.

I'm sure there was more, but by the time I'd finished the linguini, my brain had gone numb. It was like a flashback to all the miserable dinners I'd eaten with Pryce. Needless to say, I was seriously disappointed. Morgan lost half his points as punishment.

A waiter came around to take our dessert order. I took a pass, wanting only to end the torture as soon as possible. Morgan, however, decided to order a cappuccino.

"I hear Marco Salvare is working on your case," he said, looking suddenly flustered.

I lowered the wet napkin from my forehead and stared at him. "My *case?*"

"Your hit-and-run."

Was this why he'd asked me out? Because he was curious about my case? "Who told you? The cops?" At his sheepish grin, I said testily, "Did they also tell you they're giving us the runaround?"

"What do you mean?"

"They've got more information than they're telling us."

"Says Salvare?"

"Yes, says Salvare. The cops know who hit me. They're protecting somebody." I bit my tongue. Marco would hate me for telling that to a prosecutor.

Morgan leaned forward, suddenly very interested. "What has Salvare found out?"

"Nothing. That's what's so frustrating."

He leaned back as the waiter brought his coffee. "Salvare is a nutcase, Abby. He sees conspiracies everywhere. Why do you think he was kicked off the force?"

"He wasn't kicked off. He left by mutual agreement."

"Is that what he tells people?" Morgan snickered. I found myself prickling in Marco's defense.

"Don't let Salvare turn you paranoid, Abby. The cops are the good guys. Remember that."

"They're real peaches, especially when they're writing bogus parking tickets. You don't need to lecture me, Morgan. My father used to be a cop. I know all about them, good and bad. And do me a favor. The next time you have a chat with your cop buddies, tell them I'm fighting those tickets all the way to the top."

I excused myself and headed for the ladies' room, where I ripped the crackling tape from the hem, balled it up, and threw it in the trash. Let the dress hang below my knees. What did I care? Morgan had asked me out only to see what was going on with my case.

We drove home in silence. I think Morgan sensed my mood because he made no move to walk me to the door. I got out of the car, thanked him curtly, and clumped inside. As soon as I'd locked the apartment door behind me, I undressed and headed for the shower to cool my skin under a soothing stream of cold water.

"Abby?" Nikki called, knocking on the bathroom door. "Are you all right?"

"I'll be out in a minute. Pour me a big glass of chocolate milk."

"How many points did he get?"

"Zero. And he's not invited to your party."

The soy milk was waiting on the coffee table, and Nikki was perched expectantly on the sofa. "Spill."

"I can tell you how it went in two words: Pryce Osborne."

"*Pryce* was there?"

"He might as well have been. Morgan was just like him. Brag, brag, brag. Male egos! *That* is why I will never marry." I sighed heavily and took a sip of milk, then told her the most humiliating part—Morgan's reason for asking me out. "After that, I couldn't bring myself to question him about the murder case, because then I'd be just as big a fraud as he was."

Nikki was pensive for a moment, then perked up. "Let's go to the beach tomorrow afternoon. That'll cheer you."

"I have a sunburn."

"Okay, then we'll go to the outlet mall instead. Is there any better medicine than shopping?"

As it turned out, the trip to the mall was very good medicine indeed. The road we usually took had been torn up for repaving, necessitating a detour. Next to the detour sign was another one that read CPC PAVING. Vertucci's company. And what did I see parked under a tree beside the road? A white van with the CPC logo on the side. And inside the van sat Vertucci's nephew, smoking a cigarette, the radio turned up full blast.

I parked behind the van and got out. If Tony had been the one to hit the Vette, I'd know immediately by his reaction to my car. "I'll be right back," I told Nikki.

"Wait." Nikki dug through her purse and pulled out a tiny bottle of hair spray. "Here. If he tries anything funny, shoot him in the eyes."

"It's broad daylight, Nikki."

"He might have a silencer."

"You've been watching late-night TV again, haven't

you?" I strolled up to the truck and tapped on the window. "Hey, Tony."

He lowered the volume on his radio, rolled down the window, and smiled. "If it isn't the hot little lady from the country club. Where'd you come from?"

"Back there." I pointed over my shoulder. "I'm on my way to the mall with my friend Nikki."

"Nikki, huh?" he said with a leer, as if the very name conjured up a hot babe.

"Come on back. I'll introduce you."

He stepped out and started back with a swagger, then stopped when he saw my car—exactly the reaction I'd hoped for.

"Is something wrong?"

He made a big show of checking his watch. "Hey, I gotta get moving along." He saw Nikki wave to him. "How ya doin'?" he called, firing his little finger pistol at her. I saw her cover her mouth to hide a laugh as he turned on his heel and practically jogged back to the truck.

I tagged after him, enjoying his discomfort. "What are you doing sitting out here on a beautiful Sunday afternoon?"

Tony climbed into the van and shut the door, clearly eager to be away from me. "Making fifty bucks an hour."

"Not bad, considering you're not doing anything."

He took off, spinning his tires in the gravel.

I slid into the Vette and fastened the seat belt. "He's the guy, Nik. He took one look at the car and turned gray."

"So now what?"

"Now I wait for Marco to find out where Tony was that morning."

I pulled out and followed the detour signs around the construction. It wasn't until we were strolling through the mall that it hit me: The logo on the side of the CPC truck was the same logo I'd seen on the T-shirt of the man in the SUV.

All signs were pointing straight at Tony Vertucci. Just a few more pieces of evidence and I was sure I could finger him once and for all. But what would it take?

Zowie! I had it. What had Marco used to prove I wasn't parked illegally? A camera. All I needed was a shot of Tony driving that SUV, and *he was mine*.

While Nikki tried on bathing suits in the dressing room, I pulled out my cell phone and punched in Marco's number.

"Hey, sunshine. What's up?"

I was so excited I could barely get the words out. "I just talked to Tony Vertucci. You should have seen his face when he got a look at my Vette. What's more, he was driving a company truck with a logo on it that was the same as the one on the shirt of the guy who ran out of the alley. I'm *almost* one hundred percent certain Tony's our man, Marco. But I figured it would help to have a photograph of him in the SUV. I probably shouldn't use the flash. Is there film that will take pictures in the dark?"

"Whoa, there, girl. Are you telling me you're going on a stakeout?"

I hadn't actually thought of it that way, but, "Yes, I guess I am."

"I told you *I'd* find out where Tony was that morning."

"It can't hurt to have backup proof."

He sighed sharply. "You're not going to give up, are you?"

Marco just didn't get it: I would never give up when it came to righting an injustice. "No, Marco. I'm not."

"Are you going on this so-called stakeout alone or is Ethel going with you?"

"Who is Ethel?"

"Ethel is your sidekick, Lucy."

"Who is Lucy? Oh, I get it. *I Love Lucy.* Very funny. And you would be Ricky? Or his bongo drums?"

"You haven't answered my question."

I considered the possibility of having Nikki go along, and immediately dismissed it. She was not what I'd term an adventuress. In fact, she was basically a wuss. Like Ethel. But I was *not* a ditz like Lucy. "I'm going alone."

There was a long moment of silence. Then Marco said with a definite note of resignation, "I'll be there at dusk— with my camera."

CHAPTER FIFTEEN

Nikki answered the door that evening, then nearly collided with me in the doorway of my bedroom when she came to announce Marco's arrival. She pushed me back inside the room and shut the door, whispering excitedly, "You didn't tell me Marco was so *male!*"

"Shhh! His ego is big enough already."

"Forget everything I said about Greg Morgan. *This* is the guy for you, Abby."

"I have a rule about mixing business and pleasure."

Nikki huffed in exasperation. "Then hurry up with the business part. And don't give me your speech about never trusting a male, blah, blah, blah. You have to get over what Pryce did and move on. I'm telling you, do not let this guy get away, Ab." She paused to scan my black-clad torso. "You're not seriously going to wear that outfit, are you?"

"This is a stakeout, not a date, and yes, I'm going to wear this."

Nikki eyed me critically. "Maybe it would work if you tied a mint-green scarf around your neck."

"Or I could carry a flashing neon sign that says, 'Hey! Look at me! I'm on a stakeout.'" I rolled my eyes and left the bedroom.

"Hey, sunshine." Marco fired a finger pistol at me from across the living room, then blew on the tip of his finger. "I think your pal Tony is on to something here."

As he took aim at Nikki, I grabbed his finger and pulled him toward the door. "Come on, ace. You're firing blanks."

"Never say that to a guy. Take care, Nikki. Don't forget what I told you." Marco pulled the door shut behind me. "Cute girl. Is she still after that doctor?"

"That didn't pan out. Now it's a male nurse. What was it you told her?"

"Tea and honey," he replied, as we clumped down to his car. "She has a scratchy throat and the lozenges weren't working."

"She told you all that in the thirty seconds it took to get from the door to the living room?"

"She's a fast talker. How was your date Saturday night?"

I turned to look at him. "How did you know about my date?"

"You told me."

"I did?"

"Either that or I heard it in the bar."

I was appalled at the very thought. "My love life is a subject of discussion in the bar?"

"Everything is subject to discussion in a bar. Got your V8 juice?"

I turned to go back inside.

"There's some in the car," he said, catching my arm.

I stared at Marco as he opened the Jeep's door for me. "You brought Splash for me?"

"Don't look so shocked."

"I can't help it. You're being so—gentlemanly."

He gave me a look that said of course he was a gentleman. I decided I'd been keeping points on the wrong guy.

* * *

Marco drove into the commissioner's wooded subdivision but stayed clear of his house for fear of running into Blasko. About half a mile beyond Vertucci's block, he pulled onto a dirt trail that led into the woods and tucked the Jeep far enough into the brush not to be seen.

"We're going to hike over," he said, opening a can of black shoe polish, "which means trudging uphill in dark, mosquito- snake- and mice-infested woods." He told me this as he blackened my cheeks, nose, and chin. I suspected he was still trying to deter me. "If you want something to drink, better get it now. It's in the cooler behind the seat."

I peered through the window. Sure enough, there sat a small thermal cooler. No doubt there were napkins and straws inside, too.

"By the way," he said, as he sprayed me down with insect repellant, "I found out a few things about your pal Tony."

"Tell me," I said, coughing.

"He had a charge of aggravated assault brought against him in Chicago last year. Seems he got into an argument with a coworker and nearly killed the guy. But it was dismissed."

"That figures. His uncle probably used his influence to get the charges dropped, but at least it proves that Tony has a history of violence."

"You're not going to like this one."

I reached into the cooler, pulled out a Splash, twisted off the cap, and took a swig. "Go ahead."

"He was at the construction site last Monday morning."

"Then how do you explain his reaction when he saw my car today? And do we know how early Tony was on the job?"

"He was there when the crew started at seven o'clock. That puts him quite a distance away an hour before your car was hit."

I tapped the mouth of the bottle against my chin. "It

takes about twenty-five minutes to get from the road construction site to downtown. What's to say Tony didn't leave work around seven thirty that morning, drive to Billy Ryan's apartment, get into an argument, shoot him, hit my car, and drive back all in about one hour's time?"

"I had a feeling you were going to say that. Unfortunately, my source couldn't say for sure that Tony was there all morning."

"Then I say we find out. We should also see if Tony has a registered gun. And we really need to get a look at the SUV's rear bumper. Maybe you can check with the police to see if they got any good fingerprints from the apartment. Boy, would I love to get my hands on the coroner's report to see if there was a struggle of some kind."

"Whoa, Lucy. All you're after is a photograph, and then we're done. Hear me? D.O.N.E."

"At least we should take a look at that bumper. If it has yellow paint on it, that would put the SUV at the crime scene." And there was no way the cops could ignore that little fact.

"Listen to me. The first thing Vertucci would have done when he found out about the accident was to get that SUV into the shop to have it repaired. I guarantee there won't be any traces of yellow paint on it. Remember who you're dealing with."

Marco pulled a sleek black cap and gloves out of his jacket pocket, put them on, then leaned in to open the glove compartment and remove a small leather case. Tucking it inside his jacket, he gave me a critical once-over. "That baseball cap won't do. I can see your hair." He opened the back of the vehicle, rummaged in a leather bag, and removed a black knit stocking cap. "Wear this."

I made the switch, put the Splash back in the cooler, and turned for another inspection.

"Ready?" he asked.

"As ready as I'll ever be."

                    *   *   *

I squinted into the darkness of the forest, trying to keep Marco in sight as I wended my way through trees and brush, stepping on a cushion of spongy leaves and crunching twigs underfoot. The air smelled damp and woody, and got cooler the deeper into the trees we went, making me glad for the long sleeves of my black T-shirt.

After a good quarter of an hour of trekking, Marco stopped and turned, and I ran into him. He clutched my shoulders to steady me. "The house is up ahead," he said in a quiet voice. "We're on the garage side of it. I'm going to approach to see if it's safe. Keep low and wait here. I'll signal you with two flicks of my flashlight if it's safe for you to proceed."

And then he was gone.

I ran a finger under the edge of the hat, trying to reach an itch, and swatted away a mosquito buzzing my face, the only part of me not covered in repellent. A twig cracked behind me, sending my heart rate into the stratosphere. I swung around and quickly searched the blackness for a human form, then saw a squirrel leap onto a tree trunk close by.

It seemed hours before Marco finally signaled, but that was probably because my legs were going numb from crouching. I crept to the edge of the clearing, then darted across the open space between forest and house, and pressed myself flat against the bricks, heart racing from the excitement. I felt just like a female James Bond, inching along until I reached the corner, then peering around it. But I didn't see Marco.

A hand on my shoulder nearly caused me to lose bladder control. A mouth near my ear said, "Follow me."

I grabbed Marco's shirtfront and tugged his face down until I could put my mouth to *his* ear. "If you ever frighten me like that again you will sing soprano."

"If the dogs are loose, we'll both be singing soprano."

I grabbed his shirt again. "Dogs?"

"Rottweilers."

I followed him around to the back of the garage, thinking, *He's only trying to frighten me. If there were dogs, we'd hear them.*

On the backside of the garage was a window. Marco cupped his hands around his eyes and peered inside, then flicked on his flashlight and swept the beam over the cars, illuminating Tony's Mustang, then the black SUV. "Looks like your pal is home."

"I wish you'd stop calling him that. Tony is not, and never will be, my pal."

The parking space nearest the house was empty, which meant the owner of that car—probably Vertucci in his Cadillac—could potentially arrive at any moment. It wasn't a particularly comforting thought.

"Follow me," Marco whispered. He slunk along the side of the building until he could peer around the corner at the front. After making sure it was safe, we crept across the lawn to a circle of shrubbery surrounding a flowering dogwood, about ten yards from the garage. Marco knelt and took a tiny camera out of his case, while I hunkered down behind the trunk of the tree, my eyes locked on the front door.

"Notice anything odd about the house?" he asked.

"All the lights are out."

"Including the security lights." He patted a black-encased outdoor lantern planted in the ground beside him. "A big house like this, you always leave your security lights on."

"What do you think it means?"

"It means we sit tight and hope we find out why they've been shut down."

"I can see how this work could be tedious," I remarked, after half an hour of sitting on hard ground. "It helps to have a partner, doesn't it?"

He took out a pair of night-vision binoculars and adjusted them.

"Well, I think I make a damn fine partner," I said. "Look at me—wearing black, keeping the stakeout from being boring. What more could you ask for?"

"A little silence would be nice."

I threw him a scowl, and he playfully punched my arm. "You're all right, you know that?"

"I am?"

"Yeah. You make me smile."

"You hide it well."

"I'm smiling on the inside."

I had to laugh at that. Marco had the most serious expression of anyone I knew, even more so than my sister-in-law Portia, who had perfected the model's sour pout. As we waited for some activity, I started wondering about Marco. Was he somber because of his army and police training, or had he joined those forces because he was a serious kind of guy? Did Marco have a dark side I had yet to see or was he a *what you see is what you get* type? Was there a steady girl in his life, and if there wasn't, why not?

Scratch that last question. It was none of my business. But that didn't mean I wouldn't like to know. "How long has Vertucci been a commissioner?" I asked.

"Too long. The longer he's in office, the more corrupt he becomes."

"You know what I think? I think most people go into politics honestly believing they will do good things, but once they discover the power of their position, they forget their original purpose."

"And then there are those who are corrupt from the start."

"Which do you think Vertucci is?" I asked.

"The second type."

Suddenly he sat forward, his body tensing like a cat. Down the street we could hear a car approaching, but without its headlights on. It rolled to a stop at the bottom of the driveway and someone got out.

Just then, the automatic garage door began its noisy

ascent and a lone figure appeared in the opening, the light from inside illuminating his silhouette. He was shaped like a beach ball, and wore a light-colored polo shirt and dark slacks. He stepped out of the garage to meet the man who came quietly up the drive.

Marco trained his binoculars on the pair. "Blasko," he whispered. He watched the two men for a few minutes, then handed the binoculars to me. "Do you recognize the other one?"

I studied the heavy-set man. "He's familiar."

"Didn't you see him at the country club Friday night?"

"You're right! That's Vertucci's cohort, Frank Jancich. He manages County Paving Company." I watched as Jancich handed Blasko a thick envelope. Blasko opened it and thumbed through something inside. I focused on the envelope. Money!

"Marco," I whispered excitedly, "Mr. CPC just handed Blasko an envelope full of bills."

Marco aimed the camera and began clicking. I could see Blasko grinning as he folded and pocketed the envelope. Jancich said something to him, and Blasko replied with a shrug.

At that, Jancich's voice got louder, floating across to where we huddled. "Wait a minute, you son of a bitch. We had a deal. Don't go pulling that shit with me."

I couldn't hear Blasko's reply, but Jancich didn't look pleased. After much further debate, he finally gave a curt nod of acceptance, then ducked back inside. I watched Blasko saunter down the driveway to the squad car as the garage door descended behind him, putting us once again in darkness.

Marco slipped the camera in the bag and took the binoculars from me. "You just witnessed a payoff."

"Didn't I tell you so? Vertucci is paying Blasko to cover up the murder! Wow! This goes deeper than I thought."

"No conclusion jumping, sunshine. It looks suspicious,

but all we really know is that Blasko accepted money. For what purpose is anyone's guess. Maybe he fixed a few parking tickets for the commissioner."

"Come on, Marco! You saw that wad. That's a heck of a payment for fixing parking tickets. It would have been cheaper to pay the fines. Look how Blasko crept up to the house with his headlights off. He's a dirty cop, and he's working for Vertucci."

Marco was silent for a few moments. Then he said in a low, grit-your-teeth kind of voice, "There's nothing I hate more than a dirty cop."

I could tell by the chilly look in Marco's eyes that he meant it. "I feel the same way, Marco. What's our next move?"

"I'm going to find out what that bastard is up to. Let's get out of here."

We hadn't gone more than five yards across the lawn when the floodlights came on. I wasn't sure what had alerted the occupants, but I considered it a moot point when I heard the sound of frenzied barking.

"Hell!" Marco muttered. "The Rottweilers are loose."

CHAPTER SIXTEEN

W hy had I ever imagined that detective work would be fun? I sprinted across the grass, pumping my legs as hard as I could, running like the devil and all his staff were after me. The blood was thudding so loud in my ears I couldn't tell if Marco was with me or not. All I could think of was being torn to bits by those dogs.

I raced through the woods, branches scratching my hands as I held them in front of my face. I burst out of the trees onto a road and kept going into more woods. I didn't stop running for what felt like hours, until the barking had faded. Then I keeled over onto my knees and gasped for breath, extremely grateful for my exercise routine. I can't imagine the state I'd have been in if I hadn't been in good shape.

Once I'd regained my strength, I stood up on trembling legs and peered through the maze of tree trunks. "Marco?" I called in a whisper. I listened hard for several moments, but didn't hear anything. What if he'd been caught?

Wiping my perspiring forehead with a tissue, I suddenly realized my hat was gone. I looked around, but didn't really expect to find a black lump in the dark. I started walking in the direction I thought was south, and soon realized I had no idea where I was. I finally decided to stay put and wait for Marco to find me, or for daylight, whichever came first.

Sitting with my back against a tree trunk, I kept a sharp eye out for anything creeping, crawling, or slithering past. Wings flapped above me, no doubt attached to the small furry bodies of bloodsucking bats. As the hour wore on, I began to get chilled, and decided to do some jumping jacks to keep warm. The noise would also help keep the critters away.

I bounced up and down until my leg muscles cramped. Then I sat again and rubbed my arms for warmth. So far the only positive I could find in being lost in the woods in the middle of the night was that it made my evening with Morgan seem like heaven.

Suddenly I spotted a dot of light in the distance. I crawled behind a tree and watched the light move closer, praying it was Marco.

"Abby?" a wonderfully familiar voice called.

"Over here!" I waved from my hiding spot. His light found me moments later, but instead of rushing forward and hugging me in relief, he glowered down at me and said, "Where's your hat?"

"I lost it."

"Let's hope you lost it in the woods."

"Even if I didn't, if Vertucci found it, he wouldn't know who owned it."

"That's not what worries me." He offered me a hand and hauled me to my feet. "It's your bright red hair in the floodlights. Let's go."

"Can't we rest a bit? My legs are a tad shaky."

Without batting an eye, Marco swung me up in his arms. "Some partner you are."

I lay my head against his shoulder and enjoyed the ride. It couldn't have been easy to trudge through the woods carrying a one-hundred-twenty-pound bundle.

Even though I was short, I still had meat on my bones. But Marco didn't even break into a sweat. And the faint trace of cologne that clung to his neck was causing my thoughts to drift to romance of the knight-in-shining-armor variety. So when he finally set me down beside the car, I let go with some reluctance.

"Are you all right?" he asked, tilting up my chin for a better look.

I nodded, wishing against my better judgment that he'd continue my romantic fantasy with one little kiss. Instead, he handed me his handkerchief. "Better take off the polish before we get to town. You look gothically deranged."

I scrubbed my face as he started the car, thinking about that moment when Marco could have kissed me but had chosen not to. Not that I cared.

"Want to stop for coffee?" Marco asked as we headed back to town.

"That's the best idea you've had all evening."

After washing off the rest of the shoe polish in the ladies' restroom at a diner, I settled into the red leather booth across from Marco. While I sipped a decaf, he checked his camera.

"So where were you while I was wandering in the woods?" I asked.

"I saw Vertucci's Cadillac coming up the street, so I circled back. He must have phoned ahead from his car to have the lights switched on. Sorry I couldn't let you know, but you were too far ahead to hear me call, and I couldn't very well shout. You were okay out there, weren't you?"

Other than having to fend off snakes, spiders, and bats, did he mean? I smiled gamely. "Of course I was all right. I'm tough. So what did you see?"

"When Vertucci pulled into the driveway, Mr. CPC came out to meet him. Luckily, he had the dogs on leashes. The two men had quite a discussion in the garage, and Vertucci looked pretty steamed. I have a feeling that whatever information Blasko passed through CPC, it didn't sit well with the commissioner."

"And the lights were off so their meeting could take place. Do you think Blasko's putting the squeeze on them?"

Marco took out the roll of film, pocketed it, and snapped the camera shut. "Could be."

"What are you going to do with the film?"

"Develop it, then tuck it away."

I nearly choked on the coffee. "You can't be serious. Those photos are evidence!"

"Evidence of what? Blasko taking an envelope filled with money? There's no crime in that. Look, you're somewhat of a babe in the woods when it comes to the way these things work, so you have to trust me on this. If there's bribery going on, we have to keep quiet until we know how far it extends up the chain of command."

"You're not talking about all the way up, are you? Not to the chief. I've known Harrington since I was a little girl. He was always so nice to me."

"Nice guys get greedy, too. I'll develop the photos myself and put them in a safe place. Maybe the day will come when they'll be useful, maybe not. In the meantime, I can't go flashing them around, making accusations that could be considered slanderous unless I have positive proof of a crime. I don't want to lose my license and/or get sued."

I studied his serious face and finally came to the conclusion that Marco was smarter at these things than I, so I would be wise to heed his advice. I certainly wouldn't want to be responsible for anything bad happening to him.

But what to do about the murder? There had to be some way to prove positively that link between Tony Vertucci and Billy Ryan. I rested my chin on my hand and tried to ponder the matter, but my eyelids kept wanting to close.

Marco glanced at his watch. "We should get a move on it. You've got to be at work in a few hours."

I nodded, covering my mouth to hide a yawn.

Standing in front of the door to my apartment building, I said, "You've more than earned your dozen roses, Salvare."

"I told you I would."

I held up his blackened handkerchief. "I'll wash it for you."

He took it from me, found a clean corner, then used it to wipe a trace of shoe polish from above my lip. He was standing so close that I could see gold flecks in his dark brown eyes. My insides began to quiver.

"You shouldn't look at me like that," he said huskily.

I had to wet my lips to speak. "Why not?"

"I just might have to act on it." Giving me his lopsided grin, he turned and sauntered away, calling back, "Keep the handkerchief. It's a souvenir."

Damn his arrogant hide.

Nikki flung open the apartment door before I could even insert my key. "What happened?" she squealed, bouncing with excitement.

I glanced down at my scratched hands and black-smudged nails and shook my head in amazement. "You'll never believe it. I spent an hour lost in the woods after fleeing from a pack of attack dogs—"

"No, I mean, did Marco kiss you? I was watching from the window, but that darned overhang blocked my view."

Leave it to Nikki to cut to the important stuff. "Oh, that!" I gave her what I hoped was a secretive smile.

"He didn't kiss you," she said with a sad sigh. She turned around and went to the kitchen to resume scrubbing the sink. "Better put some antibiotic cream on those cuts so they don't get infected."

"How do you know he didn't kiss me?" I asked, following her into a room that positively sparkled.

"You would have told me."

"Would not."

"You always have before. Who was the first to know about Dennis Hunt kissing you in sixth grade?"

"I was twelve years old!"

"Who was the first to know that Pryce kissed like a fish?"

"I was suffering from temporary insanity. Okay, you're right. Marco didn't kiss me. But he almost did and probably would have if I hadn't warned him away."

"Right."

Ignoring her sarcasm, I scrubbed my hands, then pulled a carrot stick from the fridge and munched on it as I filled her in on the night's events.

"What if that CPC Frank guy got a look at you?" Nikki asked, furiously polishing the faucet. "With your hair you're pretty easy to recognize for anyone who's seen you before."

The carrot suddenly didn't want to go down. I grabbed a glass of water and gulped it. "You know what probably happened," I said. "A branch snagged my cap when I was running through the woods." That's what I hoped anyway. "Your voice sounds better," I told her, changing the subject.

"I've been drinking tea with honey all evening."

With Nikki that would mean honey with tea.

"Then we ran out of honey so I switched to sugar."

Not good. Nikki had a sugar-sensitive system. Two candy bars had her bouncing off walls. "How many cups are we talking about?"

"Eight, nine—fifteen."

She was on a sugar high. That would explain the feverish cleaning.

"That Marco is a wonder," Nikki gushed. "I'm going to clean the refrigerator. Want to help?"

I hied off to the bathroom to shower while Nikki worked off her buzz. Her clunking in the kitchen kept me awake until well after three in the morning. I'd have to thank Marco for his advice the next time I saw him.

Monday morning started off with a bang, literally, when the tenant in the apartment above dropped something on the floor that weighed the equivalent of an elephant. After tumbling out of bed and nearly breaking my ankle in the tangle of sheets, I was able to assess the situation with some calm and decide that neither the ceiling nor my racing heart had been damaged. It didn't, however, put me in the best of moods, especially since I was lacking a crucial three hours of REM sleep.

But the day was early yet, and all was not lost. The sky was bright blue streaked with wispy clouds, the air smelled of sprinklers being run on cut grass, and we had made another surprising discovery in the murder case. I just had to push aside my frustration that we couldn't use the evidence quite yet. Patience wasn't one of my strong suits.

With a Walkman attached to my shorts and a water bottle at hand, I drove to the park for a brisk walk, then got dressed for work with renewed energy. Today was Monday. Who knew what good was going to come of it?

I parked down the block from Bloomers, since I now had a phobia about leaving the Vette in the spaces directly across the street, and waved to Jingles, who was washing the window at Down the Hatch. When I walked into the shop, Grace was overseeing two workers installing an alarm system.

"Good morning, dear," she called over the sound of electric drills. "How are we today?" I knew she was dying to ask about my date with Greg Morgan, but her proper upbringing wouldn't allow her to be so crass.

"Hey, sweetie!" Lottie boomed from the workroom. "I've got breakfast made in the back. How did it go with doll face Saturday?" Lottie had no such reservations.

I glanced at the workmen, who had stopped drilling in order to hear my answer. Ignoring them, I stepped over toolboxes and equipment, making my way to the back through the obstacle course they'd laid out on the tile. Grace was right behind me, a cup of coffee in hand.

Lottie pulled out a stool and patted it. "Sit and tell us."

"It was," I said, a rapturous look on my face, "absolutely"—I held up my hand to signal a pause, took a sip of coffee, sighed with pleasure, and set the cup back in its saucer—"horrendous."

Both women gasped so hard I felt the air go whooshing past my face. It took a moment for them to start breathing again. Then Lottie waggled a finger at me. "You're pulling my leg."

"I swear I'm not."

"Was Mr. Morgan rude to you, dear?" Grace asked, ready to suit up in armor and go to battle for me.

"He was very gentlemanly. He was also a bore and an egotist. In other words, he was Pryce all over again. We said good-bye in the car, and I split."

The sound of power drills filled the air. Obviously satisfied that my love life was pathetically hopeless, the workers had resumed their task.

Lottie slapped the table. "That confirms it: I've lost my touch. No more matchmaking for Lottie Dombowski. I'm hanging up my spurs and riding off into the sunset. The end. Adios and good-bye."

One could only hope.

"I put the alarm system estimate for your apartment on your desk," Grace informed me, as Lottie stalked off to the cooler. "It can be installed next Tuesday. You'll just have to call to set it up."

I glanced at the estimate and gulped. No way could Nikki and I afford that. A dead bolt would just have to do.

"Have you seen the morning paper yet?" Grace asked.

"No, why?"

She slid it in front of me. Across the front the headline blazed POLICE SOLVE RYAN MURDER.

It was my turn to suck in air. Had the cops finally nabbed Tony? I gripped the paper with both hands and read the article, then looked up at Grace in amazement. "Elvis Jones did it."

CHAPTER SEVENTEEN

I read the first paragraph in silence as I ate the scrambled eggs Lottie had made for me. Had my gut feeling about Tony been wrong?

Police have arrested Elvis Jones, 53, in the murder of nineteen-year-old Bill Ryan, of New Chapel. Jones, who lists no permanent address, had been staying at the Shady Inn Motel under an assumed name. He was taken to the county jail and placed in isolation. He will be arraigned Monday.

"I'd like to know what evidence they have against him," I said, skimming the rest of the article.

Grace removed my empty plate and put it in the sink. "You'll never get the police to tell you."

But Greg Morgan might divulge a tidbit or two. I took the newspaper to my desk and reached for the phone, then drew back my hand. I couldn't call him up to fire questions at him, not after Saturday night's fiasco. I plunked my chin on my hand, thinking. Maybe Marco could help.

"I'll be right back," I told Grace, and dashed off to find him.

Marco was working in his office, his dark head bent over a ledger. I tapped on the doorframe. "'Morning."

"Hello, sunshine," he said, without looking up.

"Did you see the paper this morning?"

"Yep."

I took a seat opposite him. "And?"

"Looks like they got their man."

"Did they?"

He put down his pencil and leaned back, stretching his arms over his head as though he'd been hunched over for hours. "The police think so."

"Do *you?*"

"It doesn't matter what I think." He picked up his pencil and resumed his work.

"Come on, Marco. I'm just asking for your opinion."

"He's guilty," Marco muttered distractedly.

"Based on what?"

"Based on whatever evidence the police have."

"I think Blasko framed him."

Marco looked up at me. "You're making quite a leap there."

"Not really, if you think about it."

"At the moment, finishing these tax forms is a little more important than speculating about Elvis Jones's guilt. Besides, that's up to Jones's lawyer to prove."

But only if his lawyer knows what questions to ask. I wheeled around and started for the door.

"Hey!" he barked. "Stay out of it."

"Okay."

"Like hell you will." He was fast on my heels all the way through the bar and out onto the sidewalk, where he stepped in front of me to block my path. "Look, I've already put out some feelers to see if I can find out what Blasko is up to. So you keep out of it."

"All I'm going to do is ask Dave Hammond to find out what Elvis's charges are and who his lawyer is."

A muscle in his jaw twitched. "Why are you so determined to interfere?"

"I'm not interfering. I'm simply a stickler for justice."

"You still believe Tony Vertucci is involved."

"I'd bet my life on it."

"You'd better hope it doesn't come to that."

I stopped at Dave Hammond's office and found him preparing for court. As usual, he was in a last-minute rush to gather paperwork and case files, so I asked if he would look into the Jones matter for me when he had a free moment. He promised he would and left at a trot, suit coat flapping as he hurried across the street. On my way back to Bloomers I glanced over at my Vette and there, plastered against the windshield, was another dreaded yellow paper.

"I don't believe this!" I said to no one in particular as I read the parking ticket. I checked the time on my watch, and then scanned the street for the traffic cop, who was, as usual, nowhere in sight. Frustrated, I moved my car to a new spot, then marched to the courthouse dungeon. "I'm being harassed."

"That's what they all say." The clerk slid a form toward me. "You know the routine."

Annoyed into the bad mood I had tried to keep at bay, I walked into Bloomers to the smell of sawdust and the sound of beeps.

Grace was in the parlor serving tea and cakes to the Monday-afternoon ladies' poetry circle, but stepped out as soon as she saw me. "Did you learn anything?"

"Nothing. Dave's going to check into it for me."

"I have a bit of good news," she said, beaming proudly. "The alarm system is in." She pointed to a white plastic box mounted on the wall behind the front counter.

"I suppose I need to learn how to use it."

"It's quite simple, really." She lifted the cover to show

me how to set it and how to disarm it. Amazingly enough, it actually did seem quite simple.

"Just remember," she cautioned, "if you get here first in the morning, you have only forty-five seconds to disarm the system once you've unlocked the door and stepped inside."

"No problem."

"And thirty seconds to leave once you've armed it at night."

"Right. I can do that."

"Here are your messages."

Two of them, to be precise, both from my mother. While Lottie worked on a huge centerpiece of mixed summer blossoms for a bank lobby, I punched in my mother's cell phone number, got her voice mail, and left a message.

"How is Pearl?" I asked Lottie.

"She's doing better. She's out looking for a job today."

"Good for her. Any word from that maniac she's married to?"

"He's being strangely silent. She has that hearing tomorrow morning, you know, that providential one."

"Provisional."

"That's it. I hope Dave can free up some money from the tightwad's wallet. Pearl wants me to go with her, so I'll take an hour off, if you don't mind."

"Be my guest." Pearl needed all the moral support she could get.

The phone rang, and moments later Grace stuck her head through the curtain and whispered, "It's your mother."

I picked up my phone and said cheerily, "Hi, Mom. What's up?"

"Abby"—*pant, pant*—"I just got your message." *Pant, pant.* "What did you want?"

"You called *me,* Mom. Twice. Are you on a treadmill?"

"No, I'm on the sidewalk."

"Running?"

"Carrying. I'm outside your door. Would you mind opening it for me? My arms are full."

"I'll be right there."

Lottie shortened a lily stem and inserted it into the foam inside an Oriental vase. "What's your mother up to now?"

"Apparently she's carrying something and wants me to open the door for her. I don't know how she's holding the phone."

"She's *carrying* something?"

My eyes widened at the same time Lottie's did. "She's bringing more art!" we both cried.

I jumped up, dashed through the curtain, and got to the door just as my mother was about to knock on it with an elbow. I opened the door, and she toted an enormous bundle inside. She placed it on the floor in the middle of the room and stood back with her hands on her hips.

"Wait till you ladies see what I made. I just finished it this morning." She knelt down and began to remove the wrapping. She still had on her artist's smock.

Grace, Lottie, and I watched in morbid fascination as layers of brown paper fell away and a trio of neon-hued, anatomically correct male monkeys appeared. They were in a circle and seemed to be doing the hula, with their hands raised over their heads, palms skyward.

I glanced at Lottie, who was quietly edging out of the room. Grace stood with her hand on her chin in silent contemplation as my mother took the last piece of the puzzle from the wrappings—a glass circle—and set it on top of the monkeys' hands.

"That's a very clever table," Grace said diplomatically.

At that moment, the Monday-afternoon ladies' poetry circle disbanded and the ladies began to stream out of the parlor. I watched their faces as, one by one, they took in the dancing monkeys. It was not a pretty sight. A few gasped aloud, others covered their mouths in horror. One even shaded her eyes. And one poor old soul nearly fainted and had to be helped to the door. Within minutes, the room was empty except for the three of us. I had no doubt but that word of the table would be all over town by evening.

"Do you like it?" my mother asked, turning to smile at me.

"What's not to like?"

"What can I ask for it?"

A decent burial? "I'll have to check around to see what other, uh, monkey tables are going for."

My mother glanced around the store, arms akimbo. "Where's my pot?"

Drat! I'd forgotten to put the ivy in it. Where had I put the thing, anyway?

I was just getting ready to launch my excuse when she cried, "There it is, back in that corner! You've nearly hidden it, Abigail. Let's pull it out where it will be more visible."

I stared at the overflowing pot with mouth agape. Someone had filled it and placed it beside our antique display cabinet. I glanced at Grace, who shrugged.

God bless Lottie.

"Maureen, would you care for tea?" Grace asked, ignoring my vigorous head shaking.

"Love it." She adjusted the glass top and stood back to admire her latest work of, well, art. "Abigail, do you think it should be in the front window?"

"No! That is, not unless you want the sun to bake it. Besides, it might be too wide. Also, that window is probably too shallow, and—" Ye Gods, what other excuse could I use? I glanced around for a better location, somewhere that would satisfy my mother and not offend my customers. "How about over there, in front of the wicker settee? Kind of a tropical theme."

"Perfect." She carefully scooted her dancing monkeys across the room and positioned it just so. I knew that as soon as she was gone Lottie would move it elsewhere, possibly next door, although I doubted the Realtors would appreciate it.

"Tea is served," Grace called from the parlor.

My mother headed off in that direction. "Coming, Abigail?"

As if I had a choice.

"Your cousin Jillian is getting married," my mother announced as we sat at one of the white ice cream tables in the front window. She sipped delicately from her teacup. "You'll never guess who she's marrying."

For once my mother was right. I didn't have a clue. Jillian Knight got engaged once a year. Last year it was to an Italian restaurant owner from Chicago's Little Italy neighborhood. The year before that it was to a Parisian artist named Jean Luc who had a showing at the Museum of Modern Art in Chicago. I couldn't remember who came before Jean Luc, the English consul general or the Denver plastic surgeon.

"Surprise! Pryce's brother!" my mother exclaimed joyously. "Isn't that a coincidence?"

I nearly choked on my tea. Claymore Osborne, Pryce's younger brother by two years, was every bit as borish and snooty as Pryce. He also stood to inherit half the Osborne fortune. Jillian always did go after money. Then again, Jillian came from money—my aunt having inherited a third of an oil well somewhere in Texas—which is probably why Jillian met the Osbornes criteria. It hadn't hurt that she'd graduated from Harvard, either, although I'm not sure how much she actually learned there. She had started out in Organismic and Evolutionary Biology only because she'd thought the catalog had said *orgasmic*. "You know she won't go through with it," I told my mother.

"There's always a first time."

I didn't even try to win that one. We'd never seen eye to eye on anything.

"May I get you another cup, Maureen?" Grace the Referee asked.

"No, no. I must be on my way. I'm due for a haircut at one." She bounced up, bussed my cheek, and scurried away, calling back, "See you Friday!"

I sank back in the chair as the bell over the door jingled. "There's no way I'm going to that wedding, Grace. Not with Pryce there."

"You're right, dear. It would be awkward." Grace picked up the empty cup and carried it back to her counter.

"But if I don't go, Jillian will be hurt, and Pryce will think I'm staying away because of him. Wouldn't he just love that!" I sighed in resignation, imagining one horrible reception scenario after another. "Looks like I'll have to go."

"I've already marked it on the calendar, dear."

Dave Hammond called back midafternoon to tell me that all he'd learned was that Elvis had asked for a public defender, was in an isolation cell, and was awaiting his initial hearing. No one was willing to give out any other information.

"I don't suppose there's any way you can get me in to talk to him," I asked.

"Abby."

"Okay, just thought I'd ask. Will you let me know who his public defender is?"

"So you can pump him for information? Good luck with *that*. By the way, I've sent for the incorporation papers for the Sapling Corporation on the Harding case. That should tell us if Harding is truly involved. I'll let you know when I hear something."

I still had Elvis Jones on my mind when I stopped to pick up my coupons at Pronto Printer. I wanted to question the building superintendent at the Hampton Arms to see what he knew about the murder, but other than pretending to be an investigative reporter I wasn't sure how to go about it.

Armed with a box of bright green flyers, I started back for Bloomers and saw Lottie's four boys waiting for me outside, sweat beading on their foreheads.

"Hi, guys," I called, strolling up. "It's cooler inside."

"No, it's not," one of them said. Except for Karl, who had tipped the ends of his dark hair a white-blond color, I couldn't tell them apart. Another boy added, "Mom is on the warpath." A third hitched his thumb toward the fourth. "Karl screwed up again."

Poor Karl. He seemed destined to be the black sheep of the family. I knew Lottie should have given him a *J* name. "What did you do, Karl?"

"Nothing."

"Right," I said with a smile.

One of the *J*'s spoke: "He wants to move out of the house and live on his own."

"I'm tired of being a quad," Karl retorted. "I want my independence."

"He wants to rent that empty apartment on the next block," another brother said. "The one where Billy Ryan lived."

"I just wanted to check it out," Karl clarified.

"Now I get why you're standing out here. Your mother would never go for that plan. Here are the flyers. Divide them up and hit all the businesses in town."

I watched them head off in different directions. Then I cut through the alley next to Bloomers and approached the Hampton Arms. Karl's plan had given me an idea. I could pretend to be looking for an apartment.

As I studied the names beside the buzzers, an elderly lady shuffled out, her back humped, her gray head stuck forward like a turtle poking out of its shell, undoubtedly caused by a bad case of osteoporosis. "Excuse me. Does the superintendent live in the building?" I asked her.

She had to crane her neck to peer up at me. "Apartment 1B, on the first floor. Are you going to rent here?"

"I'm considering it."

"Good! It's about time we had someone decent move in. Nothing but riffraff anymore."

My information antennae quivered. This woman could be helpful. "I know what you mean. It's hard to feel safe in one's own home. Take Elvis Jones for instance. What a tragedy that man's life is." I waited a beat, then gave her a wary glance. "He didn't live here, did he?"

"Not in the last five years or so. He caused so much trouble they wouldn't let him lease here anymore. I wasn't surprised when they arrested him. He was always breaking into vacant apartments to hide out. Stayed in one for a week once before he was caught. You know how they caught him?" She pointed to her nose. "I *smelled* him."

On that decidedly malodorous note, I tried to end the conversation, but she wasn't finished.

"So I said to my husband, 'Henry, there's an awful stench in the air downstairs. Go see what it is.' Well, sir, you know what he found? Elvis, flat on his back on the wood floor, snoring like a steam engine, flies circling him like hungry vultures."

I clucked my tongue to show my commiseration. "Let me ask you something: Do you consider Elvis to be dangerous?"

"Good heavens, yes. Armed and dangerous, just like they say on television."

"You've seen him with a gun?"

"A big old army gun, or so he claims. He used to brandish it around, bragging about what a crack shot he was. Crack*pot* is more like it." She cackled gleefully.

With that history I was beginning to see why the police would suspect Elvis. "Do you think he killed the boy?"

"I wouldn't put it past him. He didn't tolerate young people. Said they were all worthless—like *he* was a prize."

So Elvis had the means, the opportunity, and somewhat of a motive. And what did I have on Tony? Opportunity and my gut feeling. It didn't take a full-fledged lawyer to realize that those weren't enough.

I was on the verge of conceding defeat when the woman said, "You know, it could have been those drug-gies. We see them slipping in and out of the building early in the mornings—scary-looking people, like you see on *Law and Order*. We call the police, but they're never able to catch them in the act."

My ears perked up and so did my hope that my instincts weren't wrong after all. "Can you describe any of these scary people?"

"Oh, no. They always keep hoods up to hide their faces. We never see any cars, either. They sneak in and out like a bunch of spies."

Or like cops with their headlights off? "Did you see any of those people that morning?"

"Goodness no. Monday is my bath morning. Henry has to help me, you know. These old bones don't climb in and out of the tub very well."

"Did you tell the police this?"

"Huh. Think they care what an old woman has to say?"

"Could I have your name for future reference? I'm— working on this case for a friend."

"Of course, dearie. It's Betty Summers. That's with two *M*'s. You know, I didn't really buy your story about wanting to rent here. You're too smart for this place."

I took down Betty's information, thanked her again, and buzzed apartment 1B. The name listed there was Jerry Kenderhogen. I crossed my fingers and waited, hoping I'd get as much information from him as I had from Betty.

"Who is it?" a gravelly male voice said.

"My name is Abby Knight. I'd like to see your vacant apartments."

"I'll be there in a minute."

It was more like ten before an overweight, middle-aged man stepped out of the first apartment on the right side of the hallway. He had on a navy sweat suit that looked like he'd worn it for the past ten years or so and might not have washed it for that long either. He introduced himself and led me down a narrow hallway to apartment 1F. I walked inside and looked around while he gave me his sales spiel, including a bargain-basement deal on rent.

I could see why. The ceilings were warped and stained in giant yellow circles from leaks from the apartment above; the once-beautiful crown molding had grown its own mold; the window sashes were rotted; the walls were filthy; and the creaky wooden floorboards desperately needed replacing. I hadn't even glanced at the kitchen or bathroom yet, but from where I stood, I could smell them.

"Are any of the apartments furnished?" I asked, keeping my voice pleasantly curious.

"No, but I have some items that I rent out to my tenants. To tell you the truth, a few just became available."

"Such as?"

He scratched his left haunch. "Sofa, kitchen table and two chairs, couple of silk plants."

"What color is the sofa?"

"Pink. You'd like it. I'll give you a good deal on it, too."

It sounded to me like the furniture from Billy's apartment. I opened a closet door and pulled a chain. A bulb threw a dim yellow light over the interior, illuminating three wire hangers on a wooden rod. "Isn't there another apartment available on the second floor?"

"Not until we repaint."

The thought of painting over blood made me shudder. "What about safety? One of your tenants mentioned that there was drug dealing going on."

"Who said that? Betty?" He glanced at the door, as if to see if anyone were listening. "She watches too much TV. We get a few complaints about noise. That's about it."

Right. I thanked him for the information, told him I'd consider his offer, and left. I'd learned a lot, but nothing that would directly implicate Tony Vertucci or clear Elvis. I decided that I'd have to make an overture to Greg Morgan to see what other tidbits of information I could ferret out of his prosecutorial brain.

Lottie and I finished seven of the orders by five o'clock. Three were headed for the Happy Dreams Funeral Home, so we loaded them in her station wagon and she took off to make the delivery. I cleaned up the worktable and turned out the lights as Grace turned the sign on the door to CLOSED.

"Did you set the alarm?" she asked, as she headed out the door ahead of me.

"Oops. I'll do it right now."

"Thirty seconds," she called.

"Got it."

I stood in front of the little box staring at the keypad, trying to recall the procedure: PIN Number, Enter, Set Alarm? Or was it Set Alarm, PIN Number, Enter? I tried the latter and saw the red light go on. It was armed. I had thirty seconds to leave.

I started out the door and remembered my sunglasses were on my desk. How many seconds had passed? My pulse raced as I ran to the workroom. Where the heck were the glasses?

I pulled the bag off my shoulder and dug around inside. My mother would feel so vindicated at this moment. She always told me to get a purse with compartments.

Did I need the sunglasses anyway? A little squinting wouldn't hurt.

I dashed for the door just as the alarm began to sound. If I were a burglar, the deafening noise would certainly drive me out. With an index finger stuck firmly in my left ear, I hit the Disarm key, PIN Number, and Enter, and when that didn't work tried it in reverse. To my relief, the last combination worked. Then I sat down to await the police.

My cocky friend on the motorcycle showed up first, followed by several of his pals in their squad cars, sirens blaring. I was sitting on the wicker settee, facing the door, when they came in, guns pulled. One of them was Sean Reilly.

"It's just me," I said with a sheepish grin. "I accidentally set it off. We had it installed today and I'm still learning how to—"

Reilly silenced me with a glower. He turned to his buddies and waved them off. "I know her. She's the owner." Then he leaned down and pointed a finger at me. "Learn how to work this alarm or we'll have to charge you for every call we answer. And we won't be happy answering them, either."

"Yes, sir."

His gaze shifted to the left. He took off his silvered sunglasses and stared at my mother's inventiveness. "What the devil is that?"

"A monkey table," I said sadly.

He took a long look and started to laugh. I glanced up as Marco dashed through the doorway. "What happened? Are you all right?"

"I set off the alarm."

"Salvare, did you see this?" Reilly gasped. "It's a monkey's table."

"Not a monkey's table," I corrected, "a *monkey* table."

Reilly wiped his eyes. "That's the funniest thing I've ever seen. They even have wangs! What trick shop did you find it in?"

I hung my head. "My mother made it."

That sobered him. "Sorry. Learn that alarm system, okay?" He nodded at Marco and left.

Marco sat beside me on the settee and leaned forward to look at the table. He rubbed my shoulder. "You've had a rough day, haven't you?"

I nodded unhappily. Might as well milk the sympathy.

"Why don't you come have a bowl of corn chowder and a hot ham sandwich with me?"

"Okay," I said in a little girl's voice.

I carefully set the alarm and shut the door. This was something about which I would never tell Grace.

I sat in the last booth in the back by the kitchen, where I not only had a view of everyone coming into the bar, but also of my Vette parked across the street. It sat there like a sleek, shiny lemon, glinting in the sun.

Marco tended to some business at the bar, then slid in across from me, bringing a glass of red wine for each of us. "Here's to monkey tables," he said, clinking his glass to mine.

I sipped the wine. "Merlot?"

"Yep. Do you like it?"

"As long as it's not from a box, I like anything red." I took another sip and set it aside. "So you're really going to investigate"—I leaned toward him to mouth—"Blasko?"

"I said I would. It's going to be tricky, so the less said about it the better."

"I understand."

Marco eyed me over his glass. "I suppose you've talked to Dave Hammond already and got the scoop on Elvis Jones."

"As a matter of fact, there is no scoop. No one wants to talk about him. But let me tell you what I learned today."

Marco folded his arms on the table and listened, dark eyebrows drawn down in a thoughtful frown. "Interesting," he said.

I took a drink of wine and set the glass down with a firm *thunk*. "I need to know what evidence the police have."

"You know I hate like hell encouraging your meddlesome ways, but before you go planning something crazy, like breaking into the evidence room, don't you have a friend in the prosecutor's office?"

Probably not anymore. "Good idea. I'd completely forgotten him." I ignored Marco's skeptical look as I pondered a way to approach Morgan that would save face for both of us.

Our waitress brought bowls of steaming chowder, followed in short order by plates of sandwiches and fries. The cheddar cheese had melted over the edges of the thinly sliced ham, just the way I liked it. I scooped up a finger full and popped it in my mouth.

"Ketchup for your fries?" Marco held out the slender bottle.

"Pour it on." Ah, if only Pryce could see me now. I finally sat back some fifteen minutes later, my hunger abated, my soul soothed. "Now all I need is a peaceful night's sleep and I'll be a new woman."

"Come on. I'll walk you to your car."

We waited for a van to pass, then crossed the street together. The top was up on the Vette, so when I opened the door, heat poured out. I tossed my bag onto the passenger seat, then put the top down. "Thanks for the supper," I called, starting up the engine.

He did that pistol thing with his finger and threw in a wink for good measure, then jogged back across the street.

There was no one parked behind me, so I shifted into Reverse and put my foot on the gas to ease backward. As soon as I had enough room to pull out, I stepped on the brake, but the Vette continued to roll. I pressed down harder to no avail, and as the street inclined in the opposite direction, that backward roll took me straight into the intersection, where drivers began honking their horns in protest. Did they think I meant to do it, or that I just hadn't noticed?

"Pump the brakes!" Marco yelled from the opposite corner.

"I am! Nothing's happening!"

As soon as I had cleared the intersection, I shifted into Park and cut the motor, but the car continued its slow, backward slide until it hit a Buick parked at the corner. I jumped out to see if I'd damaged anything just as Marco jogged over. Luckily, the Buick only had a slight ding.

While I pulled out a pad and pen to leave insurance information for the Buick's owner, Marco got down on his hands and knees to look underneath my car. He rose minutes later and knocked gravel off the knees of his jeans.

"Your brake lines have been cut. Call the police."

CHAPTER EIGHTEEN

W ho would have guessed that teeth could clatter in the middle of the summer? As I sat in my car with Marco, waiting for the police to arrive, mine certainly were. One thought kept running through my head: Someone wanted me dead.

The most likely suspect was Commissioner Vertucci. But then I couldn't forget Harding's threats either. I knew he was angry at me, but enough to kill me?

"I didn't have a problem with my brakes until just now," I said, "so it must have happened after I parked here."

"In broad daylight?" Marco said. "Not likely. Besides, the lines weren't cut clear through. It could easily have happened this morning. You probably had just enough brake fluid to get downtown. Is there a garage near your apartment where you can park your car at night?"

I shivered hard. "Why? Do you think this person will try again?"

"Do you want to take that chance?"

"Sometimes people rent out private garages. I can look into it."

"Good girl. And at the risk of sounding like a broken

record, didn't I tell you that one of these days your meddling would get you into serious trouble?"

Motorcycle Cop's arrival saved me from replying. He pulled up to the curb behind the Vette, climbed off, and came toward us, shaking his head at me. "What now?"

After I explained the situation, he said, "There's not much I can do but have someone check for fingerprints." He got on his radio and called the station, then came back to tell us, "Someone will be over to dust it."

Forty-five minutes later, an investigator concluded that whoever had tampered with my brakes had worn gloves because there were no prints. Another hour later, my car was on its way to Dunn's Body Shop for repairs, and I was back in the blue Escort once again. I parked in the stall assigned to my apartment. Then, armed with Nikki's masking tape and a red marker, I placed long, marked strips in strategic places under and around the car. If someone tried to mess with it, I'd know about it.

Tuesday had to be better.

The next morning I woke to high winds, crashing thunder, and garbage cans rolling down the street. The only bright spot was that the masking tape on my car was intact. I had to skip my power walk, then couldn't find a parking space downtown close to the shop. I ended up in front of a shoe store on the other side of the square.

As I stood beside the car trying to lock the door, hold an umbrella over my head, and juggle my purse, a particularly nasty gust of wind snapped the umbrella inside out. Within seconds I was drenched. Did I say Tuesday would be better?

"Good morning, Abby," Grace called as I blew in the door. Her mouth dropped when she saw me.

After grumbling a greeting, I stuffed the ruined umbrella in the copper stand by the door, plopped my purse on the counter, and started toward the bathroom to fix my soggy locks. Thank goodness Grace had bought a hair dryer.

"The electricity is out," Grace said. "If you're going to the workroom you'd better take this." She handed me a lit candle from one of the parlor tables.

Okay, so my hair was wet and hanging in strings. Was that really so bad? I decided coffee would greatly ease the situation and headed for the parlor only to have Grace remind me again that the juice was out.

"Where's Lottie?" I asked, settling for a cup of cold water.

"Giving Pearl a pep talk. Her hearing is this morning."

We unlocked the front door at nine o'clock as usual, but not one customer came in. It didn't promise to be a good day. At nine thirty, Lottie breezed in with Pearl in tow. She plopped her cousin on the wicker settee and came back to see what I was doing, which happened to be putting together an arrangement of rosy pink coneflowers, blue globe thistle, and violet blue salvia—at least that's what colors they appeared to be in the light of fourteen candles I had placed around the room.

"Hey, sweetie, how about I finish this and you go with Pearl to the hearing?"

"Me? Why?"

"I didn't know the judge was going to be that ol' geezer Duncan. He and I tangled once, and he ended up tossing me in the hoosgow. One look at his craggy hawk face and flinty eyes and I'd be a puddle of melted strawberry Jell-O. I'd hate to think what that would do to Pearl."

I studied the long stem of salvia I had just inserted and decided it was too high. "What did you tangle over?" I asked, reaching for my trusty florist's knife.

"Whether I had a right to call someone a gigantic horse's ass."

"Whom did you call a horse's ass?"

"The judge."

I couldn't imagine anyone calling Hezekiah Duncan

anything but *Your Honor* or *sir*. He looked like what I always imagined God would look like in human form. "This incident happened in private, I hope."

Lottie's eyes twinkled impishly. "Right in front of a packed courtroom."

I handed Lottie the knife. "I'd better take Pearl to court."

"That was my thinking, too. You might want to fix your hair first."

Pearl was sitting exactly where Lottie had left her, clutching her purse to her chest like a shield. Her face was ghostly white and her eyes darted nervously around the shop like a three-headed dragon might appear at any moment.

"How are you?" I asked, sitting beside her. She bit her lip and shook her head, which I took to mean not well. "Is Tommy at school?" She nodded nervously, so I patted her arm. "Relax, Pearl. You're going to be fine. I promise." At that moment, the lights went on. I took it to be a sign from heaven, and ran to plug in the hair dryer.

At ten minutes to ten, huddled under Grace's red-and-white golf umbrella, Pearl and I hurried across the street to the courthouse and took the elevator to the third floor. As soon as the doors slid open, Pearl made a strangled sound and stepped back against the wall.

Coming toward us like a charging bull was Tom Harding, malicious intent in his eyes and his attorney close behind. At once I stabbed the button to close the door, but Harding was faster. He stepped in and blocked the opening with his huge body.

"Pearl, we gotta talk," he said, as I jumped in front of her.

"Get back, Mr. Harding," I commanded, pushing against his massive chest. It was like trying to move a cement mixer. Behind me, I could hear Pearl whimper in terror.

"Pearl, you're making a mistake," Harding said. "You can't do this to me."

"Mr. Feinberg," I shouted, as Pearl sank to the floor, "call off your client or I'll yell for Security."

"Pearl!" Harding bellowed, as Feinberg grabbed his arm and tugged him out of the elevator. "You'll be sorry, Pearl!"

"You'll be sorry, too, if you don't get out of her face," I shot back, just as two security guards came running over.

Harding looked directly at me, and I could understand why Pearl feared him. He was mean all the way to his yellow eyeballs—mean and ugly, like a mad dog. Except that dogs could be euthanized for it. What kind of hell had it been for Pearl to live with him all those years?

I took her by the arm and led her out of the elevator to a bench outside the courtroom. The poor woman was shaking like she'd been dipped in an ice bath, staring at her husband with huge, terrified eyes. Harding was glaring at her from across the hall, guards on either side of him, so I moved to block his view.

"He can't hurt you here," I told her, although I wondered just how much the guards could do if he was truly intent on harming her. And what about afterward? Who was going to protect Pearl then?

Dave appeared a few minutes later, and I quickly filled him in. He briefed Pearl on what would happen at the hearing, and then we were called in. Pearl sat with Dave at the plaintiff's table, and I took a seat in the row behind. Dave laid out the case for Pearl's support to Judge Duncan, who kept darting glances at Harding, as if to check his reactions. But the man who sat beside Feinberg was completely different from the one in the outer hall.

Finally Dave got Harding up on the witness stand and fired questions at him—such as why he refused to give Pearl any money to buy food for their son, and why he was threatening her—hoping to rattle his chains. But Harding remained calm, humble, and even contrite when the situation warranted it. He was doing his best to charm the judge. I wanted to wring his neck.

In the end, however, the wily old judge wasn't fooled, and Pearl was granted temporary support in a generous amount. I was so relieved I almost clapped.

As we filed out, Harding pushed forward, sneering in my ear from behind, "You haven't learned your lesson yet, have you, bitch?"

I doubled up my right arm, and with a quick, sharp twist of my torso, connected my elbow with Harding's paunch—hard. There were a *few* benefits to being short. I glanced up to see his face contort. "Looks like you could learn a lesson or two, Harding. And I'd think twice before tampering with the Vette again." Brave words from someone shaking on the inside.

"What the hell are you talking about?" he asked through teeth clenched in pain, as his lawyer pushed him off to the side.

I left him muttering oaths and hurried to catch up with Dave and Pearl, who were about to step on the elevator. Once the doors had closed, I sagged against the side.

"Are you okay, Abby?" Dave asked.

"I'm fine." I glanced at Pearl, who was standing as straight as a flagpole. I patted her shoulder. "You did it, Pearl. You got him."

Her eyeballs rolled back in her head, and she crumpled like a rag doll.

Dave had a firm grip on Pearl's arm, while I held the umbrella over our heads, as we walked her across the street in a downpour. I stepped off the curb first, straight into a deep puddle of water. Dave steered Pearl around it, and we scooted into the shop.

"It's a victory," I announced, standing the wet umbrella in the copper pot. Lottie whooped with glee and hugged Pearl.

Grace held up a handful of coupons. "Four customers came in with these while you were gone, dear."

"Another reason to celebrate," I said. The day was looking up.

Grace started for the parlor to get us cups of coffee, then paused and tilted her head toward the floor. "Does anyone hear a squishing noise?"

"It's my shoes. I stepped in a puddle," I said.

"Better take them off and dry your feet, dear. You don't want to get a fungus."

Lottie rolled her eyes, and Dave shook his head in amusement. Only Grace would think of a fungus.

I pulled Lottie off to the side to tell her about Harding's behavior at the courthouse.

"I told you he was mean," she replied. "I'm going to try to convince Pearl and Little Tommy to stay with us for a while longer, at least until that madman gets used to the idea that she ain't coming back."

"Good idea."

We warmed up with cups of steamy cappuccino while Dave regaled the ladies with details of the hearing. By the time Pearl had downed her coffee, her color had returned.

"You're going to be all right now," I told her. "You'll have money to take care of your son, and a protective order in place."

Remembering Harding's threat, I was starting to wish that protective order covered me.

Simon was waiting for me at the door that evening, a rubber band at his feet. Nikki was sitting on the sofa in her robe, sipping a cup of tea. She glanced up at me with bleary eyes when I walked into the room. "Hi, Ab," she rasped.

I tossed the rubber band for Simon. "What are you doing home?"

"I hab a code." She coughed for effect. "It started coming on last dite. By ears are plugged and by throat is sore."

"Gee, I'm sorry, Nik. Anything I can get for you?"

"Soup. I deed soup."

I fed Simon, who thought that whenever we ate, he should, too. Then I heated the contents of a can of hearty chicken and noodle soup and carried a bowl in for Nikki. I plunked down on the far end and had a bowl myself as I filled her in on the events of the day. She was still upset over my brakes being cut, so I left out the part about Harding's courtroom threat. She went to bed soon after, and I ran for the vitamin C tablets, gulping several for good measure.

At nine o'clock that night the phone rang. I answered and heard heavy breathing on the other end. "Pervert," I yelled, and slammed it down. When it rang again, I ran to the junk drawer in the kitchen and pulled out a whistle. This time I picked up the phone and put the whistle between my lips, waiting for the breathing to start.

"Abigail?"

"Mom! Did you call a moment ago?"

"No, and why didn't you say hello?"

"I just had a heavy breather call."

"Buy a whistle, Abigail."

I looked at the one in my hand. "Okay."

"I hear you had a date last Saturday with one of the prosecutors."

This woman had eyes and ears everywhere. "It was a casual date. Just dinner and conversation."

"How did it go?"

"Not very well. He reminded me too much of Pryce."

"How is that bad?"

A beep interrupted what would have been a testy reply. "I have another call. Good-bye, Mother. Talk to you soon." I switched to the next call, hoping it wasn't the pervert again.

"Abby? Justin. Your baby's repaired. You'll be happy to know there was minimal damage."

I was as delighted by that news as I was surprised that

Justin knew the word minimal. "Bless your heart, Justin. I'll be there first thing in the morning."

Funny how a day can go so badly and then all of a sudden make a complete turnaround.

Wednesday morning I was at the track by six o'clock, even accounting for the time it took to peel off all the masking tape under the car. The weather had turned hot and muggy overnight, and even at that early hour it was decidedly uncomfortable. Afterward, I showered and dressed, checked on Nikki, fed Simon, and drove to Dunn's Body Shop to pick up the Vette.

"You must have pissed someone off royally," he commented, scratching his ear with grease-stained fingers. "You could have been killed."

I was trying my best not to think about it.

I paid Justin and drove to town, parking on a tree-lined neighborhood street two blocks behind Franklin. It was a longer walk to the flower shop, but there was no time limit for parking. I'd outsmart that shadowy ticket writer yet.

Lottie and Grace were seated at the worktable, drinking coffee when I arrived. They mumbled distracted hellos, their heads bent together over the morning newspaper.

"What's so interesting?" I asked.

They glanced at each other, then slid the paper over so I could see the headlines.

ELVIS JONES CONFESSES TO MURDER

CHAPTER NINETEEN

Forty-five seconds after reading the headline I burst into Marco's office and slapped the newspaper down on his desk. "Did you see this?"

"I saw it."

"Do you believe it?"

"Yes, Abby. Elvis confessed. Give it a rest."

"Right. He confessed. We both know how that goes: 'Sign this paper, Jones, and then you can go home,' *wink, wink*. Well, I'm not buying it. Commissioner Vertucci paid a cop to extract that confession to cover up Tony's involvement, and that cop is Blasko. I know it in my gut."

Marco shut his ledger with an irritated *fwap*. "Would you just maybe consider the possibility that Elvis Jones *did* do it? And that Tony Vertucci showed up afterward, saw the body, got scared, and ran?"

"Then Tony's guilty of not reporting it!"

After heaving a very tolerant sigh, Marco came around the desk, put his hands on my shoulders, and gently guided me to the door. "You and I both know that's not a crime, just a shame. Tony has his uncle's protection, and nothing you do is going to change that. Now, go do your flower thing and forget about this murder case. It's over. We have better things to do."

Frustrated, I left the restaurant and stood on the sidewalk, trying to decide my next course of action. I knew Tony was involved in that murder somehow, just as I knew the police would investigate no further if they believed they had their man, or even if they didn't believe it, as long as they had *someone* to pin it on. But until *I* believed it, I wasn't about to settle for a quick solution.

Before I left for lunch I called my insurance company to give them the information on Vertucci's SUV so I could file my claim. At least in one small way I could strike back.

My agent, a genial red-haired man by the name of Toby McDaniel, asked, "Are you *sure* you want to file this against the commissioner?" in a tone of voice that was meant to imply, *Are you nuts?*

"Toby, I'd file it against the President of the United States if his car had hit mine."

"Okay," he said, though he didn't sound very happy.

I made a quick stop at the hot dog stand on the corner; then, munching a cheese-covered chili dog, I hiked over to Taylor to make sure there was no ticket on my car. At least that had been my original plan. It changed the instant I found a snowy-white Lexus parked where I had left the Vette. Panic washed through me as I glanced up and down the street. Where was my car?

I hurriedly dug for my cell phone and punched in 911. Ten minutes later two officers responded, one of whom was Blasko. He got out of the passenger side and swaggered over, thumbs hooked in his belt.

"Well, if it isn't Salvare's girlfriend," he said to his partner. "Miss Busybody."

I ignored him and turned to the other cop, a decent-looking guy in his late thirties who had a pen out and his notepad open. "My yellow Corvette was stolen. 1960, black roof and interior. I left it here around eight o'clock this morning."

Blasko snickered behind me.

"Can I see your license and registration?" the other cop asked. He seemed to be ignoring Blasko as well.

I slipped the registration out of my wallet, unfolded it, and handed it to him, then removed my driver's license and gave him that also. Both men seemed surprised. Most people keep their registrations in their glove compartments, which didn't help if their cars were stolen. The nice cop went back to the squad car to radio in the information while Blasko stood there with a smirk on his face, as if he had a secret.

A few minutes later the other cop returned with my papers. "Your car wasn't stolen, Miss Knight. It was towed."

My heart sank. Someone had put a big, nasty, metal hook beneath my newly refurbished bumper? "Why was it towed? This is a residential neighborhood. Free parking!"

Blasko pushed back the brim of his hat with the tip of his thumb, his beady eyes traveling slowly up my torso. "You shouldn't have parked by a hydrant."

I pointed to where the Lexus stood. "*That's* where I parked. Do you see a hydrant there?"

"No, but I see one *there*." He pointed to an empty space halfway down the block.

"I didn't park *there*. I parked in front of that yellow house, where the Lexus is."

Blasko's upper lip curled back in anger. "Are you giving me attitude?"

I knew he was itching for a reason to charge me, but I wasn't about to take the bait. I turned my back on him and said to the nice cop, "Would you tell me how to get my car back, please?"

"You'll have to go to the city garage and pay the fine."

"Pay a fine for what?" I asked as he slid into the police car. "I didn't park illegally."

"I'm afraid I can't help you there. For that you'll need

to file a complaint." He shut the door and started the engine.

"I *have* filed complaints," I called, "and I'm really tired of this harassment!"

"You call *this* harassment?" Blasko said with a sneer, and I swung to glare at him. He adjusted his hat and said in an undertone, "Lady, this is only the beginning."

CHAPTER TWENTY

As Blasko swaggered over to the squad car, a sick feeling of suspicion crawled through my gut. It grew
stronger when he paused to smile at me before sliding
into the vehicle. He was the one who'd had my car towed.

That feeling turned to helpless frustration as I watched
them pull away. What could I do? Call the police? Blasko
was the police. He was untouchable. Just like Tony
Vertucci.

I felt numb as I headed for the city garage, a block and
a half west of the courthouse. It all made sense now—the
dead rat, the parking tickets, the threats, the cut brake
lines. Commissioner Vertucci was using Blasko to scare
me off. Or kill me.

As I passed a bank parking lot, I spotted Marco's tan
Jeep in line at one of the drive-up windows. I diverted my
course and walked up to the passenger side, opened the
door, and climbed in.

"Hey! 'Afternoon, sunshine."

I stared straight ahead, rubbing my upper arms to ward
off the chill that had invaded my soul.

Marco shook my shoulder. "What's wrong?"

"I know who cut my brake lines."

He sat up straighter. "Tell me."

I started talking, and once the whole story was out, my numbness had not only worn off, but it had turned to fury. "How dare Blasko threaten me! How *dare* he! Well, I'm not going to let him get away with it."

I grabbed the door handle to get out, but Marco caught my elbow and held on. "Where are you going?"

"To see Chief Harrington."

"What do you expect Harrington to do? Call the commissioner and tell him to lay off you? You can't even prove the commissioner's involvement."

That stopped me. I rested my arm on the open window, tapping my fingers on the side of the Jeep. "Wait a minute. What about those photos? I can show them to Harrington, tell him what Blasko said to me, and let him know what's been happening with my car. How much more proof does the man need?"

"That's a very bad idea." Noticing that the sedan in front of him had pulled away, Marco rolled up to the machine, put an envelope in the pneumatic tube, and hit Send. "Look, you have every right to be angry, but going to the chief isn't the solution. Cops protect each other, mainly because no one else looks out for their welfare. So if you go to the chief and get Blasko in trouble, ten others will make life miserable for you, and there's no guarantee you'll even be proved right. Imagine what your life would be like if the policeman you accused was cleared."

"Then I'll go to the FBI."

"Again, bad idea. They'll contact the chief before they do anything."

"So you're saying I should just back down?"

"Not *just* back down. You need to step out entirely for your own well-being." The tube came back with his receipt, which he pocketed. "You can't take on the police department. I know. I tried."

"Well, I *haven't* tried."

He pulled into an empty space at the bank and put the

Jeep in Park. "Listen to me, you're *not* Sherlock Holmes, or Lucy Ricardo, or whomever it is you fancy yourself to be. You don't even have a law degree. You own a flower shop. And you're in way over your head with all your snooping. You want the harassment to stop? Then all you have to do is give up your pursuit of this SUV driver, and you'll be left alone."

I stared at Marco in disbelief. This was the man I'd pictured as my knight-errant? "I can't believe you're telling me to take the coward's way out. Is that what you did? Did you leave the force because it was easier to step out than to fight? What about your hatred of dirty cops?"

His jaw muscles worked furiously, and I knew I'd hit a nerve. "At the moment," he said in a slow, carefully controlled voice, "my concern is for your safety, which right now is in jeopardy. Now, I'm going to put out the word that you're filing an *uninsured* motorist claim with your insurance company and paying the deductible yourself, and then it's over. End of story."

"Marco."

"What's your deductible? If you can't pay it, I'll help you out."

"Marco, it's too late. I called my insurance agent before lunch and told him to file the claim against Vertucci."

He blinked a few times, then uttered one word. "Shit."

He drove me to the three-story city garage without saying another word, which was a shame because I had quite a convincing argument prepared as to why I believed I'd done the right thing. That conviction lasted until I learned the towing fee was one hundred twenty-five dollars, and then I was starting to see his point.

I gritted my teeth as I wrote out a check and handed it to the cashier. After one near miss with my brakes, various threats, two car repairs, and two towings, not to mention those parking tickets I might ultimately end up paying, I couldn't afford any more harassment. But could I really step out entirely? Could I close my mind to that tragic image of the Ryans walking into the funeral parlor? Could I turn a blind eye to the police corruption and go on with my life as if nothing had happened?

Not hardly. I'd just have to be careful.

Marco waited with me while the attendant brought out my car. As I walked around the Vette looking for signs of abuse, Marco said, "From now on park in a metered lot. And make sure you get that dead bolt put on your apartment door. I'll see what I can do to mitigate the damage you did with the police. In the meantime, watch your back."

I took his advice and parked in the closest public parking lot, inserted five dimes in the meter, and walked back to Bloomers. But as I came across the courthouse lawn, I saw a police car parked in front of the shop and my stomach knotted. More harassment?

I took a deep breath and opened the door. Two cops were standing at the counter—Sean Reilly and Gordon, the motorcycle cop. Reilly was counting out money, so whatever they were there for, it wasn't all bad. He handed the bills to Grace, then glanced around at me and winked.

At that moment Lottie came from the back with a huge box in her arms. She placed it on the floor and said, "There you go, fellas. Enjoy!"

"You can count on that," Reilly said. The two officers hoisted the box between them and left, laughing.

"What did they buy?" I asked Lottie.

"I'll tell you in a minute. First, how was lunch?"

I decided on the spot not to mention my latest run-in with Blasko. I could only imagine the fretting and fussing that would go on, and, besides, I was getting tired of being scolded for meddling. "Lunch was fine," I said, then noticed that Lottie and Grace were grinning at me like I was about to sprout broccoli from my ears. I grabbed a brass pot and smiled at my reflection. Nothing on my teeth. "What's up?" I asked.

"Don't you notice anything different in here?" Grace replied.

Now that she mentioned it, there *was* something odd about the room. It seemed quieter somehow. I watched curiously as both women walked to the wicker settee and sat down.

"She hasn't missed it yet," Grace said quietly to Lottie.

"I thought for sure she'd notice right away." They both glanced to the right. I followed the direction of their gazes, but saw nothing unusual.

And that was the whole point. There was nothing unusual in the room, not even a monkey table. I turned my shocked gaze on Lottie. "The police bought my mother's table?"

"Yep."

My mouth dropped open. "How much did they pay?"

"They offered seventy-five dollars," Grace said. "We discussed it and decided to accept. Do you think your mother will be angry?"

"She'll be delighted. I can't wait to tell her. To think that yesterday one of those cops made fun of that table."

Grace started for the tea parlor, then stopped and turned. "I don't remember a bobby being here yesterday."

"It was—um—right after you left. He stopped by . . ."

"When the alarm went off? Yes, dear, I know all about it. The alarm company called this morning to see if everything was all right. I trust you know the procedure now?"

"PIN Number, Enter, Set Alarm." At her frown, I quickly amended it. "Set Alarm, PIN Number, Enter!"

"Perhaps I'll write it out and post it next to the keypad."

"Good idea."

We closed at five o'clock, but stayed an hour longer to finish arrangements. My coupons had brought in half a dozen customers and as many orders. We could have worked all evening, but Lottie wouldn't hear of it. She told me I looked like something the cat had dragged in. And actually, after the day I'd had, a restful evening did sound good.

Following Grace's printed directions, I set the alarm, then scooted over to the metered lot, fearing what evil had been done to my car since I'd left it. Luckily, the car was unscathed, with not a ticket in sight. Still, as I slid inside the Vette I kept expecting some demon in police uniform to spring from one of the trunks, waving his ticket book and laughing maniacally. On the drive home, I obeyed all the speed limits and pulled to a complete stop at every stop sign. I wasn't taking any chances.

Back at the apartment, Nikki was lying on the sofa in her pink sweat suit, sipping something steamy from a mug, with Simon curled up at her feet chewing on the end of a plastic straw. Nikki's cold had traveled down to her chest, giving her a hoarse voice that she thought sounded sexy. I'd have voted for froglike myself.

"Have some beef stew," she croaked. "It's on the stove. Then we can go shopping for party supplies."

So much for a relaxing evening.

I ladled out a bowl and joined her in the living room, where I told her about the car being towed and Blasko's threats. Nikki put her mug aside to give me almost the same lecture I'd gotten from Marco. Then she caught me up on all the soap operas I never watched and repeated verbatim the weather channel's forecast for Saturday, which promised to be a perfect summer evening for her party.

"Nikki, if you want to be able to talk Saturday you'd better stop talking *now* and rest your throat. Your voice is fading fast."

"Wait. Listen to me sing. It's incredible." She burst into a rendition of "Yellowbird," which ended abruptly when her mouth moved but no sound came out.

"I hate to say I told you so . . ."

She grabbed the pad of paper by the phone, scribbled something, and held it up. It said *SHUT UP!*

We took Nikki's Toyota, but I drove because she was hopped-up on cold medicine. Then we had to weave our

shopping cart through the hordes of customers who had
decided tonight was the night to stock up on everything.
After some clever maneuvering, we made it to the ethnic
food section in aisle two, which is where Nikki wanted to
start.

She had to write down what she wanted to say, so it
took some time and patience on my part to bear with her.
At one point I forgot I could talk and grabbed the pen and
paper and wrote my reply. An elderly couple stopped to
pat Nikki on the arm and give us sympathetic looks,
along with the suggestion that sign language classes were
available at the college.

Hummus, Nikki wrote, as our next item.

Hummus was in the refrigerated section all the way on
the other side of the store, past aisle fifteen. We fought
our way there; then she debated for ten minutes over what
flavor to buy, finally settling on red pepper and basil.

Tofu, she wrote next.

Tofu was in the health-food section at the rear of the
store by aisle one. I glanced at my watch. At the rate we
were going, we'd be lucky to make it home for the
nightly news.

Shrimp, she scrawled, after we'd picked up the tofu.

Shrimp was in the frozen foods beyond the refrigerated
cases and aisle fifteen—again. I gave her a perturbed
look. "We could have saved a lot of time if you had organized the list *before* we got here."

Scowling, she added another item to her list and held it
up: *crab.*

"Fish department," I ground out, turning the cart
around. Nikki grabbed my arm and tapped *crab* furiously.
Then she pointed to me.

Message received.

Once we had secured all the items on the list, we took
a shortcut up the paper products aisle only to find our
path blocked by the same elderly couple who had advised
us of the signing classes. The woman had turned the cart

width-wise across the aisle and was calling directions to her husband as he strained to reach a roll of paper towels on a high shelf.

"No, Dexter, I said the one with the *blue* squiggles." She glanced around at us with one of those *What-are-you-going-to-do; he's-a-man* looks, while poor Dexter made a slow reach for the blue one. The next thing we knew, the entire top row came bouncing down on our heads.

While the woman screeched and ducked for cover, Nikki and I started scooping them up. I chased one out into the main aisle and startled a woman picking apples out of a bin. She dropped her bag of McIntoshes, and a brawny guy with a short haircut and a case of beer on one shoulder stopped to pick it up for her. As he bent over, his bowling-style shirt slid up his back, exposing a big, black-handled gun.

I stared at the weapon in surprise. The man was carrying it the way off-duty cops and criminals did, tucked into his pants in the back, with only the handle exposed. My gaze shifted to the man as he straightened. He automatically reached around to pull his shirt down. Then he turned and caught me watching him.

I sucked in my breath. This burly brute was no cop. It was Buzz, the manager from Tom's Green Thumb.

And he was none too happy to see me.

CHAPTER TWENTY-ONE

Buzz glared at me, his beady eyes narrowing into furious slits, his fingers clenching into fists, as if daring me to say something about the gun. Then he turned and stamped toward the front of the store.

I looked around at the other shoppers, but no one seemed to have noticed either his gun or his hostile reaction. Why was Buzz carrying a concealed weapon? Was he afraid someone would hijack his Heineken? Or was he planning something more nefarious, such as a robbery?

As I stood there, trying to decide what to do about it, someone nudged me. Then a notebook appeared in front of my nose. *What's going on?* Nikki had written.

"A man has a gun," I told her quietly. "Let's go see what he does with it." I grabbed our cart and made a beeline for the cashiers, hoping to catch up with Buzz. Unfortunately, there were at least three customers waiting at each checkout line, except for the Ten Items Or Less aisle, where Buzz was at that very moment, slapping down money.

So he wasn't robbing the store. But I still wanted to know why he felt the need to arm himself. Was he

Harding's bodyguard? Was something going down at the greenhouse tonight?

As Buzz strode toward the door, I did a quick tally of my cart's contents—eleven items—and headed for the quick checkout, hoping the cashier wouldn't notice. A man in a shiny silk suit and alligator shoes saw my intent and raced me there, forcing Nikki and I to cool our heels behind him while he smugly placed his items—all fourteen of them—on the counter.

When we finally got out to the parking lot, it was just in time to see Buzz speed past in a green Thunderbird. Much to my surprise, in the passenger seat was Daryl, the multiple-pierced stock boy who had worked with Billy Ryan.

So much for Buzz's policy of not fraternizing with his employees.

"Why would a landscape store manager carry a gun?" I asked Nikki, as we hurriedly loaded our groceries into the trunk.

She pulled out her pad to scribble, *To cover his asspens.* She scratched it out and put, *Sorry. Bad joke.*

As soon as we were in the car, she wrote, *Anyway, it doesn't matter why. Remember what*—she flipped the page—*Marco said. Stop meddling.*

Remember what Marco said? How could I forget? I was still stinging from his words. *You don't even have a law degree. You own a flower shop.* As if that meant I wasn't very bright. Well, I was just as bright as he was, maybe brighter. And one day I'd prove it to him.

I turned at the next corner and headed for the highway. *Where are we going?* Nikki wrote.

"I want to see if Buzz is headed for the greenhouse."

"My groceries!" Nikki rasped, forgetting she couldn't talk.

"They'll hold an extra ten minutes."

I turned off the highway and drove through the parking lot at Tom's Green Thumb, circling around to the back of the building. Sure enough, there was the green Thunder-bird parked next to the loading dock. Beside it was a black Lincoln Town Car. Harding's red pickup, however, was missing.

"Either Tom Harding pays his employees a heck of a salary," I said to Nikki, "or Buzz is entertaining a wealthy friend."

Okay. Let's go now, Nikki wrote.

"I'd sure like to know what's going on in there."

None of your business, she wrote.

"Maybe Buzz is planning to kill someone."

She underlined her last sentence.

I knew she was right, but seeing Buzz with a gun, with Daryl accompanying him, had my inner alarm ringing like crazy. "Nikki, what if Buzz is planning to kill Daryl?"

Why would he do that? Nikki wrote.

"Because Daryl knows something, or because Buzz is a jackass. I don't know. I'm just tossing out ideas." I checked my watch and saw that I had fifteen minutes until the store closed. I drove around to the front, told Nikki to give me ten minutes and if I hadn't returned to call the police. Then I dashed inside before she could scribble a protest.

And then I stood there, staring around the huge glass structure, wondering what to do next. I finally decided to look for Daryl.

A young man with bad skin and long sideburns was stocking shelves in the pot room. "Is Daryl here?" I asked casually. "He was supposed to check on something for me."

"Daryl doesn't work here anymore," he answered without looking around.

Then what was he doing in Buzz's car? "Are you sure?" I asked.

"That's what I was told."

I couldn't very well argue with him. "Okay, thanks." I

started to walk away, then had another idea. "You didn't know Billy Ryan, did you?"

"No. I just got hired a week ago." He put the last can of rose dust on the shelf and picked up the empty box. "I heard about what happened to him, though."

"I'll bet the news shocked everyone here."

"Yeah. I guess Buzz *totally* wigged out about it."

"He wigged out?"

"*Totally.* Stan Brown—this guy I know from school— well, actually he graduated last year, but I knew him from track—anyway, he said when he got here that morning— what was it, Monday?—Buzz was freaking—throwing things around in the stockroom and swearing up a storm. Mr. Harding had to calm him down."

"Wow. Is this Stan Brown here now?"

"He works the day shift, nine to three."

Which meant that when Stan Brown arrived at nine o'clock on the morning of the murder, Buzz already knew about Billy. How?

I made my way down one of the wide aisles to the back of the store, keeping an eye on the office door near the front, half expecting Harding to come charging out again. I meandered over to the double swinging doors of the stockroom and listened for voices. Hearing nothing, I pushed one side open a crack and peered in. The room seemed deserted, so I stepped inside and looked around.

There were stacks of wooden crates, wheelbarrows, birdbaths, and fountains down the center of the long room, and a garage-type, roll-up door in the middle of the rear wall, no doubt leading to the loading dock. There was also a service door with a mesh window on a side wall, and ceiling-high, metal storage shelves covering the rest of the wall space, with fully half of those shelves filled with dark green boxes of Green Thumb brand fertilizer. There were spikes, tablets, powder, liquids, and every other possible form fertilizer could take.

I would have never guessed there was such a market
for it.

Hearing voices, I grabbed a box off the nearest shelf to
use as a prop, and turned to flee, just as Buzz and Daryl
stepped into the room through the mesh-windowed door,
both holding cans of beer.

"Hey!" Buzz barked. "Hold it!"

My scalp prickled as I imagined him pulling his big-
handled gun and aiming it at my back. I turned with
a smile. "Oh, hi! I was looking for someone to help
me. This was the last box on the shelf in the pot room,
so I . . ."

Buzz came at me—shoulders thrown back, chest
puffed out, and jaw cast forward in typical bully fashion—
stopping inches away, obviously to intimidate me. I stood
my ground, maintaining an unconcerned smile. That always flustered them.

"This area is off-limits," he snarled.

"It is? I'm sorry. I didn't know."

"Sure you didn't. It's hard to miss that big red sign outside the door."

I smacked myself on the forehead. "I must have zoned
out. Sorry." I glanced over at Daryl, but he was looking
in the opposite direction, as if he were either embarrassed
for me or for himself. At least he was alive. There wasn't
any sign of a third party, so I couldn't assign the Lincoln
Town Car to a face.

I turned and strolled out of the room, trying to appear
casual about it, still clutching the little green box in one
sweaty hand. Buzz knew who I was. Would he tell Harding I had been there? Was he calling him even now?

I hurriedly paid for the fertilizer and exited the building. If I had accomplished nothing else, at least I knew
what kind of car Buzz drove and that he had lied about
being friends with Billy. But why? Was he into drugs,
too?

"Why did you buy fertilizer?" Nikki whispered, as I

slid into the car and started the engine. "We don't have a garden."

I tossed it in the backseat. "It was my cover. I'll use it at the flower shop."

Thursday morning got off to a bad start when I discovered the pilot light on the hot water heater had gone out and I had to wait thirty minutes before I could take a shower. To add to the delay, I had retaped my car the night before, and *that* had to be removed. When I finally got to Bloomers, I found a message waiting for me from Dave Hammond saying he wanted to see me and would be available around noon. There was also a message from my mother reminding me of our Friday-night dinner.

"You bought tree spikes?" Lottie asked, as I plunked down the box of fertilizer on the worktable.

"Not on purpose. It's a long story." Which I couldn't go into because Grace was in the room. "Why don't you take the spikes for your fruit trees, Grace?"

"Thank you, dear. I think I will. My new willow isn't weeping the way it should. Maybe these will help." Hearing the bell over the door, she took the box and left us to our work.

"Do you remember the lady who ordered that seven-foot pine wreath last Christmas?" Lottie asked, as she made up a small vase of pink and white carnations.

"The wreath with the plastic bananas and grapes and neon green ribbon?" I shuddered at the memory. The woman had apparently been into smarmy tropical decor.

"That's her. She wants you to come out to her house to help her plan flowers for a party."

"She asked for me, specifically?"

"Yessiree. She said she liked your eye for color."

I wasn't sure whether to be flattered or insulted.

"Or maybe she said she liked your eye color. Anyway, she wants to hire you."

"How many orders do we have for today?"

"Not many. If you want to fit her in this afternoon I'll give her a call."

"That will work." I glanced through the small pile of orders and saw one going to the prosecutors' offices. Odd that Lottie hadn't mentioned it. Normally, she'd have me right on it, hoping for another encounter with Greg Morgan. I pulled the order—a bouquet of white and yellow roses, no vase—and had it assembled in fifteen minutes.

"I'm taking this over to the courthouse," I told her.

Lottie looked up in surprise. "I was going to do that one for you, baby."

"No problem. I'm on it."

"No, really, sweetie, let me do it. I told you I was done with that matchmaking stuff and I meant it."

"The thing is," I said quietly, so Grace wouldn't hear, "I need to weasel some information from Morgan about Elvis Jones's case."

"But Elvis confessed, didn't he?"

"Or so they say." I turned and found Grace standing inside the curtain, arms folded, regarding me with a wary eye over her half moon glasses.

"Meddling again, are we?"

"No! Absolutely not. Well, maybe. Okay, yes. But it's harmless meddling. In fact, let's not even call it meddling. Let's call it curiosity."

" 'What's in a name?' " she said, falling back on her trusty Shakespeare. " 'That which we call a rose by any other name would smell as sweet.' "

Lottie rolled her eyes at me. When Grace started spewing Shakespeare, we knew we were in trouble.

"And you know what curiosity did to the cat," Grace continued.

"I'm sure you'll tell me as soon as I get back." I slipped past her and headed for the door and the courthouse across the street, trying to still the sudden flutter of butterflies in my stomach. Why was I nervous at the thought of facing Morgan? He was the one who had behaved like an idiot.

But I was the idiot who had gone out with him. And I was the idiot who had thought he was actually interested in me.

It took four flights of stairs to banish those winged caterpillars. Then I had to pause outside the office to catch my breath. *Cool, calm, and collected,* I chanted to myself.

"I have a flower delivery," I said to the secretary with the blue glasses.

She looked at me, then at the bundle in my arms, picked up her phone, punched a number, and informed the person on the other end of my arrival. "Go on in," she told me, indicating Morgan's door.

"These are for Greg Morgan?"

"Yes." She gave me a disdainful look.

I took a deep breath and mentally prepared myself, trying to block out the humiliation of Saturday night. "Flower delivery," I said, standing in his doorway.

Morgan practically leaped out of his chair in his eagerness to welcome me. "Abby, come in." He tried to look cool as he high stepped stacks of files, but his bright red ears gave him away. "Thanks for bringing them over. I was hoping you'd come." He smiled at me, but his eyes were turned down at the corners like a choir boy who'd been caught peering under girls' skirts. Was he contrite?

He took the bundle and placed them in the only sliver of space available on his desk, next to his phone. "Would you care to have a seat?" he asked humbly.

This wasn't the cocky deputy prosecutor I knew. Curious as to the reason for this sudden personality change, I maneuvered the obstacle course and sat down across from him.

He tugged on his tie, avoiding my gaze. "How are you?"

"Just fine. And you?"

He busied himself shuffling through papers. "Embarrassed." He cleared his throat. "About Saturday night . . . You see, when I'm nervous I tend to talk too much and" — *shuffle, shuffle*—"I end up making an ass of myself."

Morgan—all star ladies' man—nervous? About being out with *me?* I was flattered and a little touched by his frank confession. It took courage to admit to being an ass. Courage was worth twenty-five points. Even being an ass, he was still five points ahead.

"It happens to the best of us," I offered generously. To save him further embarrassment, I changed subjects, right to the one I wanted. "How's that murder case coming along?"

"The Ryan case?"

Like there was any other. "I see Elvis Jones confessed. Lucky you. What kind of evidence did they get on him?"

The Greg Morgan of old returned. He leaned back in his chair and gave me a look. "You know what our office policy is, Abby. I can't give out that information."

"If it's just a matter of being in the office, let's go for lunch," I retorted, half in jest. I didn't really want to share another meal with him, but sacrifices had to be made.

Morgan scratched his ear and grinned sheepishly. "Why don't we make it dinner? I'd like a chance to redeem myself."

A multitude of snide remarks formed in my head in those seconds before I answered, such as, *Do I look that stupid?* Or, *Why not? I'm a glutton for punishment.* Or just a resounding no would do the trick. But I knew Morgan wouldn't cooperate with me unless I said yes. Besides, he looked so darned angelic in that light, and he *did* want to redeem himself, so I smiled instead. "Only if I can pick the restaurant."

"I'll pick you up, say, six thirty?"

"Deal."

I had a triumphant smile on my face when I walked into Bloomers. Lottie took one look at me and broke into a victory dance. "I haven't lost my touch after all!" she sang out, causing two customers at the counter to share puzzled glances.

"Don't get excited," I said quietly. "It's not a date. It's a meeting to share information."

Grace peered around the customers to lift one eyebrow at me. I pretended not to see her.

Lottie moonwalked to the curtain. "Call it whatever you like, baby. Lottie the Matchmaker is back in *town!*"

Grace waited until the customers had gone. Then she came up to me and put her hands on my shoulders. "Curiosity *killed* the cat, dear."

At noon, I grabbed a hot dog and dashed down to the law office to see what Dave had for me.

"Look what came in yesterday's mail on the Harding case," Dave said, handing me a folded letter.

I opened it up. Entitled ARTICLES OF INCORPORATION, the document listed all pertinent information on the Sappling Corporation, such as, date of incorporation, names of the officers, and a list of major shareholders, which, in this case, were the same: Thomas Harding, president; his attorney, Sol Feinberg, vice president/resident agent; and most impressive of all—a secretary/treasurer named Honey B. Haven.

"Honey B. Haven?" I chortled. "Sounds like an exotic dancer to me."

"I believe that's his current girlfriend."

"Don't you find it odd that his attorney is also his vice president?" I asked.

"It's certainly not a recommended practice—too much potential for conflicts of interest on the lawyer's part—but it's not that unusual. It often happens when they're good friends."

I could see Harding and the pit bull as friends. Birds of a feather. I looked at the paper again. "This doesn't say what the Sappling Corporation is about."

"Sounds like something to do with trees."

"Why would this company be separate from his landscape business?" I mused.

Dave's secretary buzzed, and he took the call. He put his hand over the phone and said, "I've got to take this. We've got Harding now, Abby. I'll have those subpoenas out to the Michigan bank in today's mail. Then we'll know what that sly fox is really worth."

Boy, was Harding in for a surprise.

I left the shop midafternoon to drive out to one of New Chapel's three gated communities for the party consultation. The exclusive subdivision was filled with big, multileveled brick homes that sat on lots of an acre or more. Most of the homes had swimming pools in the back, space for at least four cars in the attached garages, and landscaping that had to have cost the owners a small fortune.

The customer's name was Trudee DeWitt. "Double E's, double T's," she'd informed me after I'd introduced myself. "And that's just my bra measurement," she'd deadpanned.

Corny joke, but I laughed anyway. Dressed in a tube top, funky bright miniskirt, and skinny pink sandals, Trudee had nearly a perfect hourglass shape, although there was a bit more sand on top than on the bottom. She wore her platinum-blond hair pulled back in a french twist, with big gold hoops dangling from her earlobes, and lots of gold bracelets stacked at each wrist.

She walked me through a roomy house decorated with fake tropical decor and a miniature indoor waterfall and briefly described what she had in mind for her party. She also said price wasn't a factor. Stemming the urge to jump up and down with glee, I told her I'd work up a plan and drop it off.

When I got home from work, Simon was waiting by

the door, meowing as if he hadn't been fed for weeks. "You don't fool me, cat," I said as I checked the answering machine, relieved to see there were no messages. "Take a look at your belly the next time you waddle past the hall mirror."

On the kitchen counter next to his can of cat food was a note from Nikki reminding me that the party was only two days away and that we had to get the apartment ready. I looked around at the gleaming surfaces and wondered what was left for me to clean. But it was hard to miss the orange sticky notes Nikki had posted on the bathroom mirror, toilet, and shower stall.

With an hour to go before I had to get ready for my dinner date, I threw on a pair of old shorts and a T-shirt, tied a yellow bandanna around my head to keep my hair back, and tackled the bathroom with rubber gloves, a scrub brush, and bathroom cleaner. Half an hour later, I stood back to survey my work. Simon came to sit at my feet. "What do you think?" I asked him. "Will it pass inspection?"

He took off for the bedroom, which I took to be his answer until the intercom buzzed, and then I knew there was a human male somewhere in the vicinity. I pulled off a yellow glove and hit the button. "Who is it?"

"Abby, it's Greg. I know I'm early, but I was in the neighborhood so . . . surprise!"

Surprise?

Minus thirty points.

Irked, I buzzed him in, swiped a stray lock of hair from my eyes with the back of a rubber-gloved hand, and opened the door. Morgan came striding up the hall, wearing that angelic grin and casual attire straight out of a magazine. I slipped off the glove and tossed it over my shoulder.

He gave me a quick once-over. "Did I catch you in the middle of something?"

"Actually, yes. I'm getting the place spiffed up for a

party this Saturday. Come in." I stepped back to admit him.

He pulled a large, familiar-looking bundle out from behind his back and handed it to me. It was the bouquet of yellow and white roses I had made for him.

I was stunned. "You ordered these for *me?*"

"White as a peace offering. Yellow because it's your favorite color."

He knew my favorite color? "You didn't have to do this, Morgan."

"I was going to give them to you this afternoon, but then we made dinner plans and I thought—well, anyway, I owed you for putting up with me last Saturday night."

His points were multiplying; he was nearly out of the red. And now that I had let my plans slip for the party, my earlier decision not to invite him was superceded by a higher power: guilt. "Want to come to the party?"

He had the good sense to look humble. "I don't want to intrude."

"You won't be. I don't have a date yet." Why had I admitted that? I crossed mental fingers and hoped he'd decline.

"Sure. I'd love to come."

Swell. Lottie would be tickled pink. Abby was not.

"Do you want a soft drink or a beer?" I asked.

"Got anything diet?"

When I returned with a glass of diet root beer, he was standing in the middle of the living room, looking around. "So this is where Abby Knight resides."

"This is home, at least for now. Once I get my business established I plan to—"

"I had your apartment pictured like a jungle hideaway—you know, tropical plants, palm trees, vines, flowers. . . . By the way, I like what you're doing with your hair these days."

Belatedly remembering the bandanna, I tugged it off and tossed it onto a chair, subtracting ten points from his balance—five for interrupting and five for a snide comment. "I'll go change."

"Sure." Morgan sat on the sofa and reached for the remote while I dashed off to the bedroom. I hadn't even thought of what to wear, so I pulled out my standard country-club outfit of khaki skirt and white shirt, coated my lips with peach lip gloss, threw on a pair of silver hoops and I was done. No more fancy red dresses and crackling tape for me.

I had chosen a local Italian restaurant that had a quiet atmosphere and cozy, high-backed booths, where people could talk without being overheard. Morgan ordered wine for us, then toasted to fresh starts. I decided to be optimistic about it, clinked rims with him, and took a sip.

"Hi, Greg," a pretty brunette said, tossing a sexy pout at him as she passed by the booth. She didn't even toss a hangnail *my* way.

"Hey, Samantha. How's it going?"

"Hello, Gregory," the woman following her said in a sultry voice. "Haven't heard from you in a while."

"What can I say?" Morgan replied, trying to look put-upon. "That's life as a prosecutor." He twisted his head to look behind him, as if expecting more of the parade to pass by. Then, as if remembering there was already a female within bragging distance, he leaned one shoulder against the tufted leather back, holding his glass of wine in a studied but casual pose, and gave me the smile that had melted many hearts.

When I was in high school that smile would have turned me into a giggling glob of hormone-fueled goo. Now I saw it as just another Morgan modus operandi: disarm with charm.

Here it comes, I thought. *Another tedious discourse on the accomplishments of Greg Morgan.*

"So," he said, lifting an eyebrow, "tell me about Abby."

Well, *that* was different. I smiled back. "What do you want to know?"

And then he put his foot in it. "Where did you go to high school?"

I took a deep breath and maintained my smile. "New Chapel."

"No kidding! What year did you graduate?"

Still smiling, but very close to gritting my teeth I said, "I graduated with *you,* Greg. Remember? *Ally* Knight?"

He studied me for a long moment, then aimed an index finger at me. "You were one of the B team cheerleaders, weren't you?"

B Team? Now he had both feet in it and was sinking fast. Still keeping my smile, I shook my head.

"Wait. I've got it! You were in theater!"

"Wrong again." At this rate, he'd be lucky if that hole he was standing in didn't swallow him altogether.

Morgan's eyebrows drew together in puzzlement, and I thought fleetingly that he would finally admit defeat. But then he reverted to form. "Hey, I'm just yanking your chain. How could I forget a hot chick like you?"

Because you're a phony, egotistical, horse's ass, that's how. I put down my glass, slipped my purse strap onto my shoulder, and stood up. I didn't care that I hadn't been able to question him about the Ryan case, this hot chick wanted out. "I'll see you around."

"Wait. What did I say?"

Tempting though it was to march out in a huff of indignation, I decided it was only fair to let him know how clueless he was. I sat back down and glared at him. "I thought that maybe you and I could have an honest conversation, but I was wrong. You're so busy trying to impress people that you've forgotten the meaning of the word honest." I dug through my purse, extracted a ten-dollar bill from my wallet, and slid it across the table. "This is for my wine."

He shoved it back. "I don't want this. Hey, come on, Abby. Please, stay. I'll be honest, I swear."

"Why should I believe you?"

"Because I like you."

He liked me? Wow. That was quite a frank admission. Reluctantly I stayed, though I left my purse strap on my shoulder for a quick getaway.

He put both palms flat on the table. "You're right. I admit it. I was being a jerk—again. The truth is, I don't remember you from high school and I can't figure out why. I guess I don't have a very good track record, do I?" He waited for me to smile, but I wasn't in the mood, so he rearranged his fork and spoon several times, and, keeping his eyes on the table, finally said, "Can we start the evening over?"

"Can you knock off your Mr. Charming act and be yourself?"

He looked up, and I was surprised at the somberness of his expression. "I can, but I don't think you'd care for the results."

I was about to tell him that it couldn't be any worse than what I'd already seen, but he was gazing straight at me, no artificial smile, no macho posturing, and no dazzle to hide behind—revealing a startling truth: Morgan didn't like himself. This handsome hunk was basically an insecure male who thought he had to put on a big act to attract women. How I wished I'd known that in high school. "You're not giving either one of us much credit, Greg."

He dug his fingers through his hair several times before he replied. "See, here's the way it is: People like me because of what they see, and who they *think* I am. And I don't disappoint them."

"So basically you're an actor, always putting on a show so people will like you, because if they saw the *real* you they'd turn tail and run."

He took a drink of wine, a pained expression on his

face, and I knew I'd hit the nail on the head. But now that I had his number, I felt sorry for him. How sad to pretend to be more than you were.

Taking pity on him, I said, "How you live your life is your business, Greg, not mine. If you're comfortable with it, then who am I to say you should be otherwise? And if I hurt your feelings, I apologize."

"You *were* pretty brutal."

I lifted one shoulder. "I call it like I see it. That's who *I* am."

He gave me a lopsided, un-Morganlike grin. "I don't get that very often."

"What do you say we order a pizza and have an honest-to-goodness conversation?"

"On one condition: If you don't like what you see, you won't ever tell a soul, including me, by the way."

"You're on."

After that, Morgan dropped the suave facade and became human as we dickered over toppings for a pizza, then tried various means to get the attention of an overworked waitress, including tossing sugar packets into the air and trying to catch them in the bowl. We decided on a pepperoni, green pepper, and mushroom combination, and while it was baking, munched on garlic breadsticks and talked about movies. And while Morgan wasn't the sharpest pencil in the box, he did have a good sense of humor.

I was enjoying myself so much that it wasn't until we were chowing down on pizza that I remembered my original reason for agreeing to the date. "So," I said, wiping my greasy fingers on a napkin, "just between you and me, what evidence do the police have on Elvis Jones?"

He leaned forward and said quietly, "Enough to convict him *without* his confession."

"Do you have the murder weapon?"

"No, but we know from the slug that it was a .45

caliber, and we have witnesses who saw Elvis with a gun that size. We also found his fingerprints in Billy's room."

"You didn't find anyone else's prints at the scene?"

"None that matched any on file."

"What was Elvis's motive?"

"Money. Drugs. Who knows with Elvis? He might have shot the kid because he was in a bad mood."

"Didn't he give a reason in his confession?"

Morgan shrugged, as if he didn't want to say. I was betting that once Elvis had *confessed,* the cops didn't press him for a reason. They'd gotten what they'd wanted.

"He had the means and the opportunity," Morgan said. "We can *place* him at the scene."

"You can place every resident of the building at the scene."

"Come on, Abby. The evidence is there."

At least enough to convince a jury of his guilt. But there were still too many loose ends, and in my mind the murder wouldn't be solved unless they were tied up. But unless I could convince Morgan of it, the case was closed. "What if I told you Elvis hadn't acted alone?"

He picked up his glass and raised it to his mouth, saying dryly, "A conspiracy theory?"

"As a matter of fact, yes."

"And the other conspirator would be?"

I decided not to implicate the commissioner or Blasko at that point. If I could get Morgan interested enough to investigate, he'd discover their involvement for himself. "Tony Vertucci, the commissioner's nephew."

Morgan nearly choked on the wine. "You've got to be kidding."

"Not at all." I leaned closer to say, "I know Tony was at the scene that morning because he's the one who hit my car. I *saw* him run out of the alley and drive off in the SUV at the time of the murder. Yet he claims he was across town. So there you go. Find out if he's into drugs and you'll have a motive. Fingerprint him and you might be able to match one set of those unidentified prints."

Morgan looked anything but convinced. "So you're saying I should drop the charges on Elvis and start investigating the commissioner's nephew based on your claim that he was near the murder scene? I don't think so."

"I didn't say you should drop the charges on Elvis. But if you know there's another suspect out there, how in good conscience can you ignore that?"

He leaned toward me to whisper, "Do you know what you're asking me to do? Commit political suicide. As much as I'd like to help you, I can't do that. I need this job."

"How would it be political suicide? You're not elected."

"My boss is. And believe me, he could make life miserable for me, especially if I went after Vertucci's family."

"What does the word *justice* mean to you, Greg? Are you going to turn a blind eye to whatever the commissioner's nephew does because of who his uncle is?" I leaned forward. "Are you going to let him get away with *murder?*"

"He's innocent until proven guilty, Abby."

"And Elvis Jones isn't?"

Morgan steepled his fingers and rested his chin on them. "Why do you care what happens to Elvis? Why are you so involved in this case?"

"Have you met Billy Ryan's parents? You ought to talk to them. I did, and their story broke my heart. That's why I'm involved. As for Elvis, if he's guilty, then he should be punished. But so should everyone else involved, regardless of who they are. Tony Vertucci committed at least one crime that I'm sure of—a hit-and-run—and maybe helped with a murder. But as long as Commissioner Vertucci protects him, Tony will never pay unless *you* bring him to justice."

Morgan sat back. "Me? Look, Abby, I admire your

convictions, but I can't tell my boss I'm starting an investigation because a florist tells me to."

"That's it, then? You're not even going to look into it?"

He lifted his wineglass to his mouth, pausing to say, "Sorry. I really can't."

You could if you wanted to. I tore a hunk off of a bread stick and jabbed it in olive oil, trying to come up with another way to convince him.

And then it came to me: the photos.

CHAPTER TWENTY-TWO

I leaned forward and said in a quiet voice, "Would you investigate Tony Vertucci if I told you I had proof that he's involved?" It was a stretch, but I was desperate.

Morgan's throat stopped in midswallow. "What kind of proof?"

"Photos."

"Of what?"

I toyed with a bread stick as I considered how much to reveal. "A payoff involving a cop." It was vague, but it was enough to get his attention.

"Are you serious?"

"I've never been more serious in my life."

He glanced over his shoulder. "Do you have them with you?"

I shook my head

"Can you get them?"

Oops. That was something I hadn't considered. I'd have to wrest them out of Marco's hot hands. My mind flashed back to a snippet of conversation I'd had with him on that very subject: ... *I can't go flashing them around, making accusations that could be considered slanderous unless I have positive proof of a crime. I don't want to lose my license and/or get sued.*

I had a strong feeling that Marco wouldn't be happy with me right now. "They're in a safe place," I told Morgan.

He scratched his ear, looking doubtful. "I'd have to see them first."

"Can't you take my word for it? Why would I lie about them?"

"To get me to start the investigation."

"I see your point, but I still can't give them to you. Anyway, if a cop is involved, how would you get an honest investigation done?"

"We'd have to take it to the Feds."

"What's my guarantee it won't get back to the police?"

Just as I feared, Morgan didn't have an answer. "Tell you what," he said. "Let me run a 'what if' scenario past my boss and see what he says."

"You won't mention names? Or photos?"

"Absolutely not. Trust me."

Could I trust the new and improved Morgan? Did I have a choice?

When Nikki got home at twelve thirty in the morning, I was ensconced on the sofa watching Cary Grant and Jimmy Stewart flirt with Katharine Hepburn in *The Philadelphia Story,* in a vain attempt to bury myself in their clever banter and forget my own stupidity.

"Did you find my sticky notes?" she asked, kicking off her white nurse's shoes and picking up Simon, who had been winding around her legs in a vain attempt to trip her.

"Yes, Mom, I did. The bathroom is all clean. Now we'll have to bathe in the kitchen sink for the next two nights."

"Uh-oh. Someone's in a temper. Did Greg Morgan screw up again?"

"No, I did."

She spotted the roses I had stuck in a glass vase. "Wow. Did he bring those?"

"Yes, and he's coming to the party Saturday, too."

"That's not so bad."

"Yes, it is, and it gets worse."

"Wait. I want to get a glass of wine." She scurried to the kitchen, popped open a bottle, and was back in under sixty seconds. "Okay, spill your guts."

I'd already done it once that evening, but I took a deep breath and spilled again. She shook her head in awe. "I wouldn't want to be you when Marco finds out what you did."

"I don't plan to tell him."

"Aren't you going to get the photos from him?"

"Not on your life. I'm just going to hope that the threat of having photos will be enough to launch a new investigation."

Nikki lifted her glass to me. "Good luck."

I turned back to the movie where Jimmy Stewart was getting plastered. From where I sat, that was looking pretty good.

The phone rang and I grabbed it. Lottie was on the other end, informing me that Pearl was in the emergency room. One of Lottie's boys had dropped her at the Methodist church so she could attend her women's circle meeting, but afterward, she'd been waylaid by her soon to-be ex-husband and things had turned ugly. Karl had arrived to pick Pearl up, took one look at her, and drove her straight to the hospital. That snapped me out of my funk.

"Call Dave and tell him what happened," I directed. "He'll probably phone Feinberg and raise hell. In the meantime, I'll go to the hospital and take care of Pearl."

Ready to raise hell myself, I grabbed my purse and was out the door in a flash. I took Nikki's car, since I had already bound mine in tape, and found Pearl and Karl in the ER, waiting to see a doctor. Pearl was trembling all over, her face bruised and swollen, her left wrist cradled in her right hand. I sent Karl home. Then I sat on the bench with Pearl. "What happened?"

She stared at the tiled floor. "I—fell and broke my wrist."

"*You* broke it, Pearl? Or did Tom do it?"

She began to cry. That was answer enough. "Tell me about it."

"My meeting ended early," she managed between sobs, "so I went outside—to wait for Karl. Tom—must have followed me. He came at me and—I tried to get away—but he grabbed my hand and twisted it. He just kept twisting and twisting—saying I had to tell him how my lawyer knew about some sapling company."

My stomach plummeted.

Pearl took a few deep breaths and wiped her eyes with the back of her sleeve. "I swore to him I hadn't heard of no company like that, but he wouldn't believe me. He said he'd caught you snooping up in Michigan, and I was the only one who could have sent you up there."

I didn't know what to say to her. It was *my* fault she was sitting there. I was responsible. How could I have been so careless as to let Harding see me? "I'm going to get us some coffee, Pearl." I walked to the vending machine and inserted quarters, guilt gnawing at my insides.

But as I carried the steaming cups back, I realized that I was falling into the same trap that abused women did. This was *not* my fault. It was *Harding's.* He didn't have to take his anger out on his wife. He could have kicked a few tires, jogged a mile or two, or hit a punching bag. Or better yet, taken an anger management course. Why was he angry in the first place?

Because he had something to hide.

I handed her a cup and sat beside her. "You're going to have to file charges, Pearl."

"No! He said if I went to the police he'd hurt Little Tommy. I can't take that chance."

"Pearl," I said, lowering my voice, "he assaulted you."

"Nothing is worth risking my son's life."

I tried to reason with her, but after ten minutes I gave up. She was too distraught to think clearly. Once she had calmed down, though, I'd have to convince her to file charges against that madman. Harding didn't care about restraining orders; laws were for other people. But maybe a few days cooling his heels in jail would make him think twice before he bothered her again.

Suddenly, I saw Sol Feinberg striding toward us. I jumped up and blocked his path. "What are you doing here?" I demanded.

"Dave Hammond called me. I want to make sure Mrs. Harding is okay."

Right. And maybe find out what she knows about the Sapling Corporation, while you're at it? "You can't talk to her. It's unethical."

He got down in my face and sneered, "Are you telling me what I can and can't do? Show me your attorney's license."

"Why don't we call Dave and ask *him* what you can and can't do? And then you can also explain to him your relationship with Mr. Harding and the Sapling Corporation."

There was a pregnant moment of silence. Then Feinberg said, "The Sapling Corporation? What is that, exactly?"

"You tell me. You're the vice president."

"Where did you hear about it?"

"That's not important."

Feinberg suddenly got friendly. "You know, it's probably nothing more than one of my client's minor business ventures. He's always looking for small investments, and, between you and me, he loses more than he gains. But, hey, I get paid by the hour, so what can I tell you? It's business, right?" He put an arm around my shoulders. "As soon as Mrs. Harding gets treated, you take her home, and I'll make sure this doesn't happen again, okay?"

"Just how do you plan to do that? Your client is an animal."

"Trust me. We'll even throw something extra into the settlement pot for her."

"I want a guarantee of her safety."

"You'll have it."

As if I believed that.

I stayed with Pearl while the doctor cast her wrist. Then I took her to Lottie's. By the time I got back to my apartment, Nikki was almost asleep on the sofa. She sat up, stretched, and followed me into the kitchen, while I filled her in.

"Wow," she commented. "Harding is one mean dude."

I poured myself a glass of soy milk and gave Simon skim milk. "The thing you have to remember about bullies is that when they're cornered by someone tougher than they are, they cry like babies." I downed the soy, banged the glass on the counter, and wiped my mouth with the back of my hand, like a cowboy of old. "Well, I'm going to make him cry."

Friday morning started out as one of those rare summer days with everything seeming in perfect balance. The temperature was a perfect seventy-five degrees, the humidity was at a comfortable level, the wind was calm, and the sun was bright without being glaring. At the flower shop Lottie and Grace were both humming, each in her separate room, while I arranged a new display for the front window.

Then the building inspector arrived.

He was an average-looking man of medium height and build, wearing a bad toupee, a blue plaid polyester sport coat, tan trousers with cuffs, and brown loafers scuffed, dusty, and turned up at the toes. He'd walked many a mile in those shoes.

He came inside, looked around, spotted me standing at the window and said brusquely, "County Building Inspector. Do you own this shop?"

I put down a big vase full of artemisia and stepped out

just as Lottie and Grace peered from their respective rooms to see what was happening. "I'm the owner," I replied.

He consulted his clipboard, then looked up at me with humorless eyes. "I'm here to do an inspection."

"Again? I just had one done a few months ago for the bank."

He checked his clipboard again, looking annoyed. "This is Bloomers, isn't it? You're on my schedule."

I glanced at Lottie and she shrugged as if to say, *Who knows how the government works?*

Still, my antennae were quivering, so I followed him through the rooms as he peered behind, under, and inside everything, making little check marks as he went. I was confident in the outcome since the building had passed with flying colors three months earlier.

But when he started *tsk-tsking*, I started worrying.

"I've never failed an inspection," Lottie whispered, giving me a reassuring pat on the back, as I stood at the kitchen door watching the man examine the electrical outlets. "Go get a cup of coffee and relax. I've got to run down to Happy Dreams and then I'll be back."

The inspector did a full circle, including the basement, and ended up at the front counter, where he added up the check marks and shook his head ominously. "You have some serious violations. I'm going to have to shut you down."

My mouth dropped open. "Shut me *down?* What are the violations?"

He consulted his list and said dryly, "Where do you want me to begin?"

I rubbed my forehead, trying to think what to do. Lottie would know, but she hadn't returned, and Grace was serving customers in the parlor. "Okay. Just give me the list, and I promise I'll have everything fixed in a week." *I hoped.*

"I'm still going to have to shut you down."

"For how long?"

"Until I can do another inspection."

"When will that be?"

He flipped to another page. "Looks like the next open-ing I have is mid-July."

"That's a month away." My heart sank. If he shut me down for even a *week,* my regular customers would go out to the new flower and craft store, and once they started going there, what chance would I have of getting them back? I was doomed. My dream was evaporating like so much vapor. I rubbed my eyelids to keep the tears at bay.

"However . . ." he said.

I peered at him through my fingers.

"If you were to cooperate"—he gave me a supercilious smile—"maybe I could be persuaded to give you more time to fix your violations."

I dropped my hands and stared at him. So that's what his surprise inspection was about. He was shaking me down! I hastily considered my options. I could call Dave and have him file a complaint with the county, but it wouldn't be heard until they met, which might be a month away. Or I could just pay the bastard and keep the shop open.

I walked over to the cash register and opened the drawer. "How much?"

"You're not understanding me. What I'm saying is that if you *cooperate,* I'll give you some time to fix your problems."

He had me totally confused. "How much time?"

"Two weeks." He gave me that smug smile again. "Why don't you sleep on it, and I'll stop by tomorrow so we can discuss your *cooperation.*"

Completely at sea, I stood at the window and watched him climb into a white Chevy van marked with the county seal on the side. What kind of cooperation was he talking about? I paid my taxes, kept my property clean, voted regularly. Sure I had a beef with the police, but who didn't at one time or another?

Could it be the unpaid parking tickets?

I crossed that off the list of possibilities. He wouldn't know about my tickets. He worked for the county.

He worked for the *county!* And who ran the county? Five commissioners, one of whom was Louis Vertucci.

And that's who had sent the building inspector.

CHAPTER TWENTY-THREE

"You're rambling, sunshine. Take a deep breath," Marco instructed, clasping my shoulders.

I tried to breathe deeply, but I was shaking too hard. I had dashed out of Bloomers and straight down to Down the Hatch, where I was lucky enough to catch Marco coming out of his office. "It was a direct threat, Marco. If I don't do what Vertucci wants, he'll put me out of business."

Marco guided me to one of his director's chairs and pushed me into it. Then he poured a glass of water from a plastic bottle and instructed me to drink.

"Now," he said, settling into his desk chair, "did the inspector ever show you his list?"

"No."

"Did he show you any credentials?"

"No, but he was driving a county truck."

"Maintenance men drive county trucks. Did he tell you his name?"

"No."

Marco lifted an eyebrow, and I said, "My God, Marco, am I that naive that I didn't even think to check?"

"You were flustered. It's understandable, and he was

probably counting on it anyway. The question is, do you want to make this go away quickly?"

"Of course I do. But if you mean will I let Vertucci intimidate me, the answer is no."

"Can you afford to be shut down?"

I rubbed my temples. "No."

"The way I see it you have two choices: You can cooperate—and by that I'm guessing they want you to call your car insurance company and drop your claim against Vertucci—or you can call their bluff."

"Why is it so important to Vertucci that I drop the claim? It's not an accusation of murder."

"He doesn't want the insurance company investigating his nephew. At the very least, it would be a political embarrassment to have a member of his family charged with a hit-and-run."

"And at the worst," I added, "Vertucci might lose the election if his nephew were involved in a murder. Well, I'm not going to drop it, so how do I call their bluff? By asking to see the violations? What if the inspector *does* have a list? What if he is who he says he is?"

"If this is Vertucci's handiwork, then he's already accomplished his objective—he's got you running scared—so I doubt you'll see his inspector again."

"But what if I do?"

"Then you'll have more decisions to make."

I stood up and paced his office, trying to come up with a plan. "Okay, let's say this inspector doesn't fall for the bluff and gives me a list. In that case I'll threaten to contact my attorney, and if we find that the violations are bogus I'll sue the county."

"Think hard before you do that, sunshine. We're not sure how desperate Vertucci is. You could be endangering your business, your employees, and yourself."

"What are they going to do, torch the building?" I joked.

Marco didn't laugh, and that gave me a cold chill. To

what lengths *would* Vertucci go to keep me quiet? Did I have the right to jeopardize the lives of my employees?

"You know how to put a stop to this," he reminded me.

"What would *you* do, Marco? Would you call their bluff?"

"I hope I never have to make that decision."

Maybe I shouldn't be making the decision either, at least not alone. Like it or not, Grace and Lottie were indirectly involved, so they should have a say, too.

"Don't you dare give in," Lottie said, after I'd laid it all out for them. "I didn't survive in this business all these years by being afraid, and you won't either. Besides, Grace and I can take care of ourselves. We're not your average, middle-aged mamas, you know."

"If you don't stand up for yourself today," Grace added, "you won't be able to face your mirror tomorrow."

This time I didn't try to hide my tears. "What would I do without you two?"

Lottie put her arm around my shoulders and gave me a squeeze. "We stick together, baby. We have right on our side."

"Remember this, dear," Grace said. " 'Thrice is he armed that hath his quarrel just.' "

With William Shakespeare on my team, how could I fail? "So if the inspector comes in tomorrow?" I asked.

"We tell him to go to hell," Lottie boomed.

The phone rang; Grace answered it and handed it to Lottie. "It's Herman."

As I headed for the workroom, Grace said, "By the way, dear, I brought back that box of fertilizer. It seems to be mislabeled. It's not spikes at all, but powder. I know you don't use a common fertilizer here, but as I'm fond of saying, waste not want not."

I opened the box she'd put on my desk and looked inside. The powdered fertilizers I used were typically packaged in one big plastic bag, sealed with a twist tie, then boxed. But this one was different. There were three smaller bags inside, stacked one on top of the other. An odd way to package it, but then I wasn't familiar with the Green Thumb brand.

Curious, I opened the top bag and stuck my fingers inside to take a pinch. The powder was very fine and pure white, not like any commercial fertilizer I'd ever seen. "No smell," I reported. "Maybe it's bonemeal."

I looked around, spotted a salmon pink *Chrysanthemum rubellum* just starting to bud under the growing lights on a nearby shelf and sprinkled the powder over the soil. I closed the bag and stuck it back in the box, then tucked it on the shelf below the worktable, alongside giant bags of potting soil.

Lottie came through the curtain carrying a large box, the contents of which were clanking together. "I'm taking a few things to the basement," she said as she passed through the room on the way to the back stairs. I had a sneaking suspicion my mother's three-lipped pot was among the items going down for storage.

That brought to mind the weekly family dinner I had to attend that night, which reminded me that I had missed lunch. I glanced at the orders and saw that three of them were to be picked up by four o'clock, so I gave up the idea of running down to the deli and nuked a bag of popcorn instead. Then I turned on the radio and turned off all thoughts of inspector threats, gun-toting store managers, and crooked cops to concentrate on what I loved best.

Lottie's news station was on, but I wasn't paying much attention until I heard the words *Elvis Jones* and *escape*. I leaped off the stool and turned up the volume just as Lottie returned from the basement. "Listen," I told her, as the reporter continued his story.

"Police haven't yet determined how Jones escaped, but a reward is being offered for any tips that might lead to his capture. Caution should be exercised, however, as Jones is considered armed and dangerous."

Elvis had been in isolation. How could he have escaped?

I was at the country club by seven o'clock on the nose and was *still* the last one of the clan to arrive. Since the sky looked fairly threatening, I put up the top, locked the Vette, and hurried across the parking lot. Pryce and his parents were there, seated at their table near the bar, pretending not to notice me when I strode through the room. I was considerate enough to return the favor, and everyone was happy.

The bliss lasted until my cousin Jillian arrived on Pryce's brother's arm, and then the evening got dicey. Jillian greeted the Osbornes with enthusiastic air kisses, then saw us, waved frantically, and motioned for us to come over to their table. As my family dutifully rose to do her bidding, I rolled my eyes. There was no way Pryce and I could ignore each other now.

As usual, my cousin was oblivious to the tension between us, being intensely focused on the current apple of her eye. I felt sorry for Claymore, knowing what fate lay in store for him. But if he was gullible enough to fall for long legs, a sweep of reddish blond hair, and fluttering eyelashes without getting to know the calamity that was Jillian, then he deserved to be jilted.

"Isn't this wonderful?" Jillian gushed, clinging to Claymore's arm. "Now we can all have dinner together every Friday. In fact, let's have dinner together tonight!"

Both sets of parents murmured less-than-enthusiastic assents.

"Delightful," I said cheerily. Pryce gave me a look that said he wasn't any happier about the situation than I was.

His parents looked extremely embarrassed as busboys rushed to join two tables to hold us all. As our waitress transferred our glasses from one side of the room to the other, my dad wheeled out of their way, my sisters-in-law huddled with Jillian and Mrs. Osborne to discuss wed-

ding plans, Claymore, Pryce, Mr. Osborne, and my brothers watched the Cubs get slaughtered on TV, and my
mother directed the entire operation as if she were an air-
traffic controller.

"Put that wineglass here. The bread basket should go at
that end. We already have one down here. Watch that candle, you'll burn your sleeve. Where is the water boy? This
ice has melted."

During the hubbub I took the opportunity to talk to my
dad about Elvis's escape. I couldn't get the idea out of my
mind that he'd had help, but my father wasn't so sure.

"Elvis has been in jail so many times he knows the
place and the routines by heart. It's an old building,
Abby, not like these modern lockups. Could he have had
help? It's possible. But he wouldn't have needed it if he
were crafty enough."

"Okay, everyone," my mother called. "Take your seats."

I grabbed a chair as far away from the Osbornes as
possible and ended up next to Portia, who spent the rest
of the evening keeping her eye on the disappearing
mound of food on my plate. I couldn't tell if it was out of
envy or horror. She ate her usual fruit plate and edamame
beans, then sat back and patted her concave stomach with
a sigh of contentment. I sucked in my gut, decided it
wasn't worth the effort, then finished off the last of the
garlic-smashed potatoes. I knew she was silently cluck-
ing her tongue at me.

Shortly before ten o'clock my phone beeped, and I
slipped out of the room to answer it. Jillian was busy entertaining the ensemble with stories of her Parisian ex-
ploits, so my departure went undetected. I couldn't help
but chuckle. By the pained expressions on the Osbornes'
faces, I had a feeling they were having serious doubts
about their son's choice of a wife. And they had thought
I was bad!

Still smiling, I walked over to the glass doors for
better reception and flipped open the phone. "This is the

Secure Alarm notification center," a woman told me. "Your alarm was triggered at nine forty-eight p.m."

I gulped. Had Bloomers been burgled? My first thought was that Elvis had done it, but that was just my paranoia talking. Elvis was on the lam. He wouldn't be stupid enough to hang around town with a murder charge on his head.

"We've alerted the police," the woman informed me. "Will you be able to meet them at the business?"

"I'm on my way right now." I shut the phone, stuffed it in my bag, and looked up into the frowning face of Hit-and-Run-Man-of-the-Year, Tony Vertucci. He stood directly in front of me, blocking my path, looking for all the world like he wanted to wring my neck.

I took a step back and said tentatively, "Hi, there, Tony. How's it going?"

His jaw tightened. "Not so good."

"Sorry to hear that."

"Yeah, I'm sure you are."

Over his shoulder I saw his uncle striding up the hallway from the direction of the washrooms. I abandoned the idea of returning to tell my parents about the alarm, and decided to flee instead. I could call them from the shop once I knew more.

"Well, I'd love to stay and chat, Tony, but I have other plans." I detoured around him and pushed open the glass door, hoping he wouldn't follow me outside. I didn't have time to deal with him right now.

A rain shower was in progress, so I practically sprinted to my car. I started the engine, flipped on the wipers, and pulled out of the parking lot, tires squealing on the wet pavement. Driving as fast as the weather allowed, I headed up the long, two-lane road that led back to town.

What would a burglar want from a flower shop? There wasn't much of anything of street value other than a boom box and an old computer, and no one in their right mind would think we kept much cash on hand.

What about the photos? a little voice in my head whispered. *Could Morgan have let that information slip? Could word have gotten out to Blasko? Or Vertucci?* I tried to push aside those thoughts, fearing that I really was turning paranoid, seeing conspiracy everywhere.

But the little voice wouldn't shut up. *Dumb move, Abby, putting your trust in a man like Morgan.* I knew that voice was right, and I was so angry with myself I banged my fist on the steering wheel. I'd had a bad feeling about it even then, but had that stopped me from opening my mouth?

You won't mention names? Or the photos?

Absolutely not. Trust me.

Right. Trust Morgan. He'd undoubtedly blabbed the whole thing to the chief prosecutor in order to impress him, because impressing people was what he did best. His boss would have then called the detective, who in turn would have said something to the cops, and there it was, just as Marco had predicted. Make trouble for one cop and ten more will make life miserable for you. Thank goodness Marco had had the foresight to keep the film in his possession.

As I neared Maple Creek Bridge, headlights came up fast behind me. I tapped on my brakes to warn the driver to slow down, but he apparently didn't notice because he bumped me. I figured he had to be drunk. Everyone knew to slow down at the bridge, especially in bad weather. Besides being narrow and rickety, the wood had splintered in some places and chunks of it were completely absent in others. If a tire hit one of those spots just right, it could throw the car out of alignment or cause a flat. The bridge should have been replaced a decade ago, but the county had somehow never gotten around to it.

I honked my horn and tapped my brakes again, but that seemed to make the speedster angry, because he bumped me again, harder this time. He'd had to speed up to do it, so I knew it was intentional. This wasn't simply a case of drunk driving. This was also road rage, and that frightened me. Enraged drivers killed people. I read about it all the time. I needed to get out of his way quickly and call the police.

Steering the Vette over to the side of the road just before the bridge, I was digging for my phone when he hit me again, pushing my car forward at an angle, so that the right front end was hanging off the narrow, sloping shoulder and I was staring down into muddy water. Fear prickled along my spine. What if this wasn't a case of road rage? What if someone was trying to kill me?

I braked hard to keep the Vette from going over, then heard the unmistakable sound of an engine being shifted into Reverse. I glanced up at my mirror in horror.

He was getting his car positioned to ram me again.

CHAPTER TWENTY-FOUR

Praying for divine intervention, I quickly unbuckled my seat belt, pulled the door handle, and tried to escape before the maniac hit me again, but the car's angle made the door heavy and awkward. My heart was thundering as I threw my weight against it. I had to get out before he pushed the Vette into the creek. I had visions of my car rolling over and me being trapped underwater. I'd rather take my chances on land.

Suddenly, headlights came up from the other direction, causing the enraged driver to do a quick U-turn and flee up the road toward the country club, sparing me from what could have been a very ugly situation. I glanced in my rearview mirror to see if I could get a look at the car, but only two red taillights were visible.

Trembling all over, I carefully backed onto the road, then leaned my head against the steering wheel, the trauma completely draining me of energy. I heard a car door open, and then a tap on my window. A muffled, warbly voice called, "Abby? Are you all right?"

I looked around, and there beneath an umbrella stood my guardian angel—ninety-three-year-old Martha Schmidt.

"Martha!" I said, rolling down the window, trying to pull together my scattered wits. "You don't know how glad I am to see you."

"That man nearly pushed you into the creek," she said, her rheumy gaze wide with disbelief.

"Did you get a look at the driver?"

"I didn't, dearie. But I did see the car."

"Bless you, Martha! What kind was it?"

"A sedan."

"What kind of sedan?"

"A great big one."

Not much help there. "Did you see the color?"

"It was dark."

"Dark, as in black?"

"No, too dark to tell. I'm color blind at night. Would you like me to call the police? My house is just a few blocks from here."

"Thanks, but I have a cell phone."

"Are you sure you're all right, dearie? I can make you a cup of cocoa with marshmallows on top. That would fix you right up."

"I'll be fine. Thank you so much for stopping."

As soon as Martha was safely on her way, I drove off, hands still shaking, my heart in my throat. Who had been in that car? Tony? He could easily have followed me from the club. Or maybe his uncle had put one of his cohorts on my trail. Or maybe it had been Blasko.

My mind was spinning with possibilities as I turned onto Franklin and saw the police car in front of Bloomers. I pulled up behind it and hurried inside, where two cops were waiting. One of them I knew from high school, Matt Hill. The other was Reilly, and he looked so big and safe that I wanted to throw my arms around him and hold on tight. But I checked that impulse. Reilly was still a cop, and I wasn't sure who among them I could trust.

"What happened?" I asked.

Reilly spoke. "It looks like someone came in through

your fire escape door. It's been forced open. Your back rooms are a mess, but it doesn't look like the perp got any farther than that."

"What locksmith do you use?" Hill asked, unfolding a cell phone.

"Gandys."

"I'll get them out here," he said, and walked away to make the call.

Reilly flipped open a notebook and took out a stubby black pencil. "Is anything missing in this room?"

I took a look at the cash register, but it was undisturbed, as was the heavy steel safe beneath the counter. Nothing had been touched in the display window either, and all our floral arrangements were exactly as we had left them. "Not that I can tell."

"How about in here?" Reilly asked, turning on the lights in the parlor.

I checked out Grace's equipment, but everything was intact.

Next we inspected the workroom, where drawers from my desk were lying upside down on the floor, their contents scattered over the desktop and worktable. My computer monitor and tower had been pushed over but fortunately hadn't been smashed. The drawers beneath the worktable were open and the tools inside were jumbled. Potting soil from the shelf below had spilled onto the floor. And in the refrigerated case, every single container that held our fresh flowers had been tipped over, with water all over the floor and flowers strewn haphazardly. Yet our boom box sat untouched on the shelf.

"Any valuables missing?" Reilly asked. "Computer equipment? Electronic equipment? Did you keep a wallet in your desk? Jewelry? Credit cards? Take your time and look around."

I walked around the room picking up containers, closing drawers, righting the computer, studying everything carefully. Someone had obviously been looking for something, and that something had to be the photos. But there was no way I could tell the cops. For all I knew, they were behind it. "If anything was taken," I told Reilly, "I sure can't tell." And that wasn't a lie.

The locksmith arrived and Hill brought him back to the kitchen, which I had just finished inspecting. Cabinet doors and drawers had been opened, but, as with the workroom, nothing seemed to be missing.

"The burglar was looking for something specific," Reilly said. "Is there anything you kept in your desk that might have been of interest to someone?"

"I'm sorry. I can't think of anything."

"Do you have an ex-boyfriend who might be looking to retaliate?"

"An ex-fiancé, but he's as happy to be rid of me as I am of him."

"What's his name?" Reilly asked, ready to take down the name.

"Pryce Osborne," I said, imagining the look on Pryce's face if the police showed up to question him. "The second," I hastily amended, remembering he and his father shared the moniker.

The cops glanced at each other. "The second what?"

"The second Osborne to be named Pryce. And with any luck, the last."

Reilly closed his notebook and stuck it in his chest pocket. "If you think of anything else that may be of help, give us a call. Otherwise, you can pick up your report Monday."

"Actually, I do have something else to report, but it's not about this. It's a hit-and-run, and it happened this evening, on my way here."

Hill gave me a skeptical look. "Didn't you report a hit-and-run a few weeks back?"

"Yes, I did. What are the odds of *that* happening?" I picked up a desk drawer, put it back on the gliders, and shoved it closed.

"You're a regular Calamity Jane, aren't you?" Reilly said dryly, reaching for his notebook.

They listened intently as I described the scene at the bridge. "Do you have any idea who the driver might be?" Reilly asked.

I had more ideas than brains at that moment, but I also knew that launching into a detailed account of my conspiracy theory would probably make me look insane. So I played dumb, gave them Martha Schmidt's information and address, and they promised to write up a report on it. If nothing else, it would be on record for insurance purposes.

Once the locksmith had finished and all three men had left, I locked up behind them, then went back to the workroom to clean up the mess and see if I could think of anything else the burglar might have been after. The cash register hadn't been touched, so it wasn't money. Credit card numbers, perhaps? The information was on my hard drive, but that hadn't been bothered either.

I wanted to find a connection between the hit-and-run and the break-in, but without knowing for certain what the burglar had been looking for, it was impossible. Whatever it was, he had braved the alarm to hunt for it. Was he hoping for a slow response from the cops? That would be quite gutsy since the station was just across the square.

Unless he was a cop.

Could this be more of Blasko's scare tactics? Were this break-in and my near accident at the bridge meant to keep me running scared? Because they were working.

By the time Nikki got home from work, I had cleaned up my shop, secured my battered Vette with masking tape, showered, and was sacked out on the sofa in a state of total exhaustion. My nerves were shot, my neck was starting to ache—whiplash, no doubt—but my mind wouldn't slow down. Still, I was determined not to let paranoia get in the way of common sense. If someone had really wanted to kill me, there would have been better opportunities.

Nikki, however, didn't see it that way. "I think you should call Marco," she called from the kitchen, where I could hear Simon gulping down his canned food.

"What's Marco going to do?"

"Protect you." She settled into the chair, peeled down the wrapper of a Snickers, and bit off a corner. "You know, like in that movie with what's-his-name who played Robin Hood?"

"Kevin Costner, and no, I'm not going to call Marco. I can't afford to pay him bodyguard wages."

"I'm worried about your life, and all *you're* worried about is money." She rose and marched off to her bedroom to eat her Snickers in peace.

"Fine. I'll phone Marco tomorrow." But I was not going to mention the photos.

I slept fitfully that night, suffering multiple flashbacks of my trauma on the bridge, then dragged myself out of bed Saturday morning and stood under the shower for ten minutes trying to wake up. Nikki had arisen early to prepare for our party, and when I emerged at last, she was seated on the sofa in the living room, a bowl of oatmeal on her knees, listening to the local cable station's news broadcast. It was her Saturday-morning routine. She had a crush on one of the newscasters, a good-looking reporter named Ben Carmichael.

"There's a glass of juice for you on the counter," she said, using one hand to keep Simon from licking her oatmeal. "Drink it, then call Marco."

"You can be awfully bossy at times." I gulped the juice, then obediently punched in the number and reached his voice mail. "Hey, Marco, this is Abby. Call me." I rinsed the glass and replaced the phone. "There you go. I've got to go down to the shop. I'll be home around noon."

"Omigod, Abby," Nikki cried. "You'd better come see this."

I walked into the living room and sat down beside her. On the screen, Ben Carmichael stood behind the Hampton Arms next to a Dumpster, a scruffy-looking man in dirty sweats just behind him. "This is where building superintendent Jerry Kenderhogen found Elvis Jones's body early this morning. Jones had been the subject of an intensive manhunt after he escaped from the county jail two days ago. Preliminary reports indicate that he died of alcohol poisoning."

I stared at the TV openmouthed. Elvis was dead!

CHAPTER TWENTY-FIVE

I watched in disbelief as the reporter turned to the building superintendent and stuck the microphone beneath his stubbly chin. "Mr. Kenderhogen, would you describe for our viewers what you found when you came out this morning?"

Simon jumped on my lap and dropped a slimy rubber band on my knee. "Not now, Simon," I said, and put him on the floor.

Kenderhogen looked into the camera, his unshaven face arranged in a self-important frown. "Elvis was right here next to the Dumpster, Ben, flat on his back, stinking of booze."

"And you found an empty rum bottle beside him?"

"That's right, Ben. An empty rum bottle. Right beside him."

His somberness was so comical I wanted to laugh, except that it wasn't a laughing matter. In fact, I was feeling a tad nauseated.

Carmichael went on: "Police are awaiting autopsy results, but the time of death is estimated to have been between midnight and two a.m."

The scene switched back to the studio, where another

newscaster gave a capsulized version of Billy Ryan's murder and Elvis's subsequent arrest.

When they started on a different topic, Nikki switched the TV off. "Elvis must have gone on a bender last night and drank himself to death."

"Elvis didn't drink himself to death, Nikki. Someone killed him."

"But they found the empty bottle beside him."

Simon jumped onto my lap, this time carrying a straw. "Not *now*, Simon!" I said, and put him down again. "Nikki, think about it. The man has been a drunk most of his life. All of a sudden he dies from one bottle of rum? After managing to escape from an isolation cell? Which, if you've noticed, no one is explaining. I think someone poured booze down his throat and planted that bottle."

"Or it just might be that his liver gave out. Or his heart. Or he could have had a stroke."

She was right, of course. But my instincts were screaming *foul play*. Elvis's escape and sudden death were just too convenient. I picked up Simon, straw in his mouth, and plopped him on Nikki's lap. "Here, play with your cat."

On my way down to the parking lot I tried again to reach Marco, but he still wasn't answering. The back of my Vette looked even worse in daylight, especially with the masking tape wrapped around it like multiple bandages. I assessed the damage as I pulled off the tape. There was a big dent in the left fender and the bumper was scratched and bent. Otherwise, it was okay. Still, I figured it would cost over a thousand bucks to repair, and this time I didn't even have a partial plate number to track down.

I drove straight to Dunn's Body Shop, handed him my keys and plucked the one for the Escort off the hook on the wall behind him. "You know what to do," I told him with a sigh.

Grace and Lottie arrived just as I did. They had heard about Elvis's sudden demise but neither seemed surprised. Both thought I was reading too much into it. We sat in the kitchen and over coffee I filled them in on the bridge incident and the burglary. By the time I had finished, they wore horrified expressions. And I hadn't even mentioned the photos or the possible connection to the police.

Lottie was the first to react, enfolding me in a big hug. "You poor baby."

"I'm fine, really," I said, my voice muffled by her shoulder.

She grabbed my shoulders and held me at arm's length. "You're moving in with me until the police solve the burglary. Herman can drive you wherever you need to go."

"England," Grace said. "That's the ticket. My sister lives in a lovely cottage just north of London. She'd love to have you."

"I appreciate the offers, but I'll be okay." I held up my hands as they both voiced their protests. "My mind is made up."

"Then one of us will be here with you at all times," Lottie said, and Grace nodded in agreement, adding, "I'll make you a nice cup of mint tea to soothe your nerves."

I was about to tell her my nerves were fine, but I knew she wanted to do something for me, so I kept my mouth shut and went to order new flowers for the cooler. Around midmorning, however, I noticed my hands were trembling. Unnerved, I put down my knife and held out both hands, palms down. "Look at this," I said to Lottie.

"It's the aftereffects of last night, sweetie. Go get yourself another cup of mint tea and step outside for a breath of air."

"What if the inspector comes?"

"I'll handle him. Now, go on. Git!"

*   *   *

The Saturday-morning fruit and vegetable market had been set up on the courthouse lawn, so I wandered across to check out the cantaloupes, thinking that melon balls would make a nice addition to our party menu. As I was examining the fruit I heard, "'Morning, sunshine."

I turned with a relieved smile. "Marco! I've been trying to reach you. Did you hear about Elvis?"

He had on a tan T-shirt and jeans, and held a small paper bag in one hand, a purchase from the fruit stand, no doubt. "I heard," he said grimly.

"Someone killed him, Marco. I have a strong hunch that his escape was part of a plan to do away with him."

"For once I agree with you." He took a long look at me and scowled. "You're shaking."

I held out the hand holding the cup, pretending surprise. "Would you look at that?"

Marco took the tea from me and guided me to a shady spot under a chestnut tree so we could talk in private. "Okay, tell me what else happened."

I gave him the details, including my run-in with Tony at the club. Marco took a sip of the tea, made a face, and handed it back. "What did the robbers take?"

"As far as I can tell, nothing."

"Was any damage done to your shop?"

"My flowers were ruined and the back door lock had to be replaced. The burglary happened with the alarm going off, so whoever it was knew the cops would be arriving soon." I let that sink in a moment, then said, "I'm thinking this could be more of Blasko's handiwork."

Marco studied my face, mulling over the information. "I don't like what's happening, sunshine. It has me worried. Are you feeling okay?"

"A little muscle stiffness in my neck, but that's about it."

"What about the shaking?"

I held out my right hand, trying to steady it. "It'll go away."

He put his hand on the back of my neck and massaged

it with skilled fingers as he searched my face with those dark, penetrating eyes. "You're sure you're all right?"

I sighed as the tightness began to vanish. "Oh, yes. Right there. That's the spot."

"I learned something interesting about Blasko," he said, letting his fingers continue their magic. "It seems Officer Eddie Blaskovich started out his career as a policeman in a small town in Minnesota and was forced to resign two years later on extortion charges. He shortened his name to Blasko when he moved here."

Surprised, I opened my eyes. "And he was hired anyway?"

"He changed his name to keep his secrets."

"Surely he had to produce documents to get on the force—birth certificate, high-school diploma, something!"

Marco smiled wryly. "I told you it was interesting."

"What did he extort?"

"Money from a drug dealer."

"And now he's taking money from Vertucci. Is the commissioner in the drug business?"

"Your guess is as good as mine."

"Are you going to do anything about him?"

"I'll get the information to the right people as soon as I'm sure who they are. By the way, have you had any unusual visitors this morning?"

I knew he meant the county inspector. "Not yet."

His mouth curved up at one corner in that enigmatic way of his. "I told you, you wouldn't."

I glanced at my watch, then gulped down the rest of the tea. "I've got to get back to the shop and finish up. Nikki is expecting me home by noon."

"That's right. You're throwing her a party tonight."

How did he know? Had Nikki mentioned it? Now what was I to do? I'd already invited Morgan. "Listen, if you're not busy, why don't you stop by?"

"Thanks, but I've got something else going tonight."

A date perhaps? I felt that jealous imp rear her head and quickly stuffed her back down again. "Well, have fun."

"Hey," he said, "take care of yourself."

"I'll do my best."

When I walked into Bloomers, a two-foot-high specimen of a badly abused *Ficus elastica dora* was sitting on the floor beside the counter.

"Trudee DeWitt dropped it off," Grace informed me, coming out of the parlor. "She said it needed your tender loving care."

"I'd say it needs emergency resuscitation." I took the ailing fig tree to the workroom and set it on the table. The poor plant had lost its lower leaves and the rest were yellow-tinged and drooping sadly. I stuck my finger in the soil and found it soggy. A glance at the bottom of the pot showed a tangled mass of roots growing through the drainage holes.

I untangled the roots as best I could and pulled off the old green plastic container, then took a clay pot from the bottom shelf on the back wall, lined it with new, dry soil, and replanted the ficus. After filling in around the roots with more soil, I reached for the box of fertilizer under the table.

"Grace, did you take that box back to Tom's Green Thumb?" I asked, sticking my head in the parlor. "It's not in the workroom."

"You put it on the undershelf, dear," she said as she finished filling her espresso machine.

"That's what I thought, but it's not there. Maybe Lottie moved it."

"What did I move?"

I turned around as Lottie came into the room. "I can't find the box of fertilizer Grace brought back."

"Sorry, baby. I haven't seen it."

"I must have overlooked it."

But after a thorough search we still hadn't found it.

"Well, now we know what the thief took," Lottie said.

"Why would he steal a box of common fertilizer?" Grace asked.

"That can't be what he was after," I said. "It's not like there's a lack of fertilizer in town. He must have been looking for—" I caught myself about to tell them about the photos. Thank heavens I hadn't. I wasn't up to a scolding.

"Looking for what?" Grace asked.

"Money."

"In the workroom?"

Lottie reached for the ringing telephone, then covered the mouthpiece with her hand. "It's Dave Hammond."

I picked up the phone at my desk, glad for a reprieve from Grace's questioning. "Hi, Dave."

"You're not going to believe this, Abby. You know that subpoena I sent out on the Sappling Corporation? I got the paperwork back. There's over a million dollars in that account."

I was flabbergasted. "Harding made that much selling trees?"

"Whatever he's selling, it sure is lucrative. This is going to make a huge difference in Pearl's settlement."

"Have you told her yet?"

"I called, but she's out. Pat yourself on the back, kid. Your little trip to Michigan paid off in spades."

I hung up the phone, elated. Wouldn't Pearl be excited when she heard the news!

The phone rang again and I answered.

"My caps are crushed!" Nikki shrieked in my ear, on the verge of hysteria.

"Your caps?" I shuddered, picturing her chatting with guests minus her front teeth. "What the heck did you eat?"

"Not *those* caps! My Shitakes! I'm having a mush-room emergency."

"Calm down, Nik. I'll stop at the store and get more."

"Hurry! My stuffing's getting soggy."

I hung up and turned to find Lottie and Grace waiting for the disaster report.

"It's just Nikki having a meltdown," I said. "Pre-party jitters."

"Why don't you go home, dear? We'll take over here," Grace assured me.

"Is lover boy going to be there tonight?" Lottie asked with a wink.

"I'm afraid so."

She patted me on the back. "Relax and have fun tonight, baby. After last night, you deserve it."

I fired up the Escort, which now had air-conditioning thanks to Justin's tinkering, and drove to the grocery store on a mushroom run. On the sidewalk in front of the store was a display of garden plants for sale, and stacked nearby were boxes of Scott's brand fertilizer, right out in the open, where anyone with devious intent could cart one away.

So why would a burglar break into Bloomers to steal one lousy box?

CHAPTER TWENTY-SIX

The rest of the day Nikki and I spent preparing for the party, and by the time the first guest had arrived, Nikki had on a little black party dress, I had donned a black silk top and matching slacks, our music was playing, and our buffet table was ready. Out of the twelve people invited, eleven had showed up, including Dr. Gorgeous and his wife, and Nikki's new beau—a somewhat geeky but courteous male nurse named Scott, whom I cleverly interrogated and decided I liked—and, of course, Greg Morgan, who was an instant hit with the women. Since I was preoccupied with my hostess duties, I was more than happy to hand him over.

By nine o'clock the party was in full swing: Funky music blared on the stereo, our guests were talking and laughing in small groups, our hor d'oeuvres were disappearing at an alarming rate, and the sangria flowed like a river. Plucking an empty plate from the buffet table, I slipped out to the kitchen for my last batch of cheese puffs, and while they were heating, I washed the dishes stacked in the sink.

"Here you are," Morgan said, coming into the kitchen. "I haven't had a chance to talk to you all evening."

I pulled the baking sheet from the oven and turned. "Cheese puff? Be careful; they're hot."

"Thanks." He picked out one of the bite-sized pastries, then quickly transferred it to the other hand, blowing on his fingers.

"I told you they were hot."

Morgan popped the bite in his mouth, then took the spatula off the counter and began sliding the appetizers onto the empty plate. "I ran up that test balloon we talked about the other day. My boss said he'd have to see the photos before he would consider an investigation."

Just as I'd feared, he'd spilled the beans. "You know, Greg," I said testily, "I remember specifically asking you not to mention those photos."

"How was I supposed to run it by him without mentioning them?" He gave me a wide-eyed innocent look, obviously believing that would make me soften. It didn't. I was steamed, and to show him, I turned my back and began scrubbing furiously on a baking dish soaking in the sink.

Truthfully, it was my fault as much as Morgan's, since I was the one who had mentioned the photos in the first place. But I wasn't about to admit it and let him off the hook. He had betrayed a confidence and deserved to be rebuked.

"Come on, Abby, what's the big deal?" he said, putting his hands on my shoulders. "I didn't tell him *who* had the photos."

"Well, thank you for that!"

"Abby," Nikki said, stepping into the kitchen, "we need more cheese puffs. . . . Oh, sorry. I didn't mean to interrupt."

"You're not interrupting," I said quickly. Morgan removed his hands. We both must have looked as guilty as sin.

She glanced from me to Morgan. Then a look of realization spread across her pixie features. "You're telling him about someone trying to kill you last night, aren't you?"

"Nikki," I said, with a light laugh, "no one tried to *kill* me." The last thing I wanted was for Morgan to spread word of my mishap around the courthouse.

"What do you call it when someone tries to run you off the road?"

"It was just a little bump. I survived."

"You nearly ended up facedown in the creek." She turned to Morgan and finished with, "And while that was happening, someone broke into her store and stole a box of fertilizer."

I took the plate of puffs and thrust them at her. "Here, Nik. Don't be a stranger."

"A box of *fertilizer?*" Morgan asked, turning those baby blues on me.

"It seems to be the only thing missing. Strange, isn't it?" I stuck the baking sheet in the soapy water and turned to find Morgan staring at the floor, his brow wrinkled in thought. "What's wrong?" I asked.

"We had a box of fertilizer in the evidence closet that we had collected from the Ryan murder scene. Someone from Tom's Green Thumb came to claim it the other day." He shrugged. "Coincidence, I guess."

Coincidence? My inner antennae quivered uneasily. "Why would they want Billy's fertilizer? You didn't release it, did you?"

"Not me. One of the detectives—Williams—signed off on it."

"He released murder evidence?"

Morgan lifted one shoulder. "It was a box of fertilizer."

"Didn't anyone question why a store that sold fertilizer wanted a used box back?"

"Look, Williams isn't an idiot. Obviously, he decided it wasn't important to the case."

"*He* decided? For God's sake, Greg, you're handling the case! Did you at least have the contents analyzed?"

At that moment, Nikki barged in, dragging Scott behind her. "Hey, you two stick-in-the-muds, come join us for karaoke."

"We'll be there in a minute, Nik."

"Yeah, right. I know you too well, Ab. You'll hide out here until it's over." Nikki turned to Scott and whispered, "She hates to sing in public. What about you, Greg? Can you carry a tune?"

"Not *now,* Nikki," I said in a firm voice, but the damage had been done. Morgan had an escape hatch.

"Can *I* carry a *tune?* I'll have you know in college I had the lead role in *Music Man.*"

"Who'd you play—Marion the librarian?" Nikki taunted, and Morgan took off for the living room to prove her wrong.

"Thanks a lot, Nikki," I snapped.

"Don't mention it." She was having such a good time she didn't even catch the sarcasm.

The stereo began blasting a Billy Joel song, with vocal accompaniment provided by Greg Morgan, leaving me to entertain a host of questions and several theories, and no one to run them past except myself. I gathered up the sides of an overflowing garbage bag, put a twist tie on it, and slipped out of the apartment. I bypassed the trash room and took the bag down to the Dumpster, needing to clear my head with some fresh air.

I had been wrong about the burglar's objective. He'd been after the fertilizer. It was simply too coincidental that a box of Harding's personal brand was missing from Bloomers and another had been reclaimed by someone from Harding's store. But if I assumed the same person had taken both boxes—either Harding, or someone working for him—why was it so important to have them back?

A gusty wind sent swirls of leaves around my feet as I carried the bag across the parking lot. I held the Dumpster's heavy top open with one hand and shoved the black bag inside the bin with the other, pushing down an old, discarded silk plant. I started toward the building, then came to a quick stop.

A silk plant.

Billy Ryan had silk plants in his apartment, not potted plants, as the evidence sheet had listed. The superintendent had told me so himself. Billy also had an empty box of fertilizer. But he wouldn't have needed fertilizer for a silk plant. So what had been in the box?

I smacked myself on the forehead. I had seen the powder with my own eyes, but I'd never considered that it could have been cocaine. *Harding* must have been Billy's supplier, and Billy, in turn, had been selling to others, like Tony Vertucci, to support his habit.

Something must have happened to anger Tony that morning—maybe Billy had tried to blackmail him by threatening to tell Tony's uncle about his habit. My guess was that Tony had only intended to threaten Billy, but things had gotten out of hand. It was clear to me now why the commissioner had wanted to cover up Tony's hit-and-run: An insurance investigation would have turned up incriminating evidence, and a scandal would have ruined Vertucci's political career.

I shook my head in astonishment. Fertilizer. The Sappling Corporation. What a perfect cover. No wonder Harding had wanted his box back. He'd probably sent Buzz to break into Bloomers to get it.

I couldn't wait to tell Dave. The implications for Pearl's divorce settlement were enormous. If Harding were to be convicted of dealing cocaine, he'd be charged with a Class-A felony and serve thirty years in jail, no probation, and Pearl would get the house, the store, and most of his money. She and her son would be set for life. All we had to do was prove Harding's involvement.

Elated, I crossed the parking lot and started up the stairs, but I halted halfway. How was I going to prove anything? My box was gone, and so was the evidence box. I didn't want to call the cops because I didn't know who to trust.

I sat down on the stairs, thinking hard. What I needed was another box from the stockroom at Tom's Green Thumb. I checked my watch. Nine forty. I had just enough time to get out to the greenhouse before it closed.

I dashed up to the apartment and pulled Nikki off to one side. I was going to tell her about my mission, but she was having so much fun I couldn't see any reason to put a damper on it. "We're almost out of ice. I'm going to run out for another bag. Can I take your car?"

"Sure." She handed me her keys and followed me to the door. "This is a great party, Ab."

"Good."

"I just wanted to tell you I appreciate it." She gave me a hug.

"Thanks, Nik. I know you do. I'll be back in twenty minutes."

I hopped in her car and took off, dialing Dave's number with one hand. I got his machine and left a message, then called Marco. His voice mail picked up. "Marco, I'm on my way to Tom's Green Thumb. I know what was taken from my shop and why. Call me."

The parking lot at Tom's Green Thumb had thinned out to just a few cars. I checked my watch as I pulled up close to the glass double doors. I had ten minutes to sneak into the stock room, lift a box, and get it up to the cashier without being noticed. Too late, I remembered I should have brought a hat to hide my hair. A search of Nikki's glove box, console, and trunk turned up a pink bandanna, which was nearly as bright as my hair, but as I was desperate, I folded it into a triangle and tied it around my head. At least the rest of me was in black.

I stood to one side of the doors, holding onto the scarf to keep the wind from whipping it off, until I saw people coming out, then I darted past them, through the open doors and over to the left, as far away from the office window as I could get. I stuck to the outside row of plants, where the taller ones were kept, and halted near the back wall, behind a table of decorative grasses so I could watch the door to the stockroom. A glance at my watch showed eight minutes until closing. I couldn't afford to watch long.

The door swung open and Buzz came out. I ducked, then raised my head and watched him walk toward the front and disappear behind the office door. The stockroom door opened again as another employee came out, a young man with a box on his shoulder. I waited another minute and no one else appeared.

A last call for customer checkouts came over the store's loudspeaker. *It's now or never, Abby.*

I dashed to the door, slid inside, grabbed a small box from the nearest shelf, and backed out, casting a quick glance around the stockroom as I did, relieved that it appeared to be deserted. Then I turned and skirted the edge of the store once again, emerging at the front near the farthest cashier's station.

Only two lines were open. I chose the shorter line and stood behind a middle-aged woman buying a flat of assorted flowers, each of which had to be rung up separately. An employee waited by the glass doors, ready to lock up behind the last customer, which, if my cashier moved any slower, would be me. I kept glancing over at the office door as I waited. *Come on,* I silently urged the cashier. *Faster.*

The customer ahead of me looked around with a smile, then saw the box in my hand.

"Oh!" she said, turning back to the cashier, who was about to ring up the total. "I forgot fertilizer. Can you wait just a moment while I go get some?"

At that moment Buzz stepped out of the office and looked around. My stomach lurched as his head rotated in my direction.

I slipped past the woman and walked rapidly to the doors, ditching the box in the garbage can outside, praying that would be enough to stop Buzz's mad pursuit. I hopped into Nikki's car and tried to put the key in the ignition, but my fingers were trembling so hard I couldn't do it. I glanced out the windshield, through the glass doors, and saw Buzz. He was heading straight toward me.

Muttering frantic curses, I grabbed the key with both hands and finally inserted it. As the double doors swished open, I threw the car into Reverse and backed up all the way to the road, gravel flying every which way. I took off and didn't look back.

Once I was speeding down the highway, traffic flowing all around me, I pulled off the bandanna, drew in a shaky breath, and let it out slowly, trying to steady my nerves. That had been too close for comfort. And now what was I to do? There was no way I dared go back in that store.

Frustrated, I banged my fist on the steering wheel.

Then I remembered the mum.

I parked Nikki's Toyota in front of Bloomers and let myself in. The alarm beeped and I quickly checked Grace's sticky note on the wall for the instructions to disarm it. The last thing I needed was to further annoy the cops. I locked the door, turned the lights on in the workroom, put my purse on the desk, and used the phone to let Nikki know I'd be a little later than planned.

"Is everything all right?" she shouted above the background noise.

"It's fine, Nik. I just—"

"Speak louder. I can't hear you."

"I said I just have to get something from the shop, then I'll stop for ice and be home."

After shouting good-bye, I put the phone in its cradle and took the mum from beneath the growing light. There were still traces of white powder on the soil, so I scraped some off with my floral knife and put it in the middle of a piece of clear cellophane wrap. I folded it up envelope style, taped it, and tucked it in my leather bag.

A muffled *thunk* from the front of the shop made me pause.

I listened for a long moment, trying to determine its source. Had something fallen off a wall? Had someone shut a car door outside? When all remained still, I put the mum back on the shelf and went to the sink to clean my knife.

Suddenly, the bell over the front door gave a half jingle, as if the wind had blown the door open a crack. But that wasn't possible. I'd locked it.

Cautiously, I put down my knife and started toward the display room, but came to a sudden stop inside the curtain when I heard a quick *tink,* as though a hand had clamped onto the bell to prevent it from making any noise. Then I heard the door close ever so gently.

Someone was in the shop.

CHAPTER TWENTY-SEVEN

I stood there facing the curtain, my heart beating a frantic tattoo as I considered my options. There wasn't time to pick up the phone and call the police, and even if there were, what if the intruder was Blasko? Call the cops on a cop? I thought not. My best move was to escape out the back and beat it down to Marco's bar.

I reached for my purse and eased it off the desk, praying the keys inside wouldn't rattle. Then I sidled toward the kitchen, hugging the leather pouch to my chest. I had just reached the doorway when the lights in the workroom went out.

I spun around, expecting that the intruder had entered behind me and found the light switch, but then my gaze was drawn to the curtain, where streetlamps illuminated the silhouette of a man moving through the outer room. No one was in the workroom. Someone had cut the lines from the alley. I was dealing with at least two men.

I backed into the kitchen as the silhouette moved closer to the curtain, outlining a flat head just like Blasko's. Whether he was merely trying to scare me or do something worse, I wasn't inclined to wait around to find out.

I had two choices: Either take my chances in the alley,

hoping the second man had gone around to the front, or hide in the basement and use my cell phone from there. I liked the first choice better.

I moved quickly to the back door and lifted a slat of the blind, giving a start at the sight of the dark-colored sedan parked outside. I don't know why it surprised me. I should have expected Vertucci would get directly involved sooner or later. He wasn't a man known for patience, and since his threats and intimidations hadn't worked, he'd obviously decided more drastic action was needed. It didn't bode well for me.

Suddenly, the shadowy figure of a man appeared just outside the door to my left. I dropped the blind and turned, panic-stricken, feeling for the knob of the basement door. I plunged down the steps in the darkness, staying to one side so the old wood wouldn't creak, feeling my way with a sweaty palm against the cold cement wall.

Above me, someone walked across the kitchen floor. The back door opened and shut again. I heard the murmur of male voices. Both men were inside now.

I reached the bottom and continued forward, one arm clutching my purse, the other outstretched, trying to get my bearings in the pitch-blackness. Shuffling slowly so I wouldn't topple any of the stacks of clay pots, I came to the first of a row of metal shelves along the wall and worked my way down to the furnace room at the far end. Upstairs I heard a heavy *thunk*, that sounded like the cooler door shutting, then footsteps moving around the workroom.

It seemed an eternity until I located the doorway. I felt my way around the small room, discovering the hot water heater, the gas furnace, and finally an old coal furnace back in the corner that Lottie had been wanting to get rid of for years.

Willing myself to ignore the spiderwebs, I wedged in behind the old furnace, dug in my purse, found my cell phone, and with trembling fingers punched in Marco's number. It rang once, twice, three times. Then a warning beep sounded in my ear.

My stomach knotted. In the confusion of Friday night, I'd forgotten to recharge the phone.

Come on, Marco, where the hell are you? The warning beep sounded again, just as his voice mail picked up. I left a whispered message telling him where I was and what was happening, then I disconnected to the sound of the third warning and dialed 911.

The footsteps had shifted to the back end of the building. The men were in the kitchen. How long until they searched the basement?

The phone issued a succession of warning beeps just as the dispatcher answered. I had seconds left. "I need help," I whispered. "I'm at Bloomers, on Franklin."

"Who's calling?"

The basement stairs creaked.

"Abby Knight," I whispered frantically. "It's an emergency."

The phone went dead, but I would have had to hang up anyway. The voices were getting nearer. I sank down, pulled my black shirt over my hair, curled up as tightly as possible, and prayed.

A stack of pots toppled onto the cement floor. A harsh, raspy voice said, "Give me the goddamn flashlight, you idiot."

That was Harding's voice! Harding, not Vertucci! Then whose car was in back? And who did the flat head belong to?

Buzz!

Buzz must have alerted Harding to my visit to the greenhouse, guessed I was onto them, and followed me to Bloomers. Then it had to be *Harding's* sedan, not Vertucci's, parked in the alley. It had probably been *his* black Lincoln I had seen behind his store.

Why had they come? They'd stolen my box of fertilizer,

and Buzz had to know I hadn't made it out of Tom's
Green Thumb with another. Surely they didn't know
about the minute amount of coke I'd pinched from
the box.

A beam of light suddenly swept across the furnace
room. I curled up tighter and held my breath, fully expecting to be discovered. A second passed, then another.
A spider crawled across my hand and I had to clench my
teeth to keep from shuddering.

The light moved on.

"She ain't down here," Harding snarled. "You got any
more bright ideas?"

"She has to be down here. We searched everywhere
else. Why don't we just turn the juice back on so we
can see?"

"I cut the lines, is why."

Wedged into that small space with my shirt over my
head, I started feeling clammy and short of breath. My
claustrophobia was coming on. *Deep breaths, Abby.
Don't succumb.*

"How about in the coolers?" Harding snapped. "Did
you look in the coolers?"

"'Course I did. I'm not a moron."

"Whose fault is it we're here, then?"

"How many times are you gonna bring that up? I told
you it was an accident." The voices receded as they
started up the stairs.

What was an accident? Why was it Buzz's fault they
were here?

I waited until I heard them in the front of the shop.
Then I rummaged in my purse, located the package of
cocaine, and stuck it behind the furnace for safekeeping.
With the purse strap looped around my neck to leave my
hands free, I eased out and felt my way to the stairs, stopping at the bottom to listen. There was no sound from
above, but I played it safe and gave them several more
minutes.

I took one stair at a time, pausing between each step to listen. At the top I waited, my heart in my throat, listening until I was sure no one was there. Then I made a dash for the door.

Suddenly, a heavy arm wrapped around my head and a big hand clamped over my mouth and nose.

"Thought you was clever, didn't you?" Harding sneered, as I struggled to pull his hand away. "Not by half, missy. Not by half." He swung me around to face the stairs and gave me a push. "Now we'll see how brave you are."

I grabbed the old wooden railing to keep from pitching headlong into the basement. Harding was right behind me, prodding me between the shoulder blades, almost as if he was hoping I'd stumble and fall. It was all I could do to stay on my feet.

Buzz clomped down behind us, shining the flashlight on the steps so Harding could see where he was going. I turned at the bottom to face them, and Harding shoved me down onto the cement floor, where I crab walked backward until I hit a stack of pots against the wall. "What do you want?" I shouted, trying to sound angry instead of scared out of my wits.

Harding crouched over me, his horsey face a shadowy outline in the dark, the sweat of his body combined with my own terror making me want to gag. "You know exactly what I want."

"You bought a box of fertilizer from us last week," Buzz said snidely from behind him, shining the light on my face. "We know because we got you on tape."

"So?" I held a hand over my eyes to cut the glare. "I paid for that box. And if that's what you came for, you're out of luck. It was stolen two days ago. But then you knew that, didn't you?"

Buzz snickered, and Harding threw him a silencing glare. "Don't play games with me," Harding sneered. "You took something from that box."

"Only a pinch. I sprinkled it on a plant, but it didn't look right, so I closed the bag and put the box on the shelf. And that's the last I saw of it."

Harding grabbed me by my upper arms and pulled me up as if I were nothing more than a rag doll. "You took more than a pinch. You took a whole damn bag."

"Why would I do that?" My voice was trembling, and I hated that he could see how frightened I was. It was just what the bully wanted. "I thought it was bad fertilizer."

Harding gripped my arms tighter, causing tears to spring to my eyes. "You're a lying bitch. You know what I do to lying bitches?"

I had a pretty good idea and it wasn't something I wanted to experience. *Come on, Marco, check your messages!* "If there's a bag missing," I said, trying not to wince as his grip tightened, "check with your cohort back there. Ask him how he paid for that new Thunderbird."

Harding shoved me against the wall and swung to face Buzz, while I sank down amid pieces of pottery and rubbed my arms, trying to bring back the circulation.

"What!" Buzz demanded. "Are you accusing *me?* You gotta be shittin' me. If it wasn't for *me,* you wouldn't be able to run your little side business."

"I don't hear him denying it," I said to Harding, hoping to stir things up further.

Buzz jerked his gun from the waistband of his pants and aimed it at my forehead. I thought he was going to shoot me on the spot. "Just say the word and I'll get rid of her."

As I stared up at that big black barrel, praying silently for either a quick, painless death or divine intervention, the phone began ringing upstairs. It was probably Nikki, wondering where I was. I suddenly remembered how she had thanked me for throwing her the party, and fresh tears came to my eyes. Nikki, my lifelong buddy, my best friend in the world. Would I ever see her again?

The jangling of the phone seemed to make Buzz even

edgier. I watched his trigger finger twitch in anticipa...
and even in the faint light I could see the excitement in
his beady eyes, the anticipatory lick of his lips. He
wanted to kill me. He would take pleasure in watching
me die. All he needed was one word from Harding and
I'd be a goner.

Harding shoved the weapon aside, and I nearly sobbed
in relief. "That's your answer to everything, ain't it?" he
snarled at Buzz.

"No, it ain't my answer to everything. Why do you
keep saying that?"

"Because you never use your head, that's why. You just
act. Like some kind of animal."

"*You're* saying that about *me?* I can't believe you're
saying that about *me!*"

Harding grabbed the flashlight. "Shut your trap and go
get the rope from my trunk."

"Look, the kid jumped me first. What was I supposed
to do?"

The kid? He had to be talking about Billy.

And suddenly the pieces came together. Buzz had shot
Billy. Billy must have tried to blackmail Harding, so
Harding had dispatched Buzz, probably to scare him. But
where did Tony Vertucci fit in?

Harding backhanded Buzz, drawing blood. "What
don't you understand about shutting up?"

There was a long moment when I thought Buzz was
going to turn the gun on him. Instead, he stood there dab-
bing his cut lip with the back of his left hand, glaring at
the big ugly farmer, until Harding said, "Are you gonna
get that rope or not?"

Buzz tucked the weapon back in his pants and with a
sullen look said, "I can't see the steps."

With an exasperated sigh, Harding turned the beam
on the stairs. And as Buzz climbed toward the kitchen,
one thought ran through my head: I couldn't let them
take me out of Bloomers. Once Harding had me at the

greenhouse, my odds of staying alive would drop dramatically. My only hope was to get away from Harding while Buzz was gone.

My thoughts darted madly in all directions, searching for some way to get out of that basement. *Distract him,* my inner voice said.

Harding perched on a step to wait, keeping the flashlight on me. I pretended to scratch my forehead with my left hand while I casually lowered my right hand to the floor, my palm resting on shards of pottery, feeling for one I could use as a weapon. "Was Billy Ryan dealing for you?" I asked, hoping he'd keep his eye on my face and not my hand. "Did he threaten to expose you? Is that why you sent Buzz to see him?"

"Shut up."

"Just answer one question, then. Where does Tony Vertucci fit into all this?"

"I don't know what the hell you're talking about."

"Tony Vertucci. Commissioner Vertucci's nephew."

I could see by his perplexed look that he truly had no idea who Tony was. Marco had been right all along. I only hoped I'd live to congratulate him.

My fingers closed over a long, pointy shard. I had my weapon. The next thing I had to do was get to my feet so I could run, and I didn't have time to spare. Buzz would be back at any moment. "My leg is cramping. Do you mind if I stand?"

"Sit still."

Okay, back to the drawing board. Maybe I could get Harding down on my level. "Look, Harding, you don't want a murder charge on your head, so let me go. If Buzz was the one who killed Billy Ryan, turn him in. Be a hero. We can go our separate ways, and I'll pretend this incident never happened."

"You think you're clever, don't you?"

"I'm just trying to be reasonable."

"*You* need to mind your own *business!* Everything was

going along fine until you stuck your nose into *my* business."

"I was trying to help Pearl," I offered in a small voice.

"*Help* her? Pearl didn't want that divorce. You talked her *into* it."

I sat there quietly, trying not to look as terrified as I felt. Nothing was working for me. *Where are you, Marco?*

"What gives you the right to interfere in my life?" he shouted, pushing to his feet. "What gives you the goddamn right? You think I'm just some ignorant farmer, don't you? You think I didn't know you were snooping in my stockroom."

He kicked a clay pot and sent it skittering across the floor, twirling like a dervish. "You want to see what's in my stockroom? Well, missy, you're gonna get your chance." He gestured with the flashlight. "Stand up."

My heart jumped to my throat. "Why? Buzz isn't back."

"Just stand the hell up!"

I slipped my purse from around my neck and placed it on the floor, figuring that if I had the chance to run, the less baggage to hinder me the better. And just in case he managed to get me out of Bloomers, at least there would be some sign that I had been there. I rose and pretended to adjust my slacks while I tucked the piece of clay into my waistband. "You know, I called the police while you and Buzz were ransacking my shop. They're probably here now. Maybe that's why Buzz hasn't come back. He saw them coming and took off."

Harding swept the light around the basement walls. "There ain't no phone down here."

"I have a cell phone. Listen. Do you hear anything upstairs? Maybe the police have Buzz in custody already." I could only hope.

Harding scoffed at me, but I could tell there was a smidgen of doubt in his mind. And, really, where *was* Buzz? "You don't have a cell phone."

I started to tell him it was in my purse, but then I changed my mind. I had a plan. "I dropped it behind the furnace when I hid from you. If you don't believe me, check for yourself."

"You really think I'm stupid, don't you?"

I was counting on it. "Look, I'll prove it to you," I said, and started for the furnace room.

"Hold it!" I glanced back to see him shine the light on the landing. He was nervous. "Get back here. We're going upstairs."

That wasn't part of my plan. "At least let me get my phone," I said, backing toward the doorway.

"Shit, don't you *ever* listen?"

My heart was pounding as he stalked toward me. Quickly, I felt for the shard, knowing I'd have to stab him hard if I hoped to escape. I found one end of it only to have it slip through my sweaty fingers and drop down the back of my slacks.

Harding reached for my arm, and I knew I had to act. I doubled up a leg, and kicked my foot straight into his groin with as much force as possible. With a groan he grabbed his crotch and sank to his knees.

Now or never, Abby! Trembling all over, I grabbed the handiest pot and brought it down on his head, shattering the pot into huge chunks. For a moment Harding stared at me, and I thought I was going to have to hit him with another pot. Then his eyes rolled up and he keeled over onto his side. The flashlight fell out of his hand and rolled toward me.

I shined it on him. Harding lay motionless, and a big green pot lay around him in three sections, one with a banana-yellow spout, one with a vivid-orange spout, and one with a hot-pink spout. I'd have to remember to thank my mother. On second thought, I probably shouldn't mention it.

Then I ran.

I got to the top of the stairs without encountering Buzz,

which was somewhat of a surprise—how long did it take to pop a trunk and grab a rope? I bypassed the back door and ran into the workroom, where I tripped over something bulky and fell on the floor beside it. I scrambled around on my hands and knees and took a look. It was Buzz, sprawled flat as if someone had beaned him.

Without stopping to wonder who or why, I jumped up and ran—straight into a hard, male body.

CHAPTER TWENTY-EIGHT

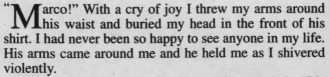

"Marco!" With a cry of joy I threw my arms around his waist and buried my head in the front of his shirt. I had never been so happy to see anyone in my life. His arms came around me and he held me as I shivered violently.

"It's okay, sunshine," he said, stroking my hair. "It's okay. You're safe."

I knew that, but my body didn't. My teeth were clattering together, and I felt like laughing hysterically, or sobbing uncontrollably—or both at the same time. What I really wanted to do was to beat the tar out of Marco. I pulled back a fist and tried to sock him in the gut, but he blocked me.

"What's that for?" he asked, holding my wrist.

"W-why d-didn't you answer my c-calls?" I managed, unable to stem the chattering.

"I tried! I kept getting your voice mail. I phoned here, too, but no one answered."

"Th-that's bec-cause I was in the basement trying to escape a k-killer!" I heard the stirring of clay fragments from belowstairs and panicked, gripping Marco's arms. "He's still d-down there. Do something!"

Marco repeated my words to someone in the room. I looked around and saw the bobbing glow of a lantern as Reilly strode in from the kitchen carrying a temporary light, several cops behind him. I saw all those blue shirts and nearly started sobbing again. Reilly snapped out orders, sending more cops down the basement steps. Then he crouched beside Buzz and felt his neck for a pulse.

"Who is he?" Reilly asked me, as Buzz began to move.

"B-buzz, the store manager at Tom's Green Thumb. Tom Harding is in the basement."

At Reilly's puzzled look, I tried to coherently clarify the situation, but for some reason my words tumbled out every which way. "Harding and Buzz are running a drug operation out of his stockroom, and I accidentally bought a box of cocaine thinking it was fertilizer and then someone stole it, but I still had some on the chrysanthemum, and now it's downstairs behind the coal furnace, and by the way, Marco, you were right about Tony Vertucci. He wasn't involved in Billy Ryan's death. It w-was B-b-buzz." I stopped talking and started rubbing my upper arms, which had suddenly gone cold. So had my feet. And hands. Icy cold.

"Take it easy, sunshine. You don't have to tell it all at once."

Marco was right. What was the rush? I felt weak all over and looked around for a chair. "I think I may be going into shock," I told him. "It's been a rough night."

Marco eased me down into my desk chair, took off his shirt, and wrapped it around my shoulders. "Sit tight. I'll get you some water."

More police came through the back door, flashlight beams bouncing off the walls as they lifted Buzz to his feet, handcuffed him, and took him away. I drank thirstily from the glass Marco handed me, and then, while Reilly took notes, I gave them an accounting of the events, starting with my arrival at Bloomers.

When I had finished, Reilly shook his head in amazement. "You're a brave lady."

Marco gave my shoulders a gentle squeeze. "Yeah, she's something else."

At that moment, another cop came over with the cellophane package and handed it to Reilly.

"That's the powder from the fertilizer box," I told him.

Reilly held it up to the lantern, then gave it back to the cop and told him to put it in an evidence bag. "We've got enough for a warrant," Reilly told him. "As soon as you get it, take a van over to Tom's Green Thumb to seize the evidence. I'm heading back to the station to do the booking." He paused at the door to look back at me. "You're a chip off the old block, kid. Give your father my regards." He gave Marco a quick salute and said, "I'll leave the lantern here and catch up with you later."

"Thanks, Sean," Marco said.

"You know, I liked that Reilly right from the start," I said, as the back door closed.

"Are you feeling better now?" Marco asked, and at my nod, he crossed his arms and leaned a hip against the worktable, studying me with those penetrating dark eyes. "Good. Then explain to me how Harding knew you were here."

"He followed me from Tom's Green Thumb."

"You told Nikki you were going for ice. They don't sell ice there."

"How did you know about the ice? Did Nikki call you?"

"Stick to the subject. Why did you go to Tom's Green Thumb?"

I recapped my conversation with Greg Morgan about the fertilizer and my discovery in the Dumpster. "When I figured out what Harding was selling, I decided I'd better pick up another box for evidence. And just for the record, I did call you to tell you about it. But then Buzz spotted me in the store and I had to ditch the box. That's when I remembered the mum." I pointed to the plant sitting under the growing light.

Marco crouched in front of me. "You had no business going to the greenhouse by yourself. You could be dead right now, do you know that?"

I shivered at the thought. "But I'm not dead. You saved me." I put my hands on his face, thinking that he was the sexiest man I'd ever met, even wearing that tight undershirt —or maybe *especially* wearing that tight undershirt. "The cavalry arrived just in the nick of time."

"This isn't a B movie, Lucy. Through a very fortunate series of events you are still alive, no thanks to your meddling." He took my hands in both of his. "I want you to swear to me that you'll never meddle again."

"I never cared much for swearing. It shows such a lack of imagination."

"Abby!"

His expression was so earnest I had to capitulate. "Okay. I won't meddle." I really hated that word anyway.

"That applies to interfering, snooping, and prying."

"I get the picture." He hadn't said anything about giving advice. "Believe me, Marco, after tonight, I've had my fill of danger."

"Good," he said. And then he kissed me. Just like that, Marco leaned over and planted one on me—a warm, firm, manly kiss that curled my toes. I pulled back a few inches to stare at him. Was that an "I'm so happy you're safe kiss," or had our relationship moved to a new level?

I was just about to ask him when I heard someone come in the front door. Marco was instantly on his feet, helping me up.

"Abby?" Nikki shrieked, and seconds later the curtain was thrown back and she came running over, still in her party dress but minus her shoes. She hugged me tightly, pressing my ear against her silver pendant. "Omigod, Abby, are you okay? Is she okay, Marco? Was she robbed?"

I untangled her arms and freed my head rubbing my gouged ear. "I'm right here, Nik. You can talk to me."

She looked to Marco for confirmation.

"Nikki!" I said. "Look at me. I'm fine. Where are your shoes?"

She looked down at her feet and wiggled her toes. "I couldn't drive in them. The heels were too high. And by the way, Abby, all that tape on your car? That's got to stop. I ruined three nails trying to get the door open."

"I'm sorry. How's the party?"

"It's over. After I talked to Marco I was so worried I sent everyone home."

"You sent Scott home for *me?*"

"Ladies!" Marco called, breaking into our chatter. "I have a suggestion. Let's adjourn to Down The Hatch for some bubbly. Abby needs sustenance, and there's a bottle of excellent French champagne with her name all over it. My treat."

"As much as I appreciate the offer," I said, "there's one hitch. I don't like champagne."

I waited for his rebuff, but Marco only said, "That's because you haven't had the *right* champagne. I guarantee this bottle will make you a convert."

"What about the bubbles?"

He hooked one arm through mine, the other through Nikki's, and guided us to the door. "I promise you'll like the bubbles, too."

CHAPTER TWENTY-NINE

We trooped down the street to Marco's bar and scooted into the back booth, Nikki across from me, while Marco went to pop the cork. He came back with a large green bottle and three fluted glasses. He slid in beside me, poured the wine, and handed out the glasses.

"A toast," he said, raising his glass, "to Abby's health. May she never meddle and put herself in jeopardy again."

"I'll second that," Nikki said.

Not to be outdone, I said, "To Marco—for finally turning on his phone! And for waylaying that big brute Buzz. And to Nikki for abandoning a boyfriend and her shoes for me."

We clinked glasses. Then I closed my eyes and took a sip, jumping slightly at the tingle of bubbles that sprayed my nose and fizzed on my tongue. The wine went down easily, and I had to admit that once I adjusted to the bubbles, it wasn't half-bad. In fact, upon further consideration, three further considerations, to be exact, I decided that I kind of, sort of, liked it—enough to finish the glass and ask for a refill. Wouldn't the Osbornes have been impressed?

"So why didn't you answer my calls?" I asked Marco.

"You can wipe that suspicious look off your face. I was tailing Blasko."

"For your information, that was a curious look. Did you get anything on him?"

Marco took a mini voice recorder out of his pocket and laid it on the table. "Oh, yeah. We had a little showdown tonight, Blasko and I."

"He saw you following him? Some PI you are, Salvare," I teased.

"I *let* him see me, Lucy."

At Nikki's snicker I said, "Don't laugh. He calls *you* Ethel."

"Ethel!" Nikki said indignantly.

"So what happened next?" I asked.

"It didn't take much goading to get Blasko to admit he was harassing you. Those bogus parking tickets, the cut brake lines, the towing—all his work. Also, Elvis's escape. Seems he had orders from the commissioner. I couldn't get him to confess to Elvis's death, but I suspect he had a hand in that, too."

"He actually told you that?"

"I suppose he figured since I was on the outs with the police, if I accused him of anything, it would be his word against mine."

"I'm surprised he didn't pat you down."

"He did. He didn't find anything."

Marco's skill was amazing. "You were right about Tony," I said. "He wasn't involved."

"Not directly. Tony went to the apartment to buy drugs and found Billy dead. That's why he ran. His uncle tried to conceal that *and* the hit-and-run because he couldn't risk the damage to his career."

"Now all three men can be charged," I said. Maybe justice would be done after all. "But what about Detective Corbison? *Was* he on vacation?"

"Yes, and when I checked with him, he couldn't remember why he'd called you. But getting back to the

story, as soon as I was able to turn on my phone, I got
your message and tried to call your cell phone. When I
couldn't get an answer, I phoned your apartment and
Nikki told me you hadn't come back from your ice run."

Nikki leaned her chin on her fist, staring at him with
wide eyes. "Then what did you do?"

"I went to Bloomers and found Buzz heading for the
basement with a rope."

"And you punched him out?" Nikki asked.

Marco hunched one shoulder, as if he did things like
that all the time.

"Omigod, Abby," she said, grabbing my hand across
the table. "Do you know how romantic that is? He saved
you! You're wonderful, Marco, even if you did call me
Ethel. You owe him big time, Abby."

"Actually, Nikki," I began. "I was the one who—"

Then I heard, "There she is!" and I looked up to see
Lottie and Grace hurrying toward us, with Lottie fairly
shoving people out of her way.

Knowing I was in for a few hugs, I stood up and was
instantly engulfed, after which Lottie held me by the
shoulders to gaze at me, her chin trembling as she pressed
back tears. Then she enfolded me once again. "My poor
baby!"

"I'm okay, Lottie."

Sniffling, she turned me over to Grace, who, after hugging me, tilted my chin, turned my head from side to side,
then stood back to look me over. "She appears to be in
one piece," she said to Lottie, who was noisily blowing
her nose.

"How did you know to come down here?" I asked
them.

"Nikki phoned us," Grace explained. "I called Lottie and
we both hurried to the shop and found that horrible mess in
the workroom. Naturally, Lottie feared the worst."

"You did, too," Lottie said, still sniffling. "We called
the police and they said to check for you here."

"Ladies, have a seat and join us," Marco said, rising. As Lottie and Grace slid in beside Nikki, Marco signaled the waitress, who came over with more glasses and another bottle.

"I want to hear the whole story," Lottie said, holding out her glass to Marco. I did likewise. That champagne was really growing on me.

Nikki smiled dreamily. "Wait till you hear Marco's part. It's so romantic."

Marco grimaced. "I'll be back later."

"Speaking of romance," Grace said, pausing to sip her wine, "your cousin Jillian came into the shop this afternoon, dear. She'd like you to do the flowers for her wedding, which I believe she intends to hold in a field of daisies under a canopy of white roses."

"Right. Like she'll go through with it," I said. "And when is this glorious event supposed to take place?"

"On the Fourth of July. She thought fireworks in the background would be a nice effect."

"That sounds like a Jillian plan," I said with a resigned sigh.

"Fireworks start after dark," Nikki said, perplexed. "If she has the ceremony in the dark, how will anyone see the daisies?"

"Or the bees," Lottie added. "I hate bees."

"You and Nikki's cat," I said.

"Your cousin will be coming in to see you on Monday morning," Grace informed me. "Also, Trudee DeWitt would like that party plan you promised her. And your mother called twice looking for you."

"Make that three times," Lottie said. "She wanted you to know she's created the *ultimate* work of art and she's bringing it over on Monday for the unveiling."

So I had a veiling and an unveiling set for Monday morning.

Marco slid in beside me. "Have you told them about your vow?"

I tried to discourage him with a frown, but he ignored me. "Ladies, Abby has sworn to never meddle again."

I narrowed my eyes at the Italian hunk beside me. "You had to tell them?"

"You betcha. Now say it once for them: *I promise I will never meddle again.*"

Rolling my eyes, I repeated the words, and then everyone started in with their own admonishments. I sat back and let them go at it, loving them all for caring about me. I was too exhausted to argue anyway. I needed rest, a whole day of it. Everyone else—my mother, Jillian, Trudee DeWitt—could wait until Monday. I could handle anything on a Monday.

Read on for an excerpt from

another Flower Shop Mystery

by Kate Collins

Slay It with Flowers

Available from Signet

J ust for the record, I am not, in the true definition of the word, a meddler.

According to my dictionary, a meddler is one who involves herself in a matter without right or invitation. *Phffft*. Isn't me at all. I am a naturally curious, caring individual strongly opposed to two things: tyranny and injustice. That strong sense of right has been with me as far back as third grade, when I first strode the halls of Morton Elementary School with my "Hall Monitor" sash strapped across my chest.

I inherited these traits from my father, Jeffrey Knight, who was a sergeant on the New Chapel, Indiana, police force until a felon's bullet put him in a wheelchair. He firmly believed that his badge stood for honesty and right, and because of that he refused to play politics, which took a lot of courage but cost him many promotions. He has always been my hero.

But after the previous week—when my beloved 1960 yellow Corvette and I were run off the road, my flower shop was burgled, and a homicidal garden center owner decided to put a stop to my breathing capabilities—even my father had determined that I'd put my safety in jeopardy once too often.

As my assistant Grace, who has a quote for everything, was fond of saying, "If we don't learn from history, we are doomed to repeat it." Grace was usually right.

That week was behind me now. The bullies had been caught, the innocent cleared, and I had sworn off what my friends termed my "meddling," a vow they did *not* have to twist my arm to get me to make.

This particular Monday started at the customary time of eight o'clock in the morning—or ten minutes past four by the clock on the courthouse spire. The clock had stopped running in either 1997 or 1897, but none of our elected officials was willing to take a stand on the matter—or find someone to fix it. When asked, their usual response was, "What clock?"

I pulled the Vette into a space two doors down from my floral shop, landing it directly in front of the town's local watering hole, the Down The Hatch Bar and Grill, owned by the sexiest man who has ever worn a uniform, Marco Salvare, a former cop turned bar owner who dabbled in PI work on the side. Out front, Jingles the window washer was already hard at work with his trusty squeegee. Jingles was a friendly retiree whose goal in life appeared to be to keep every window and door on the square squeaky clean. His nickname came from his habit of jingling coins in his pocket. I wasn't sure if anyone actually knew his real name.

I gave Jingles a wave, then continued down the block, stopping on the sidewalk outside the old brick building that housed my shop to gaze up at the hand-lettered sign that proudly proclaimed my ownership. Even after two months, I was still in awe. Me, Abby Knight, a business woman. All grown up and in debt up to my eyebrows.

I traced a finger across my left eyebrow. The ring was gone. I had truly crossed the threshold into adulthood.

Bloomers is the second shop from the corner on Franklin

Street, one of the four streets that surround the courthouse square. The store occupies the first floor and basement of the three story building, and has two bay
windows with a yellow framed door in between. The left
side of the shop houses our flowers and the right side is
our coffee and tea parlor, where customers sit at white
wrought iron tables and watch the happenings on the
square.

The courthouse, built in 1896 from Indiana limestone,
houses the county and circuit courts, plus all the government offces. Around the square are the typical assortment
of family-owned shops, banks, law offices and restaurants. Five blocks east of the square marks the western
edge of the campus of New Chapel University, a small,
private school where I would have graduated from law
school if I hadn't flunked out.

Because I *had* flunked out, I'd had to rethink my career
plans to find something I could do successfully. It had
been a very short list. Then I'd learned that the quaint little flower shop where I'd once worked part time was for
sale—a stroke of luck for me because I loved flowers
and actually had a talent for growing things. So I used the
rest of my grandfather's college trust as a down payment
and had an instant career, which mollified my stunned
parents. It also saved the owner, Lottie Dombowski, from
bankruptcy caused by her husband's massive medical
bills. Now Lottie works for me doing what she loves best,
and I work for the bank, trying to make the mortgage payments.

Inside the shop, Grace Bingham was preparing her
coffee machines for the day. As soon as I stepped inside
and shut the door, she sang out in her crisp British accent, "Good morning, dear. How are we today?"

Grace spent years working as a nurse and sometimes
still spoke in first person plural. I met her the summer I
law clerked for Dave Hammond, a lawyer with a one-
man office on the square. Grace was his legal secretary at

the time. After she retired and found herself with too much time on her hands, I persuaded her to work for me at Bloomers. It was a perfect fit.

"We are in a good mood," I called back. "The sun is shining, the temperature is just right, and it's Monday. The only way it could get better is if twenty orders came in overnight." I peered into the parlor. "They didn't, did they?"

"No, dear, only five."

Grace handled as many tasks as I cared to load on her. Since she was an expert tea steeper, coffee brewer, and scone baker, her main job was to run the parlor. It was one of our many efforts to lure in more customers. We were in dire need of more customers, especially now that a gigantic floral and hobby shop had opened on the main highway.

At that moment Lottie came bustling through the curtain from the workroom in back, a bundle of white roses in her ample arms, her usual pink satin bow pinned into the short, brassy curls above her right ear. It was a daring look for a forty-five year old mother of a highly embarrassable seventeen-year-old boy. Even more daring considering that she had *four* highly embarrassable seventeen-year-old boys. Lottie's opinion on that was simple: Suck it up.

"Oh, good, you made it before Jillian did," she said to me as she stocked a container in the glass display cooler.

The gray clouds were moving in. I almost expected to hear ominous music in the background. "Jillian is coming? Now? Something dreadful must have happened to get her up before noon."

Lottie rolled her eyes. "She's got another bee in her bonnet about her wedding plans."

Grace handed me a rose-patterned china cup filled with her gourmet coffee, fixed just the way I liked it with a good shot of half and half. "Drink up, dear. You'll need the fortification. You know how tiring your cousin can be."

Grace phrased it so politely. My term would have been "pain-in-the-ass," which Jillian had been since she hit puberty and discovered that boys adored her. Jillian Knight was twenty-five, tall, gorgeous, and one year younger than me. She was also the only other girl in the family, which was about all we had in common.

My father was a retired cop. Jillian's was a stock broker. My mother was a kindergarten teacher. Jillian's mother wielded a five iron at the New Chapel Country Club. I paid the mortgage on a floral shop. Jillian got paid to shop for other people's wardrobes. As children, my brothers Jonathan, Jordan and I worked for our allowances. Jillian allowed their maid to work for hers.

The only justice in our separate worlds was that my two brothers became successful surgeons, while Jillian's brother waited tables in a Chicago diner. For years, our families spent all holidays together, and that had given Jillian and me a sibling-like relationship: we loved each other but didn't get along.

"I'm telling you, Abby, don't pay for that bridesmaid dress," Lottie warned.

I waved away her concern. "Jillian won't call off *this* wedding. She wouldn't dare."

"Ha! Look at her track record."

Lottie had a good point, Jillian got engaged once a year — it seemed to be a hobby of hers. Her list of ex-fiances read like a travel brochure: an Italian restaurant owner from Chicago's Little Italy; a moody Parisian artist named Jean Luc; an English consulate Sir Something-Or-Other; and a Greek plastic surgeon with an unpronounceable name. This was the first time she'd ever made it to the actual choosing-of-the-flowers stage.

Jillian's current groom-to-be was Claymore Osborne, who, coincidentally, was the younger brother of my former fiancé, Pryce Osborne the Second. Claymore was every bit as boorish and snooty as Pryce was, but that didn't matter to Jillian. What mattered was that Claymore stood to inherit half the Osborne fortune. Jillian always did go after money.

The wedding was set for the Fourth of July, three weeks away. At first Jillian wanted to hold it in a field of daisies, but having none in the area suitable for a wedding ceremony, she settled for a hotel ballroom in Chicago that she believed had daisies in the carpet. Somewhere.

On top of choosing me as a bridesmaid, Jillian had also asked me to do her wedding flowers. I had agreed because Jillian's wedding would most certainly be lavish, and that meant expensive flowers, which translated into money to pay my bills. I really needed to pay my bills.

"Here are your messages, dear," Grace said, handing me a small pile of memos. "Lottie has breakfast ready in the kitchen."

Monday breakfast was a tradition at Bloomers, and I was already drooling in anticipation. There were four messages: three from my mother and one from a client named Trudee DeWitt, or "Double EE Double TT," as she called herself, who needed to know when I was coming over to consult with her on decorations for her party.

The three messages from my mother all said the same thing: "Call me. Urgent." Nearly all her messages claimed urgency. One of these days, I've told her, it really will be urgent and then won't she be sorry? The Mother Who Cried Wolf.

I took the memos and the coffee and headed for the workroom, a garden-like haven where I've spent some of my happiest moments. As soon as I stepped through the curtain I had to stop to inhale the aromas—rose, lily, eucalyptus, buttered toast, scrambled eggs. It didn't get any better than that.

I dropped the messages on my desk—a messy affair littered with a computer, printer, phone, a pencil cup shaped like a grinning cat, a few framed photos, and assorted office items—and went to the kitchen to grab a plate of food. While I ate, Lottie and I went over the orders and discussed the coming week so we could make a list and call our suppliers. After washing my plate in the tiny kitchen sink, I tacked the orders on the cork board and sat at my desk to call Trudee.

I had just punched in her phone number when I heard the bell over the front door jingle, and a moment later the curtain parted and the bride-to-be swept in. "Abby!" she cried dramatically when she spotted me, brushing a silken strand of copper hair off her face. Jillian never did anything without drama. "Thank goodness you're here!" She threw her long, tanned arms around my shoulders and sobbed hideously, ignoring the phone pressed to my ear.

"Trudee? This is Abby Knight. You called?"

"It's horrible, Abby. I just can't bear it," Jillian wept. She lifted her head from my shoulder to stare me in the face, and since she was taller than I am—everyone is taller than I am—it required her to bend her knees to put us at an even eye level. She cupped my head with her hands. "Abby, you have to help me."

Kate Collins

The Flower Shop Mystery Series

**Abby Knight is the proud owner of her
hometown flower shop. She has a gift for
arranging flowers—and for solving crimes.**

Acts of Violets
Mum's the Word
Slay It with Flowers
Dearly Depotted
Snipped in the Bud

"A spirited sleuth, quirky sidekicks,
and page-turning action."
—Nancy J. Cohen

**Available wherever books are sold or at
penguin.com**

ELAINE VIETS
Josie Marcus, Mystery Shopper

Dying in Style

Mystery shopper Josie Marcus's report about Danessa Celedine's exclusive store is less than stellar, and it may cost the fashion diva fifty million dollars. But Danessa's financial future becomes moot when she's found murdered, strangled with one of her own thousand-dollar snakeskin belts...and Josie is accused of the crime.

High Heels are Murder

Every job has its pluses and minuses. Josie Marcus gets to shoe-shop...but she also must deal with men like Mel Poulaine, who's too interested in handling women's feet. Soon Josie's been hired by Mel's boss to mystery-shop the store, but one step leads to another and Josie finds herself in St. Louis's seedy underbelly. Caught up in a web of crime, Josie hopes against hope that she won't end up murdered in Manolos.